W9-BOO-851

SCOTT FREE

SCOTT FREE

VIN PACKER

CARROLL & GRAF PUBLISHERS
NEW YORK

Scott Free

Carroll & Graf Publishers
An Imprint of Avalon Publishing Group Inc.
245 West 17th Street, 11th Floor
New York, NY 10011

AVALON
publishing group incorporated

Copyright © 2007 by Marijane Meaker

First Carroll & Graf edition 2007

Library of Congress Cataloging-in-Publication Data is available.

ISBN-13: 978-0-78671-867-2
ISBN-10: 0-7867-1867-6

9 8 7 6 5 4 3 2 1

Printed in the United States of America
Interior design by Maria Fernandez
Distributed by Publishers Group West

To remember Bob, Ernie, and Tom.

BEFORE

"Look here. Jessica, I've made a decision. I'm going ahead with the change."

That was how it began, or how it ended, with Scott announcing it at breakfast on a Saturday morning. He didn't have to go to work, but she did. Southgate Insurance was open until noon. All employees were expected to be present, even a field investigator like Jessica.

She poured him another cup of coffee. Vassilaros. He never drank any other brand. He had always been the particular one of the pair. Certain things seemed programmed into him, as though he'd come out of the womb set in his ways, from little things to this major one he was about to deal with—he felt an entitlement.

"Look here," he'd begun the debacle. Look there? She was always looking there—at him—at handsome, slender, blue-eyed him. There were plenty of men with twenty-nine-inch waists and little hard round buns, tall and muscular. Go to any gym and there they were on treadmills, hanging from bars, lifting weights. Not one with a face like Scott's. Jessica was fifteen years younger than he was, but even in his forties he was someone women turned around to see a second time, and certain men as well. Scott was this gorgeous hunk who belonged to her, all two hundred and fifty pounds of her.

At Southgate they called him "Jessica's jewel." Popular as she was, as much fun as she was, didn't they still ask themselves how she'd ever landed him? Like many overweight people Jessica had perfect features, so that a casual observer was bound to picture her thinner, then wonder why she had let herself go. With a husband like Scott House, too. It wasn't just his looks. He had a PhD from Princeton. He wrote. He taught. His father was the eminent scholar Bolton House. Only Jessica knew, and had always known, the edgy, other side of Scott.

"Did you hear me, Jessica?"

He knew she had. He knew she realized just what he was announcing in such a casual-sounding voice. He made it seem as though he could be talking about a change of address, a change of clothes, a job change.

It was a summer morning, the windows open and the sounds of children playing, their dogs barking as the *New York Times* was tossed to driveways from a car cruising down Frost Lane. In their little enclave, near the water in Bay Shore, New York, all the streets were named for popular, predictable poets: Frost Lane, Longfellow Lane.

"I heard you," she said.

There was a book of poems beside his plate. Not a popular, predictable one but Frank O'Hara. There was the Larry Rivers drawing of O'Hara on the cover. He was naked except for a pair of combat boots, his long penis hanging down above them.

Scott read all the time: at the table, on the toilet, in the tub, and even right before the announcement of the end of their world.

"Well?" Scott said.

"So you're finally going to do it to yourself? To me and Emma?"

"I'm sorry."

"No, you're not."

"No, I'm not. Not for myself. But I'm sorry for you and Emmy. I'll move out if you want me to."

"You know I don't."

"I'll have to eventually."

"When do you plan to begin?"

"I've already begun."

"Oh. Just like that."

"You knew it was coming."

"I never really believed you'd go ahead, Scott."

"I have no choice."

"No choice," she said bitterly.

"Let's not start, Jess."

"If it was another woman, if it was anything but what it is, I could talk with someone about it. Somebody who'd been through it with her husband, or her boyfriend, or brother."

"There's a support group called—"

She cut him off. "I don't want to join a group!"

He shrugged. "Then suit yourself."

"This isn't fair to Emmy."

"What wouldn't be fair to Emmy would be for me to live a lie."

"I have an idea she'd choose that over this if she was old enough to understand."

In the living room Emma House was watching a cartoon on TV.

Jessica realized it was the last time they would appear to be the typical normal family, mother and father having a second cup of coffee, their baby in the next room giggling at a dancing duck on television.

Then Jessica would drive to work, walk into the office the way Auden described how suffering took place while someone else was eating or opening a window: she would return phone calls and answer e-mail with trembling hands, knowing that the day would come when she'd have to tell them at Southgate.

"I just don't know what I'm supposed to do," she said. "I don't know where to begin, Scott, who to tell, how to explain it."

"You don't have to think about that yet. It'll take time."

"And meanwhile?"

"Meanwhile we'll carry on as usual, if that's agreeable to you."

"I don't know what else to do," she said.

"There is something else. Don't call me Scott anymore."

"What do I call you?"

"It won't be hard, Jess. No radical name change," he said. "But please start trying to think of me as female. Call me Scotti."

ONE

Scotti seldom wore pants anymore. That hot August morning she was in a knee-length pleated skirt, a white silk blouse, and gold chain, her long blond hair held back with a pink scarf. Her face had the same dichotomous quality Princess Di's used to have, or Streisand's: sometimes striking, other times almost homely. She still walked in a somewhat ungainly, striding manner. Her voice was modulated to a pleasant low tone, not as deep now. She had worked on that, hard. She was still surprised when she saw her reflection, but satisfied with how she had changed in three and a half years.

By noon the tables under the blue-and-white VIP tents at the Hampton Classic were filled. A smiling man with thick black hair, sporting a white linen blazer, dark pants, and a white cap, was wheeled into the Lasher Communications tent.

"That's Len Lasher, CEO of Lasher Communications," Scotti said, "and that's Sea Love's owner with him."

"The redhead?" Jessica asked.

"No. I think the redhead is an employee of Lasher's. Our man is behind them."

"Don't call him 'our man,' please. I hate him!"

"So do I, Jessica. Hate his guts."

They were talking about Edward Candle.

Scotti House had been investigating Candle all spring. Jessica had spent April and May at a spa, losing weight in earnest for the first time in her life, never mind her mother-in-law's crack that it was too little, too late. She was down forty pounds, out of caftans and into silk pantsuits.

Until this scorching end-of-summer morning at the horse show, Jessica had never seen Candle.

He was in his fifties, although he looked younger, balding slightly, over six foot, and lean. He had a kindly face, belying all that Scotti and Jessica knew about him. He looked gentle and intelligent, like someone who very well might have named his two show jumpers after a pair of poems by Charlotte Mew: Sea Love and the late Farmer's Bride.

There was a racing horse named after a Mew poem, too: Arracombe Wood, who had been killed in the same way as Farmer's Bride.

No one had told Scotti the horses were named after poems, but she knew Mew's work well. What other explanation was there for those three names, from a rather obscure poet's work?

Candle's game was to collect the insurance on horses that couldn't measure up. He didn't do the job himself. The man who did it for him, Scotti had learned, lived nearby in Montauk.

This was the annual presentation of the Hampton Classic, and both Scotti and Jessica had the fear it would be the last time Sea Love would jump anywhere.

It cost Candle about $75,000 a year to keep Sea Love. The rumor among equestrians up and down the East Coast was that the chestnut mare had performed badly again all summer. The horse had no wish to relinquish her autonomy, no malleability. She never had, for the three years Candle had owned her.

Edward Candle was a weekend guest of Len Lasher's at Le Reve, Lasher's home on The Highway Behind The Pond. The local newspapers reported that Candle would soon have his own home in East Hampton after years of visiting there summers.

"Why is this Lasher in a wheelchair?" Jessica asked Scotti.

"He has multiple sclerosis."

As Jessica watched Candle fuss over him, pour champagne for him, grin down at him, and pat his back, she said, "Too bad MS isn't catching."

Jessica House was a full-time investigator for Southgate Insurance. She had hired Scotti part-time after Scotti moved from Bay Shore to East Hampton and worked some days at the library. Scotti was not a trained investigator, but propinquity, her innate curiosity, and Jessica's conviction that Scotti could nail Candle had prompted her to make her ex an assistant. The fatal "accident" Farmer's Bride had in Montauk had cost Southgate $300,000. Five years before that, another insurance agency had paid out $250,000 when Arracombee Wood died.

Now Sea Love was being kept at the same farm that had housed Arracombe Wood.

Scotti's contact was somewhere in the crowd. He was a groom named Fultz. Jessica hoped she could thank him personally. He had given Scotti enough evidence to convict Candle. Jessica had already turned it over to the police.

It had cost Southgate plenty to pay off Fultz and get the goods on Candle and his hired horse killer. But it would save Southgate a good deal more. Sea Love was insured for $350,000.

Before Scotti had located Fultz, she had spent hours with riders, grooms, and stable workers, current and past, from Hang Hollow Farm.

Jessica didn't want to wait to see Candle's photographs in the newspapers, or shots of him dodging reporters when the police began closing in on him. She wanted to get a good look at the creep when he was off guard, socializing with his fancy friends: people like the Lashers.

"I haven't thought of Charlotte Mew in years," Scotti said as they strolled around the grounds near the LCI tent. "Remember the first time I read her to you? We were in a sailboat off Fire Island. I read you 'Farmer's Bride.' Do you remember it?"

"I never had your knack for remembering and memorizing poetry," Jessica said.

"'She sleeps up in the attic there / Alone, poor maid. 'Tis but a stair / Betwixt us. Oh! my God! the down / The soft young down of her, the brown, / The brown of her—her eyes, her hair, her hair!'"

"Now I remember," Jessica said. "See if you can remember what you said after you read that poem to me."

"Nope. I can't."

"You said that Charlotte Mew drank a bottle of Lysol and killed herself."

"Well, she did." Scotti laughed. There was nothing any amount of hormones could do about that laugh. Her voice coach would wince, throw her hands up, and cry, "Sotto, Scotti! Sotto!"

Scotti looked at her watch. "Ten to one. I was hoping we could see the children ride. The lead line class starts at two. The Lasher party will go down for that. The little girl rides in it. Lasher will probably go with them."

"How old is the child?"

"Three years younger than Emma. Six," Scotti said.

That could have been Jessica's cue to say something about their daughter, but she didn't. She had a perverse streak in her. All the years Scott had begged her to try getting off some weight (for her health, never mind the rest) she had waited until the divorce to book herself at the spa. Now that Emma refused to see Scotti or talk with her on the phone, Jessica hardly ever mentioned their daughter. Scotti had to ask for information, always, which she finally did.

"How is Emma doing?"

"She hasn't changed her mind about not wanting to see you."

"I don't mean that. I mean how is she?"

"Okay. She wants a cat. I can't breathe with a cat. I promised her fish."

"Fish? Why not a dog?"

"Who's going to walk it? I have enough to do as it is."

"Can't a dog hang out in the yard?"

"Who's going to fence it in?"

"I can do that."

"You'll break your fingernails."

"That's one," Scotti warned.

"I couldn't resist it."

"You never can, Jess."

"I didn't mean anything."

"You never do."

It was then, just as things were getting sticky between them, that a short, slight man tapped Scotti on the shoulder.

"Have you heard anything, Ms. House?"

Jessica thought he was talking to her.

Scotti said, "Hello, Fultz."

He was in blue jeans and a T-shirt, with a ponytail tied with a piece of rope behind his head. He was shaking his head, grimacing as he ignored Jessica and spoke directly to Scotti. "Sea Love is dead, ma'am. It was done last night."

"No!"

"Electrocution," said Fultz. "I thought you should know."

Then he was gone, lost in the crowd.

At that moment the Lashers left their tent. The hawk-faced redhead was pushing Lasher in the wheelchair. Candle walked beside the chair, laughing at something Len Lasher had called up to him. Jessica got a good look at Edward Candle, proving what she had come to know working for Southgate: they never looked sinister.

TWO

Nell Slack liked to hear about the Lashers. In a cold November rain she was in Mario Rome's van and he was taking her to LaGuardia to catch an early evening flight. He'd chauffeured her to and from the airport five or six times, and he had explained that the Lashers took precedence. That was his agreement with them.

She was the kind of woman Mario Rome wished he had valued when he was younger, instead of the drinkers and dopers who had patronized The Magic C, a bar he'd owned in New York's East Seventies. Even though he loved full, long hair and she had the cut of a waif, she had the cheekbones, eyes, mouth, and kindly manner of a lady, and no matter how foolish the idea might be, he was immensely attracted to her.

"Are you driving for the Lashers tomorrow night, or can you meet my flight?" she asked him.

"I'll be there," he said. "I don't drive the Lashers much at night now, unless Delroy needs me."

"That's a new name."

"He's like a traffic manager at Le Reve. A gofer, really, but he keeps track of everybody, or he used to, back when Mr. Lasher traveled a lot. Delroy Davenport. He looks like some kind of jungle parrot with his bright red hair, this big nose, and eyes so brown you'd swear they were black. Now he runs the house, or he thinks he does. We call him Mrs. Danvers."

"Why?" she asked.

"She was this character in the old movie *Rebecca*. Judith Anderson played her. She was a servant in this mansion called Manderly. She was very possessive of the place, and the master."

"Is this Delroy effeminate?"

"No. He's just possessive of the Lashers and Le Reve. He's Len Lasher's main man now. He does everything but—" he let the sentence dangle. He was going to say "but wipe his ass." But she was such a lady, he couldn't . . . and anyway now that Mr. Lasher was so ill, Delroy probably did wipe him.

"Is Mr. Lasher's MS worse?"

"It's got his legs now. I haven't seen much of him since summer."

"Poor man."

"That's one thing he's not: poor." Mario laughed. But he felt badly for Len Lasher, too. A big wheeler-dealer like that suddenly crippled. It was sad. . . . Still, he ran Lasher Communications same as always. Even that very week, Lasher was working on a merger with Standard Broadcasting. Delroy had told Mario the MS only made him sharper: the legs might not work as well anymore, but the mind never stopped.

"Do you get along with Delroy?" Nell Slack asked.

"Well enough. He used to be this nerdy kid whose aunt owned Knitwits, a shop in the back of a hardware store in Sag Harbor. When she was sober, she taught knitting there. When she wasn't, Delroy'd teach it. Ten, eleven years old he could knit scarves, afghans, sweaters. By the time I met him he was busing tables at The American Hotel. They called him 'Needles.' His specialty was dog sweaters then."

Nell Slack chuckled. Mario liked that soft, happy sound. He liked telling her things. She was a good listener.

He said, "I remember Delroy when his aunt died and he didn't have rent money. Then one summer he caddied for Mrs. Lasher, and the next thing you knew he was working for them. They moved him into this little farmhouse down the road from Le Reve. Now he's part of the household."

"Lucky him."

"And he used to hate the rich," Mario said. "One time his aunt delivered four of his dog sweaters to this estate in Georgica. There was a cocktail party in progress. They asked her in and fed her martinis while they dressed their dachshunds in the sweaters. She left there soused and drove into a tree, probably died instantly. Delroy blamed them for her death."

"No wonder he hates them."

"He'd hang around this place called Dirty Eddy's on Newtown Lane where the workers all got coffee mornings. He'd try to find out more about the accident, who all was there, how it happened exactly. But nobody wanted to talk to him about it. Nobody'd ever talk to him, anyway. Only I would. I felt sorry for the poor schmuck. When he got with the Lashers and began hiring drivers he'd call me."

"You were nice to him, Mario."

"He never forgot. When they need a van at Le Reve, I get the job."

"And I bet you meet a lot of fascinating people."

"Don't bet on that, Miss Slack. Mostly I cart their luggage from the Hamptons to the airport and back. And every morning, Monday to Friday, I take their six-year-old daughter to Invictus, this private school he founded for her, so she doesn't have to mix with the riffraff. Then I pick her and her six little classmates up after school and drop them off . . . so much for fascinating people."

He told Nell Slack about the field trip the seven little girls went on, guess where, to Vienna! She began to laugh that soft way again and he stole glances at her face in the mirror.

He told her how Invictus had assigned a book called *My Dancing White Horse*—all seven little girls were crazy about horses—and after they read the book they were flown to see the famous white Lipizzaners and the site of the Spanish Riding School of Vienna, mentioned in the book.

"When I was a child," she said, "I loved horses, too. But of course I never owned one. I never dreamed of owning one. I just read about them."

"Deanie can't read enough horse stories," he said. "Naturally she's got her own pony. This man named Edward Candle gave it to her."

There was no reaction to his name. Last summer Candle has been arrested as a horse killer. It was in all the newspapers.

She began talking about *My Friend Flicka*. He couldn't remember the last time he'd actually listened to a woman, unless it was Lara Lasher giving him directions, or complaining about some petty disturbance the rich could always find to keep their lives from being perfect.

As he headed into LaGuardia she said, "My return flight is on Delta tomorrow night, nine o'clock from Richmond."

"Got it. Another fast trip, hmmm?"

"Yes. I hate these overnighters. One department store looks like another. I even forget what state I'm in sometimes. I like to think you'll be there when I get back."

She didn't have to say that.

"I look forward to it, too," he managed, his heart pounding suddenly.

When he helped her out of the van and handed her garment bag to her she looked all over his face. "Until tomorrow night, Mario."

"Yes, ma'am."

"You can call me Nell."

"I'll be waiting . . . Nell."

THREE

Nell Slack wheeled her garment bag into the terminal. She went past the Delta check-in and turned right to go down the escalator where incoming baggage was collected.

Liam was by the Rent-A-Car desk, frowning and pacing, even though she was early. When he looked up and saw her, he grinned and held out his arms.

If one had to guess, just by looking, who the Italian was—Mario or Liam—hands down, Liam would get the vote.

Mario had a small nose, light blue eyes and straight brown hair, but Liam Yeats had dark eyes and olive skin, curly black hair and a crooked nose.

Unlike Mario Rome, there was nothing soft about Liam, not in his eyes nor in his body, no paunch predictable in his future—he was too restless and high-strung. He had a suspicious, jealous nature, which was why he was familiar with most tranquilizers. Before his new affiliation with Affirm, an organization for positive thinkers, he had flirted with Scientology, astrology, and Buddhism.

His dark eyes lit up at the sight of Nell.

As he embraced her he said, "I can't wait for your hair to grow back. That's what I miss: that silky red hair!"

"Give it time, love. Take it step by step."

"How'd you do?" Liam asked.

"I know a little more about the houseman. His name is Delroy Davenport. I can't ask too many questions at one time."

Liam wheeled the garment bag. "The car's across the way. Section B. Anything we can use?"

"He wanted to talk a lot about Delroy this trip. I let him. He *did* tell me Deanie loves horse stories and has her own pony."

"I checked out Invictus," said Liam. "There are a fleet of workers over there already putting up Christmas decorations."

"Outside? I thought they didn't want any attention called to the place."

"The decorations are inside. Tomorrow see if Rome takes the same route to school every day. Can you do that?"

"Probably."

"See if he picks up and drops off the girls in the same order daily."

Nell Slack said, "Save it for now, sweetheart. I'm tired."

They ran through traffic to the underground garage while he said, "I've got us a nice room for the night at the Hyatt. Let's hurry. The luggage is heavy."

"That little garment bag is heavy?"

"My luggage," he said.

"Oh, that luggage. That luggage is always heavy." She reached for his free hand, swung it, and laughed with him.

FOUR

"Del? I'm going into the village for a few hours to Christmas-shop."

"Yes, Missus." Delroy Davenport was sitting in his nook (once a closet) outside the master bedroom, reading a copy of Patricia Highsmith's *This Sweet Sickness*. He read and reread her novels. Lara Lasher had no clue why.

"When Mr. Lasher wakes up, tell him I'll be back at four."

"I will, Missus."

Lara would never get used to male help in the upstairs, a few feet from the bedroom she used to share with Len. She had moved down the hall to the guest room, at his suggestion. He needed too much help now and he couldn't count on his bladder or his bowels.

Len did not want the hospital bed in the downstairs. He preferred to be out of sight to everyone except Delroy and the nurses. He was cautious about word of his condition spreading before the merger was set and signed. MS could explain some of what was happening to him, but he did not have MS. He had amyotrophic lateral sclerosis, commonly called Lou Gehrig's disease. There was no way to live long with ALS. There would have been no merger with Standard Broadcasting if it had been known that Len would not be around to run things.

Delroy had been sworn to secrecy. He was the only member of the household staff who knew the truth. Was that what made him sit there cracking his knuckles sometimes? He used to knit, but Deanie had hurt his feelings when he'd made her a scarf with a horse's head on it, and misspelled the name of Deanie's pony.

"You can't even spell Pécheresse!" she'd scolded him.

"I've never learned any French," he'd answered, red-faced, pained by her rudeness. "And I don't know what it means!"

"It means 'sinner'! I'm six years old and I know what it means!" (That little outburst was the last time Len had spanked Deanie.)

Edward Candle had named the pony. Who knew why he would call it that? Everything Candle did was a mystery to the Lashers. Since the revelation of his insurance scam Lara would not even allow Deanie to go to the Candles' house and play with Candace Candle.

Obviously Delroy needed something to do with his hands! He chewed his nails, too. Her drove Lara up the walls: always present like some giant, restless jungle animal.

Lara escaped into East Hampton Village a lot. In her thirty-seven years she had never imagined being tested this way. A short, thin brunette, she had not been a true beauty but she had always maintained that certain look women have who can afford top haircutters, designers, and personal trainers. She had a relaxed manner that came from a lifetime of knowing Daddy would take care of it. Then Len would. There had always been someone to take care of it . . . until now. Now, except for her therapist, there were only the servants, who didn't know Len's illness was not MS, but the fatal ALS.

She had told Dr. Mannerheim, "It's not just Len's death I can't imagine. I can't imagine not having anyone to count on. Lately, all I think about is what needs to be done."

Before she left for the village that day, there were a few more instructions, things to do Delroy knew enough to do without being reminded, but that was her way now: she gave the orders. Save for the petty details Delroy handled, she supervised everything. By the time she drove the white Range Rover into town, she would know Martha was in the kitchen preparing dinner, Andy was in the package room wrapping gifts that had to be mailed before the tenth of December, Deanie was with her friends at a matinee ending at four ten when Mario would pick her up in his van. Delroy would be with Len, bathing him when he awakened, dressing him in the dark suit she had laid out on the chaise: the suit, the underwear, dark socks, white shirt with the striped silk tie from Polo, white Belgium linen handkerchief, and handmade John Lobb shoes.

"Delroy?" she said. "Anything I can get you from the village? Do you have enough to read?"

"Thank you, Missus. I do."

"Oh, and Del? Tell Mr. Lasher that Mario is free tomorrow to drive him around to stores." She flashed a smile at Delroy. "Mr. Lasher likes to do his own Christmas shopping. He'll tell you what he wants, and you can bring it out to the car for him to see."

"On Sunday, Missus?"

"I know. You never miss church. But stores like Eileen Fisher are open now Sunday afternoons, and some I'll call. They'll open for Mr. Lasher."

"I could drive him in the Jeep myself, Missus."

"No, you'll need Mario." She rarely let Delroy take the Jeep. He had too many privileges as it was.

"Fine, Missus."

Not really fine. Delroy was always pushing to drive the Jeep, and he disliked sharing his care of Len with anyone.

But Len took to Mario because Deanie did. Deanie said Mario could do impressions, talk just like Daddy, whose *r*'s were *w*'s (a slight flaw that had always endeared Len to Lara). Mario could pull dimes out of his ears, too. He made Deanie laugh.

So never mind that Delroy would rather be the only one to take Len shopping. At this stage in Len's illness, there needed to be two men along in the car anyway, one to sit beside Len: Delroy, who was younger and stronger. And Mario, who drove better.

"Missus?"

"What?"

"Won't Mario notice the Mister's speech? It's got worse."

"Good point! Call the Hampton Jitney limo instead. That has a window between the driver and the passengers. The driver can wait outside while you bring the merchandise to Mr. Lasher. Thank you for calling that to my attention."

"It's my job to protect the Mister, Missus."

"Yes, and you're good at it, Del."

"I am. I know I am, Missus. That's all I think about."

"Well, toodle-loo, toodle-loo," Lara called out, remembering how Len had loved her saying that, how early in their courtship he had said, "Who says 'toodle-loo' anymore? Only you do and I love that farewell of yours! It's rare."

She'd laughed and said, "Only you say it's 'ware.'"

FIVE

Delroy was still thinking about something that had happened over a month ago. On a rare night off on Thanksgiving, Delroy saw her in a bar on the waterfront at Hampton Bays.

Hampton Bays wasn't really the Hamptons, which was why Delroy liked it. People didn't know him there. None of the locals there had known him when he was a zero called "Needles." Back then he was this outcast whose Amish parents had disowned him, a nerd living with his aunt, knitting dog sweaters, busing tables, driving carts down the greens, always on the fringe of life.

His favorite place in Hampton Bays was where fisherman and truck drivers hung out, open every day of the year, even Christmas. The owner sold bait and gas out back.

Women didn't often go into By The Bay, and those who did never looked like this one. She was no movie star, but she had a certain bold style. She was dramatic, throwing her head back and letting go this loud laugh. Silky blond hair held back with a red scarf, long, slender legs, the nose just a bit long, the mouth wide with straight white teeth. She wasn't a local, for sure, and the young fellow she was with got proofed before the bartender would serve him.

At first Delroy figured it was her son. He'd arrived before her: watching the door, waiting for her, then jumping up to embrace her.

"You're late, Scotti!"

"No, Max, you're early. You're always early. You're compulsive!" chucking him under the chin, a good foot taller than he was.

But as Delroy watched them, he knew they weren't related. They were too involved, always touching and grinning at each other. As he studied them in the bar mirror he wondered if they were lovers. They laughed a lot and drank a lot, and got stared at by the lone losers drinking there on a holiday night.

Forbidden love intrigued Delroy. He imagined they had sneaked away to be together: this kid with the slick black hair, wearing a navy blazer, white shirt, and red bow tie. Her with a skirt showing her knees.

Delroy was fascinated by them, and when they finally left the place, so did he.

The kid got into a 1940s-style station wagon, the kind with real wood sides. She had a black Saturn. The kid gave a toot to his horn, backed out, and headed west, while she sat behind the wheel for a moment. Then she started the engine and drove straight into a post in front of the place.

Delroy walked across to her car, motioned for her to roll down the window, and said, "Where are you going?"

"Eas Hampin." Too drunk to pronounce it, but she had this deep, sexy voice. Marlene Dietrich in that old movie Delroy had seen on tape, when she'd sung, "See what the boys in the back room will have—"

"I'm going to East Hampton myself. You better leave your car and let me drive you there. If the cops get you on a DWI you'll be sorry."

He had to help her. Pour her into the front seat of the Lashers' Jeep, on one of the few times he had permission to drive it. Lara Lasher knew Delroy had no Thanksgiving invitation. She felt sorry for him, and guilty that they occupied so much of his free time. How could he have any friends?

"Thank you, *chéri,*" the woman said.

"I had an aunt who drove drunk. These people let her. She got into an accident and died."

"Sorry to hear that."

He snapped on the radio.

She said, "I owe you big for this."

"You don't owe me anything."

He glanced at her. Even drunk she had a classy way and an authority to her voice when she wasn't slurring.

"My name is Delroy Davenport."

"I'm Scotti."

"Have you got a last name?"

"Not right now." She chuckled. "But I'm glad you came along." She put her long fingers on his knee. "I've always depended on the kindness of strangers," another husky chuckle.

"Thanks, Leroy." Her hand went back to her lap.

"Delroy, not Leroy. Was that your boyfriend?"

"Max? Nooooo."

"I thought maybe you were robbing the cradle."

"He's my dear old pal." Slurring, thick-tongued.

"Where in East Hampton?" he asked, fearing she would pass out before she could tell him the address.

"Springs. You know Springs?"

"Sure."

She hummed along with the song on the radio, and then her head fell against his shoulder.

He let her sleep. Southampton. Bridgehampton. He waited until they had left East Hampton Village and were near Springs Fireplace Road.

"Where do you live in Springs?" he shouted at her.

She sat up straight. "I have to go," she said. "Wee wee."

He pulled over where there was an empty field.

"Go ahead," he said. "I'll wait for you."

She opened the door of the Jeep and sat there. He realized she probably couldn't get down without help so he told her he'd come around and offer a hand.

"Don't!"

"You'll fall," he said.

"I can manage," she said.

"I'll help you find a place," he said. "I won't look."

The moon was full and bright, and he could see clearly as he jumped down from the Jeep and went around to her side, in time to see her peeing.

"Oh, my God!"

She said, "Don't say I didn't warn you." She brushed her hair back with her hand, the hand that wasn't holding a tiny, fat penis, her skirt hiked up, legs apart, high heels dangling.

He got back into the driver's seat and waited for her to shut her door. He was perspiring, his heart thumping.

"Don't say I didn't warn you," she said again.

"Did you finish peeing?"

"Yes," and she pulled the door shut.

After he started the car he said, "Did you have something done or were you born that way?"

"I'm a transsexual," she said. "I'm a work in progress."

She pronounced it "pwog gwess," sounding like the Mister.

Delroy said, "I can't believe this!"

"I gathered as much."

"My God!"

"Cork it," she snapped.

"I just never had something like this happen."

"Neither did I, Leroy. Neither did I."

"Delroy."

"What difference does it make? Leave me on the corner of Accabonac Road and Old Stone Highway."

"On the corner? You can hardly walk."

"I'm sobering up. Fast."

"You know it doesn't matter to me."

"That I'm sobering up?"

"I mean what you are. It doesn't matter to me that you're a transvestite."

"I'm not a transvestite. I'm a transsexual."

"Whatever you are. That's your business."

"Do you know the corner of Acabonac and Old Stone?"

"Of course."

"Let me off there, please, thank you."

They drove in silence for a while. She lived somewhere near Green River Cemetery, where many artists were buried. That was where Mr. Lasher wanted to be buried. Delroy was arranging things there for him. When Mr. Lasher could still get about he'd bought a half acre behind Jackson Pollock's grave.

Delroy glanced across at her. She was staring straight ahead. At School Street she said, "Turn right."

"I know the way."

She sighed and he said, "Well, they did a good job on you. You would have fooled me except—"

"All right. Enough."

He stopped where she'd said to and with a little effort she got the door open and jumped down. She turned around.

"This never happened," she said.

"I don't think I'll ever forget it."

"We're never going to see each other again."

"I was just doing you a favor. I don't care about any of it. It's not my business."

"You got that right."

"How the heck did I know?"

"Keep your shirt on," she said in a softer voice. "I appreciate what you did. Thank you. OK?"

He was leaning over, looking down at her.

"OK," he said.

He reached across and helped her shut the door. He waited while she walked, only a slight stagger.

He headed off Old Stone Highway onto Neck Path, shaking his head, knowing he'd never forget that night. Never forget her. Him. Herhim.

He was remembering it all yet again when he heard the Mister.

"Water, please!" (wa wa eese!)

"I'm coming, sir."

"Where's Mrs. Lasher?" (issus ash?)

"Shopping, sir. She'll be back by five."

"Read to me?" (eed ew ee?)

"Yes, sir," said Delroy.

Delroy was a Patricia Highsmith fan. He even had two old letters from her, sent from Switzerland. When he'd read her obituary in the *New York Times* he had wept, cut it out, and put it inside his Bible with a single rose he'd bought at Wittendale Florist.

Lasher used to call Highsmith "Lowsmith." He would say, "Let's see what kind of weirdo Lowsmith's got up her sleeve for us this time!"

The Mister probably enjoyed her books because they took his mind off his troubles. But Delroy liked them because of all the characters who did unexpected things and were out of step. They comforted him. He felt out of step himself, but not that far out. Not as far out as Edward Candle, who looked and talked like a mild-mannered college professor, all the while hiring thugs to kill horses for the insurance. Highsmith would have understood Candle. Delroy wasn't sure she would have understood Scotti.

He propped the Mister up against the pillows and sat beside him.

"Aceyar ooday?"

Mr. Lasher was asking if Delroy had gone to the graveyard that day, to make the secret arrangements. It was easier when he used his machine to talk for him, but it took too long. Anyway, Delroy already knew what had to be done at the cemetery.

"I'm taking care of it, sir," he said.

Delroy had been up at Green River several times, not just to be sure everything was shaping up as the Mister wanted it. Delroy knew Scotti lived somewhere near there, but he didn't know where yet. He was always hoping for some sort of serendipity that would bring them together.

SIX

The moment Scotti walked in the door, her mother said, "Someone very rich is going to die soon. You should see what's going on at the graveyard."

"Uh-huh. Did anyone call named Mario Rome?"

"Is he the one you met in your writers' workshop?"

"Yes, Mother." She was forty-eight, back living at home since she had begun dressing as a female full-time. She regretted that she lived there every time she walked through the front door. Immediately she was blasted with the latest news from the Green River Cemetery next door. Her mother walked Baba, the bulldog, there daily, and she had become the graveyard's Liz Smith, filled with gossip about the Hamptonites people joked were "dying" to get into the prestigious cemetery on Accabonac. "Mario Rome said he'll come for you at eight o'clock," Mrs. House said. "Did you hear what I said about someone rich dying?"

"Who?"

"I said *someone*. If I knew I'd tell you. This lovely young man was there with some gardeners from Hrens, making very elaborate arrangements."

Scotti put her Dana Buchman coat on a hanger and stuck some Christmas-wrapped packages up on the closet shelf. Then off with her boots.

Her mother said, "I heard whoever's dying bought a lot of land behind Jackson Pollock's grave. He's going to landscape the whole area. Pine trees, bushes. This young man was asking Hrens if they could put in flowering plants with little notice."

Myrna House took a drag on her cigarette and continued, "I heard him say whoever he works for could hang on until spring or die at any moment." She blew a smoke ring straight at Scotti. Three years ago Scotti had given up smoking when she was having her beard removed, each hair blasted with electricity over the dozens of hours it took, after the year of electrology on the arms, hands, back, and stomach.

"I know this young man and Mr. X are very rich for another reason and that is that Baba didn't bark at him," her mother said. "You know what a snob Baba is. He barks his head off at the colored, the poor, and anyone speaking any language but English. We went by a funeral for this major artist last month and Baba was like a little lamb."

Baba looked up from the rug when he heard his name, opened his eyes, closed them, heaved a rapturous sigh, and let his head collapse back on the doggie bed.

"I have to take a bath and get ready for my date," Scotti said.

"You have an hour and a half but no time for me."

"I don't want to hear cemetery gossip tonight, Mother. Tell me something else."

"What happens around here? Nothing. Every single friend of mine is in Florida now."

"You can go to Florida."

"And leave you at Christmas? It was bad enough when I left you at Thanksgiving. You had a hangover when I called the next day. You said so yourself. Drinking with Max Bernstein. No wonder! You sounded like death warmed over."

Death warmed over wasn't even close, Scotti thought. Her mother slid her eyeglasses back on her white-haired head and snapped off the six o'clock TV news using the remote. Her feet were propped up on the footstool, in the red booties similar to the ones she was knitting for Scotti's daughter.

Scotti said, "I'd like you to go to Florida, Mother. I'll be just fine."

"Who is this Mario Rome?"

"I hardly know him. I told you: he's in my writers' workshop. He seems like a nice fellow . . . You could go to Sarasota. You loved it there last year."

"Last year Ellie Foxworth was alive. I'm not going to Florida by myself."

"You have other friends there."

"They're with their families. People spend holidays with their families. That's why I spend Thanksgiving with Emma and Jessica."

Mrs. House was not fond of her daughter-in-law. She had never been able to understand why her handsome son had waited so long to get married and then chosen this fat female fifteen years younger. Emma was the only reason she continued to see Jessica.

Scotti said, "Okay. We'll have a nice Christmas. Then, if you'd like to go to Florida, go." Scotti picked her bag up and started upstairs.

"Is this Mario Rome an Eyetalian?"

"I guess he is."

"Watch it! Eyetalian men are all over you, right off the bat."

"Are you speaking from experience?"

"I've been told that in Italy they walk down the street grabbing their crotches."

"I'll have to take my chances."

"It could turn ugly, Scott, if he finds out."

"He's not going to find out!" What happened at Thanksgiving was never going to happen again. Even though Scotti could not remember all of it, she remembered the tall red-headed man coming around the side of the Jeep, then exclaiming "My God!"

Mrs. House said, "This Mario Rome said to dress for bowling."

"What?"

"That's what he said. You seem to drift toward lowlifes, never mind how you try to change yourself."

"There's not that much to do out here in winter, I guess."

"What happened to a good movie and dinner?"

"That sounds fine with me, but I didn't ask him out, he asked me out. He gets to choose."

"What happened to inviting a man home to dinner?"

"Someday I might."

"If a man meets me at least he'll know you're from an ordinary family, much like anyone else's."

"Instead of from another planet?'

"Well? People don't think of your kind coming from just folks. I'm only trying to help you out, Scott."

"I appreciate it."

Scotti did, too, never mind the slings and arrows that accompanied the concern. Few members of Metamorphs, her support group, got help of any kind from a parent. Hysterics, threats, banishment was the usual treatment, and it rarely changed with time.

When Scotti went into Manhattan for Metamorph sessions she heard all the horror stories. Her own father's farewell letter seemed mild by comparison, although his adamant rejection of her new identity had crushed her as well as shocked her. As brilliant as he was, Bolton House could not understand transsexuality. He felt somehow insulted that she was giving up her male identity. The anger he felt she had expected from her mother, not him.

In the beginning Mrs. House was more bewildered than belligerent. She said she should never have let Scott dress up when he was little, try on her hats, shoes, carry around her handbags. She said she should have made him play sports more, get his nose out of those books. He was too much like his father, Myrna House had thought. Then, when the truth was out, she blamed Jessica. It never would have happened if Jessica had gone on a diet and made herself more attractive. Jessica, she said, was the one who made Scott queer first, and next this hybrid.

She shouted after Scotti, "You could watch the news with me, you know. Why do you always go up to your bedroom?"

"Because I have so little time to read, Mother. And I don't want to die of secondary smoke inhalation." Max had recommended a book called *The Master Key*, but Scotti couldn't get past a scene in the middle where a child was kidnapped. It was too graphic and grievous. She usually liked the same authors Max did. Thea Astley, Barbara Vine, Elizabeth Jolley.

Her mother's clock cuckooed seven times.

Bowling! Even when she was Scott she had always avoided bowling and bowling alleys!

Mario had told everyone in the Ashawagh Hall Writers' Workshop that he was working on a murder mystery. It was set in the late nineties, when he'd owned The Magic C in New York City. The title of his book was *Recovering from Cynthia*. It was about an ex-girlfriend who had swindled him.

In the late '70s Scott had sneaked off to discos and gay clubs, looking for himself. At the same time he was reading everything he could find about transsexuals, beginning with Christine Jorgensen's sex change. Jorgensen's surgeon had become so swamped with applications for operations once the news broke in 1952, the Danish government finally restricted the procedure to Danish applicants.

For many years Scott could not admit to himself that it was the only solution to his own plight.

Scotti had been surprised when Mario Rome came into the library a few afternoons ago, said something about tickets, a "charity thing," ending with, "No big deal. We'll just be a pair of writers out looking at life together."

She could handle that.

He'd told her he was returning books for a friend: Len Lasher.

That was a name everyone at the East Hampton Library knew. Mr. Lasher was a big contributor to the library. An honorary building patron, although he never attended planning meetings. But his checks arrived in the mail regularly. Every now and then someone would point out a write-up about him in *Fortune*, or *Barron's*, *Time*, *New York* magazine, *Newsweek*. It was always passed around to the employees.

Len Lasher, who pronounced Rockefeller "Wockefeller" and claimed he wasn't "wealy wich," disarmed you with his baby speech and tycoon ambitions.

Le Reve, the huge brick Tudor house on The Highway Behind The Pond, was often pointed out to tourists fascinated by celebrity.

Scotti's interest in Lasher stemmed from the Candle case. The actual horse killer had plea-bargained, told all, and Candle was forced to plead guilty. His sentencing was still pending.

Many of the cases Jessica worked on, and a few Scotti had helped her with, were never really over for Scotti when they ended. She was always intrigued with any follow-ups, even if it meant little more than keeping track of the principals in newspapers, on the Internet, and on TV.

Candle's little girl, Candace, often came to the library's story hour, as the Lasher child did.

If Scotti actually did end up at the East Hampton Bowl that night, the idea that Mario had some connection with the Lashers would be part of the draw. She was still curious about Edward Candle, whom she'd first seen last summer at the Hampton Classic.

Scotti was her mother's child, too, despite the family consensus that it was Bolton House she was most like. From him she'd acquired her love of reading, her appreciation of wine, a quieter, more WASP-y feel for life than Myrna House's, but people, and people's secrets, held Scotti in thrall the same way her mother was captivated by the inhabitants of the Green River Cemetery.

SEVEN

When Mario handed over the tickets at the door, he was given two wicker baskets with red and green ribbons tied to the handles. Inside, nestled atop a white linen napkin, was a box lunch of crustless turkey sandwiches, pate and crackers, fruit, cheese, and cookies, and a throwaway camera that took twenty-seven pictures. There was also a white, cone-shaped paper hat with HAMPTON HOME BENEFIT written down the side in red.

"We don't have to bowl," Mario said. "I thought it might be fun here tonight."

"It looks like it will be."

Scotti was relieved, delighted, sorry she hadn't worn her good gabardine pants and a cashmere sweater instead of the jeans she had on with a cotton pullover from the Gap.

She wished she'd worn more makeup, too. She was careful to be conservative in East Hampton. MTF transsexuals often overdid it in the beginning. Scotti saved the impulse to let herself go for visits with Max Bernstein and his wife, or nights alone at the opera with Max.

The bowling alley was decorated with balloons and streamers, several Christmas trees with tiny gold lights, and many evergreen wreaths with red bows.

Mario had on an old tweed jacket with gray flannel pants. He'd said,

"I got these tickets from a friend." He checked her coat and led her into the alleys.

She liked his looks. She liked men who had handsome, weathered faces and bodies no longer that slender but not heavy, either. Dr. Bolton House had been rail thin and pale-faced, his rimless glasses always slipping down his nose. Scott had been this beanpole kid who later joined a gym in his teens. He'd done everything to look and act like a male. He never felt like one, though. At first, Jessica was the only one he told that to. She claimed it was all in his head, and he'd answered, "That's the problem."

While Mario went to get their drinks, Scotti looked the crowd over. She doubted even one of them had ever been in the Hampton Bowl before this evening. Some of them were actually bowling. A few women giggled as they slid partway down the alleys with the balls still stuck to their fingers.

The men were more intense, but no less amateurish.

Mario waited about an hour before he let it drop that it was Len Lasher who'd passed on the tickets.

"He's not a friend. I shouldn't have said he was. I work for him, chauffeuring. Part-time."

"What's he like?"

"He's pleasant enough. Self-absorbed, like the rich are. But now he's got MS. It's slowed him down. Still, over at Le Reve they say he just swung the biggest deal of his life, with Standard Broadcasting. He always comes out on top."

Scotti bowled a bit, badly, and so did Mario. They ate the supper in their baskets while he blamed himself for ending up alone in life. She liked his honesty.

He said, "There was a time when I thought I was the car I drove, the clothes I wore, and the women I took out. It was all surface. So were the women I was attracted to. Except one. Cynthia. She was deeper. She took off with my entire savings. I went to pieces. There weren't that many pieces, either. I was on the shallow side."

Then he waited. It was Scotti's turn. She told him as much as she dared: that she'd married someone the opposite of her, an insurance investigator who didn't smoke or drink (except on special occasions) or dance . . . someone who'd never liked discos, someone always settled, while she'd been wild and immature for far too long.

"It's hard for me to imagine you wild and immature," Mario said. "What's your book about?"

"I just finished an article on the wines of the Languedoc, in France. I have to get back to the book. But talking about it sabotages it for me."

"I know what you mean."

How could she talk about it? It was mostly about Scott: how he always knew he was in the wrong body, how he always felt a stranger looked back at him in the mirror, and how he was attracted to other males, but unable to be excited by two male bodies together. Gay men Scott knew had called him "homophobic." That was a favorite accusation for anyone with gender conflict.

"Let me know when you read in class. I don't want to miss it," Mario said.

"I don't know if I can read aloud."

"You don't have to, but it helps. I was in the class last year and after I began to read aloud I began to really work."

The woman who ran the workshop wrote a brief comment after she read four chapters of Scotti's memoir.

Your conundrum (of course you've read the Jan Morris memoir called that?) almost works but we need more show and less tell. *Out of the Night* is not a good title for this, either . . . Rose Tremain wrote a novel some years back about a female to male switch, *Sacred Country*. Worth reading. And you should read aloud in class, Scotti. Don't worry about subject matter. It's not a judgmental group. But if you're shy in that way, you can always say it's fiction and not a memoir.

They talked over the noise of the crowd, standing by themselves, leaning against a wooden railing overlooking the alleys.

Suddenly a woman called out "Mario?" and then snapped his picture with one of the cameras they all had.

She had practically no hair, but she had great bones and style. The haircut seemed deliberate, not the result of chemotherapy. She had on jeans, pointy-toed cowboy boots, and a lacy peasant blouse. Large gold hoops in pierced ears. A fat leather belt cinching her waist.

Mario introduced Scotti to Nell Slack.

He seemed amazed to see her there.

"But you gave me a ticket," she protested.

"I gave you two. I thought—"

"That I'd come with someone?"

"Yes. Or call. Something."

"I should have," she said.

His face was red. "I never dreamed . . ." In an instant Scotti saw his eyes soften, saw that he was stunned and dazzled by this woman.

"I'm very late, too," Nell Slack said. "I'm sorry, Mario." She put her basket on a chair, grinning up at him. He was shuffling his feet and looking everywhere but into her eyes.

"This is Scotti House," he said again.

Then Nell Slack understood that he'd brought Scotti there.

"Oh, dear," she said to him. And oddly, stepped back and snapped another picture of him.

"Look," he said, his composure coming back weakly. "Let's the three of us enjoy ourselves."

"I can't stay, really," she said. "I just popped in to say hi!"

"Did you drive yourself?"

"Yes."

"But have a drink with us," Mario insisted.

Scotti excused herself and went back to the ladies' room, by the bar.

She combed her hair and washed her hands, stalling while she thought of what she should do. Leave. Obviously she was in the way.

She took her time and when she went back, Nell Slack was gone.

Mario threw up his hands in a helpless gesture. "I screwed that one up, all right."

"Is she someone you're interested in, Mario? You can tell me. We're just two writers out on the town, no strings."

"Thanks." But his face was crestfallen, eyes sad.

Scotti realized she'd left her bag back on the sink. Even after all these years wearing female attire, she still often forgot her bag. She went to retrieve it, and when she emerged this time she saw Nell Slack again. Nell was down at the other end of the bar, in a corner. A tall, black-haired fellow was helping her into a brown suede coat. He led her toward the door, his arm firmly around her waist.

Scotti watched them leave and then returned to Mario.

"Did your friend say she came alone?"

"No, but I'm sure she did."

"I like her looks, Mario."

"So do I."

From where Mario and Scotti stood there was no view of the bar or the door.

Fast worker, Scotti thought, but didn't really believe Nell Slack had just met someone there. And what was all the picture taking about?

"She hires my van sometimes when she's traveling. She's a product demonstrator in department stores," Mario said. "I think there's some kind of spark there. Maybe I imagined it." He chuckled.

"She did go out of her way to take your picture."

"That she did. That she did."

Scotti relaxed and began to enjoy herself. She could use a friend, and that was what he was going to be.

EIGHT

Later, when he drove her home, they listened to music on the radio. A golden oldies station. Suddenly the Village People were singing an old disco number from Scotti's teens: "YMCA."

Scotti could almost smell the dirty-socks aroma of poppers, and see the boys in flannel shirts and tight, ripped jeans, their faces joyful and sweaty, bodies gyrating, everyone singing along under the dancing beams of light on the crowded floor.

Scott had lived in those clubs as a teenager, lying about his age, telling no one, all the while feeling that it was the one place where he felt free. It was never sex he was searching for.

Years later, after he met Jessica, who was one of his students before they became close friends, he told her about it. She claimed that was proof Scott wasn't gay, that both she and Scott were just undersexed. When Scott would complain that he hated his body, Jessica would say, so did she hate hers.

She'd say, "Forget our bodies! They make us miserable!"

Thanks to his friendship with Jessica, his age, and the advent of AIDS, Scott began avoiding the discos, leather bars, and the uptown "bird circuit," where all the gay bars were named after birds.

He spent most of his time with Jessica, and finally gave in to her wish to get married and have a child.

After Emma was born, Scott accepted a position as headmaster at Regis School for Boys. Students and faculty both were buzzing about a professor in the science department named Virgil Loeper. A father of three, married for fifteen years, with a PhD, he was in the process of becoming Virginia Loeper—Ginny.

In his letter, "To All Concerned," he spoke of the Allen Institute, where he belonged to the Metamorphs.

Scott would see Loeper around campus: this dowdy, bespectacled, fiftyish "female" who dressed in severe dark women's suits, with gray hair pulled back in a bun, carrying her briefcase, calling back greetings to students in her deep voice.

Without speaking to Loeper about it, Scott soon made an appointment with Dr. Marvin Rush, who headed the institute. Jessica pleaded with Scott not to go ahead with it, accusing him of self-hatred, imploring him to just accept what he was without becoming "a freak."

"I'm already about as freaky as anyone can get."

"You have a responsibility to Emma."

"I have a responsibility to let Emma know no matter what any of us become, we'll always love each other. That's what family is all about."

Then Scott entered the Gender Identity Program, and for the first time encountered others like him. He was amazed to find there were few young men in the program, and most of the ones his age and older were not handsome or even slightly effeminate; more often they were large, burly fellows whose secret no one would guess.

Before he was accepted for gender reassignment, Dr. Rush guided Scott, exploring his stability, clearing up any misconceptions or extravagant expectations. For two years, once he began taking hormones, the only time he did not dress as a woman was when he visited Emma. The headmaster at the Regis School made some crack about Scott "catching it" from Ginny Loeper, but he did not fire him. He simply wouldn't renew Scott's contract. Scott began depilatory treatments, the estrogen he'd taken softening the beard enough to make the electrolysis less painful. He continued twice-weekly sessions with Rush, supporting himself by editing textbooks.

"You could stop now, Scotti," Rush said when nearly everything was done but the genital surgery. "For some it's enough just to be living life as a female, or a male. There are pre-ops who have no intention of becoming post-ops."

"You mean the campy Chicks With Dicks?"

"I've heard of them. I don't mean them, Scotti."

"I'm going to take all the steps. I'm not a transvestite."

Dr. Rush said, "It's odd that some transsexuals look down on the transvestites, the transvestites look down on the transsexuals, the homosexuals figure they're a peg above both of you, and the heterosexuals think all of you are freaks."

"I don't look down on anyone," said Scotti, "and right now I'm not any of those. I'm half-and-half."

Rush passed Scott an envelope. "Always carry this letter from me, in case you're ever in an accident or a situation requiring sex verification. You'll need it until you're a post-op. But start now to establish your new identity. A driver's license, charge cards, that sort of thing."

The letter announced that Scotti House was a member of the Allen Institute Metamorphism Program for Gender Reassignment. She was becoming a female.

It was the beginning of the end of Scott.

The genital surgery could have followed a year later. But three more years had passed and Scotti was still in debt from the breast-implant surgery, the work on her face and neck, and the expense of her wardrobe. Ernest Leogrande, MD, of Trinidad, Colorado, was the best surgeon, the only one Scotti wanted to operate. He had given Max the two requisite mastectomies, and the penis Max was so proud of.

Until Scotti could afford Leogrande she would pay off her credit cards, live with her mother, work at the library, and edit textbooks. She might even finish her memoir.

When the song finished playing over the radio in Mario's van, Scotti said, "I haven't heard that one in a long, long time."

"'YMCA.' That was the fag anthem," Mario said. "Sometimes some of them would come to The Magic C for our Sunday afternoon buffets. That was one song they always liked. That and Irene Cara singing 'Fame,' with that line: 'We're going to live forever' . . . ironic, seeing what happened to so many of them."

Finally, they were at her mother's house. Mario climbed down from the van and rushed around to the passenger side to help Scotti out.

On the doorstep he grinned down at her. "I can't imagine you ever hanging out in discos."

"I've changed."

"I hope I have, too. Do you want to have drinks or dinner occasionally? Winters are deadly out here."

"Sure."

"I'll call you."

She wouldn't have encouraged him if she'd thought he was even remotely interested, or vice versa.

She didn't want a romantic relationship until after Step One: the surgery.

Step Two was meeting someone you knew you would be taking Step Three with, sooner or later. Step Three was what Metamorphs called "outing" yourself.

Jessica had wanted to try living with Scotti for as long as possible. They had never been very active sexually, so that would not be missed. But Scotti felt it would be too hard for Emma to accept. Scotti just hadn't imagined, ever, that their daughter wouldn't even want to talk on the telephone with her.

Transsexuals who married seemed to be happiest when they'd known their partners before the reconstructive surgery. Usually their partners supported them through the ordeal, wanted it for them as much as they wanted it for themselves.

Max Bernstein, for example. He'd met his wife, Helen, at Smith College, fallen in love with her, and agreed with her they did not want to live as lesbians. Max swore he could only be happy as a male, and Helen just wanted Max, whatever he was. Courts in New York State did not recognize sex-changed individuals as legal marriage partners.

But the Bernsteins were happy as clams, except for two major flaws Max said Helen had.

The first was her aversion to opera, which Max adored. Particularly Wagner, who Max suspected had cross-dressed. Max had presented a paper on Wagner's famous "Letters to a Seamstress" at Metamorphs. It was about Wagner's legendary fondness for costumes, satins, and silks.

Helen Bernstein's other imperfection was the reason Max had gotten so bombed with Scotti on Thanksgiving. Helen was a terrible cook. Even something as uncomplicated as turkey was a disaster in Helen's hands.

NINE

It was the afternoon of Christmas Eve and the Thacker Quartet was playing at the library. But that wasn't the real reason for the crowd that was gathering near three o'clock. Jack Burlingame was reading from his latest thriller, *You'll Die at Christmas, Carolyn*. Burlingame was not a local, so this was a special occasion. More people arrived than had been expected. Most of the librarians were rushing around finding extra chairs.

Scotti was left alone at the front desk, checking out books beyond the time she was required to. A line had formed, and at the end of it, there he stood—the man who'd brought her home from Hampton Bays on Thanksgiving night.

She remembered very little about that ride. If he had told her his name, she did not remember it. But who could forget the size of him, the beaky nose, and the fire color of his hair? At the end of Thanksgiving evening, after Scotti and Max had left the Bernsteins' to have a drink at By The Bay, they'd noticed him standing at the bar.

"Look at the schnoz on that guy," Max had remarked. "Remember my old nose?"

"All I remember is your boobs." Scotti had laughed. "I'd have killed for them!"

Max was the only post-op still in the program. The Metamorphs liked to tease Max about using the support group solely to bitch about his wife's cooking. Helen simply did not have a talent for it. The reason Scotti and Max had left the Bernsteins' was the argument that had ensued after Helen served the guests a turkey that bled when Max carved it. Max was furious. He had muttered to Helen (but everyone there had heard), "After all I've gone through for you, you could at least learn to cook!"

Like most FTM Metamorphs, the change made Max look younger than thirty-six. He looked so much like a kid, the bartender had carded him.

It had been eons since Scotti had had that much to drink, and that little to eat. Not only was the turkey inedible, but the sweet potatoes were rock hard, the creamed onions were burned, and the salad was soggy from being overdressed.

The next day, Scotti had her first blackout in years. She had awakened on her bed, fully clothed, hungover, her Saturn, she found out after making a few phone calls, still in the parking lot in Hampton Bays.

All Max could tell her about the evening was that he had the fight with Helen, a great time in the bar with Scotti, and at the end they had waved good-bye as Scotti got into her Saturn. Max didn't remember seeing the redhead with the big nose in the parking lot.

The keys to her Saturn were in her coat pocket. She took a taxi to By The Bay, and saw that she must have hit a post there. She got into her car and drove back to East Hampton, trying hard to remember anything about the man.

She only remembered having to urinate, being unable to get down from the Jeep, then his exclamation: "Oh, my God!"

She had another blurry recollection of stumbling toward her mother's house, grateful that her mother was at Jessica's.

Had he put her out of the car? Or had she summoned forth the good sense not to let him see where she lived?

Then he was standing in front of her, at the library desk.

"Well, hel-lo," he said.

"Hello."

He put down a Ruth Rendell book, and pushed an old copy of *Edith's Diary* toward her. A Patricia Highsmith that was oddly without a murder in it. On top of the book, he placed the plastic library tag, saying, "This is one of the few books of hers I don't own." Then softly, searching her eyes before she could look away, "And how are you today?"

"Fine, thanks."

The computer produced the name Len Lasher.

She looked up at him. "This isn't yours."

"I work for Mr. Lasher. I'm his manager."

"Usually Mario Rome checks out books for him."

"Usually. My name is Delroy Davenport, if you remember."

"I don't. I'm sorry, Mr. Davenport."

"I never figured you for a librarian."

As the date registered on the book slip, he said, "I thought you might be in show business."

"We've never met, Mr. Davenport."

"I know. It didn't happen . . . but it did."

"You've made a mistake. I'm so sorry." She smiled briefly at him.

He shrugged, a smile tipping his lips. "I wondered if we'd meet again."

Scotti could feel the rush of blood from her neck to her face.

"Have you read *Edith's Diary?*" he asked.

"No."

"There's a line in it I like. It won't take me long to find it. It might appeal to you, too. I'll try to locate it." He began turning pages.

"Not now, please. We're very rushed now. The desk is closed, too."

The Thacker Quartet was playing "Hark, the Herald Angels Sing."

"I'd like to stay for the Christmas program," he said, "but I'm expected back at Le Reve."

"Too bad."

"Did you have a Thanksgiving program, too?"

She kept her eyes down. "No, we didn't."

"Some people prefer that holiday."

"I suppose some do."

"I certainly do. I have good memories of it. Is there a men's here?"

She pointed to the unisex bathroom near the reference room.

"Thank you, Scotti," he said. "I didn't get your last name."

"House."

"Scotti . . . House." He said it as though he were committing valuable information to memory.

She went down to the end of the counter and shuffled some papers. She watched him lumber toward the bathroom. She had planned to stay to hear the quartet, but that would be impossible now.

Max had said, "You were lucky he was going your way. Did everything go okay?"

She hadn't wanted to tell Max. He would feel responsible, and he already felt bad about the dinner Helen had ruined. They had invited their neighbors, who knew nothing about Max's transformation. They wouldn't have dreamed that Max had been born May Bernstein, and that sitting across from him was the former Scott House.

Max and Scotti had known each other for eighteen years. They were best friends.

Although they lived only about an hour's drive from each other, they didn't get together very often. Max was a computer expert who traveled constantly, helping corporations update their equipment.

Younger, they sometimes hung out together, drinking buddies in gay bars. The handsome boy and the tomboy girl. Both pretended to each other they were gay. Anything beyond that they denied, even to themselves.

"It's like old times," Scotti remembered Max saying at the bar in Hampton Bays.

And it was. Too much like old times.

A blackout like old times.

A stranger like old times.

That hadn't happened to Scott very often. He had never hunted for a male partner, for any partner.

But there were occasions when he had drunk too much and given in to an insistent sexual suitor.

It always shamed him.

It was after one such encounter that he had agreed with Jessica: they should get married.

TEN

"You know I don't like pink!" Myrna House whined. "I never wear it."

"I didn't know you didn't like it, Mother."

"When did you ever see me wear pink? It's an old ladies' color."

"I'll return it, Mother."

Scotti bent over and tried to take the cardigan. Her mother snatched it back. "Never mind. I'll wear it."

"If you don't like the color, it's easy for me to take it back."

"Then I'll have to hear about how you had to take it back. I'd rather break my rule about never wearing pink."

"I didn't know you had a rule about never wearing pink."

"Scott would have remembered it. Scott listened to me."

Mrs. House reached for a cigarette. They had gone through the obligatory Christmas Eve gift-opening, and the wrapping and ribbons were strewn about the floor. The television was turned low, a church service on the screen with priests officiating at an altar.

Scotti had received a note saying she was subscribing to *Reader's Digest*. There was also a bottle of '92 Vosne-Romanée burgundy (bless her mother's heart!) which Scotti knew Amagansett Wines & Liquors had recommended.

Besides the sweater, Scotti had bought her mother a bag from Coach, to replace the shabby Kmart one she always carried, and a new L.L. Bean parka, so Myrna House wouldn't have to wear her long dress coat on walks.

Mrs. House blew out some smoke and turned up the sound on the TV, before beginning her commentary on Christmas.

"This will be my last one, for sure. I won't be around next year. I hope you'll take the trouble to find a good home for Baba. I know you won't take him."

"I can't take care of a dog and work all day."

"I just wonder who you'll give him to. Not a lot of people want old dogs. The caretaker at the cemetery today said he loved bulldogs, Baba in particular, but he's on his last legs, too. Oh, and he told me something else. That grave I mentioned that's being prepared? It's for Len Lasher. Lasher Communications. You know who that is?"

"Of course. But he's not dying."

"It's hush-hush, Scott. There's a whole half acre with room for his family when they go. It's all beautifully landscaped. They've dug the grave in case the weather gets so cold the ground freezes, and they've covered it over."

"Maybe it's for one of his parents."

"It's for him."

Usually her mother's gossip had some truth to it, but Scotti doubted that Len Lasher was dying. People with MS lived for years, and anyway, Mario would have mentioned it.

"You don't find it interesting, but the old Scott would have. I remember how he'd tease me, say I was the town crier, chuck me under the chin, all the affectionate ways he had that you seem to have lost."

"Oh, Mother, cork it!"

"Yes, that was what he always said. 'Cork it!'"

Along with all the other changes Scotti's daily dose of hormones had brought (softer skin, thicker hair, budding breasts, testicles atrophying), her mother's attitude had changed toward her as well. With Scott she'd behaved in a kittenish fashion: seductive, flirtatious, playful; but Scotti inspired peevish, sulky behavior, like some older sister's acting out of sibling rivalry.

"You never visit Daddy's grave, do you, Scott?"

"Scotti. Please . . . no, I don't visit his grave. I don't see the point in visiting graves."

"You pay your respect that way," said her mother. "I visit Daddy's grave to make sure they've weeded around it, too. I want that in my will. I want my grave cared for."

"Okay, Mother."

"Someone who can't remember pink is a color her own mother never wears may not remember to take care of her mother's grave, either."

That was when the phone rang.

It was Mrs. Perry, head librarian.

"I'm sorry to call you on Christmas Eve, dear, but we have a problem. You have a door key, hmmm?"

"Of course."

"A Delroy Davenport called. He says he works for Len Lasher. He left a book in the bathroom. There's an envelope in the book that Mr. Lasher needs tomorrow. Of course, we're not open."

"And I'm the one nearest the library."

"Exactly, dear."

"What am I to do with the envelope?"

"Mr. Davenport will meet you tomorrow, at the library, whenever you say. He said he knew you."

"Why don't I just drop it off at the Lashers?"

"He wants to meet you at the library. We don't know what's in that envelope, do we? It could be that Mr. Davenport needs the envelope, not Mr. Lasher. Or maybe Mr. Davenport doesn't want Mr. Lasher to know he was careless."

"Can't he wait a day until the library is open?"

Mrs. Perry picked up on the angry tone. "After all Len Lasher has done for us, I don't see how we can refuse a small favor for his manager."

"All right, I'll go there."

"I am sorry, Scotti. . . . Here's the number he wants you to call when you're ready. Tomorrow morning, Scotti. Please."

Scotti took down the number and hung up.

The phone rang again and Scotti answered it.

She had the feeling it could be Davenport.

"Hello?" she said sharply.

"I know it's late, but I'm taking a chance you might like a little cheer on Christmas eve. This is Mario Rome. I'm at Hydra. May I buy you a drink?"

Scotti laughed, relieved. "I'm leaving now."

Hydra was a Greek place just outside East Hampton Village. Scotti used to hang out there when she was working on the Candle case. Gus Garvas, the owner, knew all the local gossip. His wife made the best pastitsio and saganaki Scotti'd ever tasted.

After she hung up, her mother said "You have to go to that library now?"

"No. Tomorrow. Now I'm meeting Mario Rome in Hydra."

"So much for Christmas with family."

"We've had Christmas, Mother."

"You know, Scott, men don't like women who are available at the last minute. And on Christmas Eve, of all times. It shows what he thinks of you."

"I won't be late," said Scotti, grabbing her coat from the closet.

"He's going to get the idea you're desperate."

"That's me," Scotti chuckled.

ELEVEN

Len Lasher was no different dying than he'd been living: he liked to organize and orchestrate his daily life. Yesterday, with Delroy's help, he and Lara had trimmed the three downstairs trees. He did not want one upstairs.

On Christmas Eve at noon the servants had been invited in for gift-giving and champagne in front of the tree in the living room. Then all but Delroy went home to be with their families.

Now, Christmas Eve, Lara, Len, Deanie, and Delroy (feeding Len) were together for a light supper the cook had prepared for them ahead of time.

Then Deanie had opened some of her gifts under the library tree. Just Deanie, Len ordered, so all attention could be focused on her.

"Has it been good so far?" Len's speech synthesizer asked Deanie. He was sitting up in a recliner, a thin flashlight fastened to a headband, pointing to letters which ultimately made words, spoken in a robotic, inflectionless voice. Deanie came out "En nee."

Deanie sat on a footstool, facing her father. "Santa should have come tonight after everyone's asleep."

Len was working out an answer for her. She was a thin little dark-haired image of Lara thirty years ago. Lara recognized some of her own mannerisms already: particularly that pout Len used to call Lara's "pickle puss."

Lara said, "Deanie, Santa is coming twice this year. He just came and then after you're asleep, he'll be back."

"Maybe I'll get my gold locket."

Len's machine mutilated the words, "More coming, Peaches."

"The party dress doesn't fit me."

Lara said, "The dress can be altered, honey."

It was a gift sent by Edward Candle, his only contact with the Lashers since last summer. Lara had felt like sending it back, but Len decided it was not Lara's gift to return. It was Deanie's, and Deanie did not know the details of Candle's arrest, just that he had done "something bad." It was no surprise to her parents that Deanie chose to keep the Christmas gift.

The dress had been designed by Carolina Herrera: white organdy with short sleeves and tiny pin tucks on the bodice and sleeves. Already, like Lara, Deanie would have a hissy fit when something she wore wasn't exactly right.

The robotic voice said, "Tomorrow we'll see what else Santa has for you."

"I hope it's the locket!"

Of course, the Cartier locket would be one of the gifts.

Before Martha took Deanie off to bed, Deanie said, "The birthday of Baby Jesus is tomorrow, too."

"It's the same thing as Christmas, honey. Christ . . . mas," said her mother.

"I know that. But it's Jesus's birthday more than anything else."

Len made the grunts that substituted for laughter.

Lara didn't think it was funny. It was a hangover from Deanie's early kindergarten/first grade schooling at Holy Family Academy in New York. A nonpracticing, nonbelieving Jew, Lara didn't put up a fight over Deanie's schooling until later.

Len had let the Catholics take over those valuable years because he'd promised his mother, on her deathbed. It wasn't until Deanie started saying things like "Jesus died for our sins" in casual conversation at the dinner table that Len began to agree with Lara the school was a mistake. When the ALS began to show itself, at first mildly, they moved year-round to East Hampton. Len got the idea to found a small private school for Deanie and a few other friends' daughters.

Still, the church had made inroads. Every now and then Deanie would say or do something that would have warmed the hearts of all the priests and nuns who'd had her in their care.

Len tried to speak independently of the machine, but even Lara couldn't understand the babbling when Len was tired. She nodded toward the instrument with a wink and a pat to his shoulder, what was left of it—it was bone and little more now.

She hated hearing him over the synthesizer. She could not bear to hear animal noises from this man who had won her with his eloquence. Even with his lisp, even when he was whispering to her or shouting at her, language had been his forte. (He couldn't stand people who pronounced it "for-tay.")

Len had gone from poor boy to tycoon counting on what would come out of his mouth. It didn't matter that he couldn't pronounce his *r*'s. His calling her "Lawa" only endeared him to her.

The doctors couldn't say how long Len would last. It could be six or seven months more. One didn't die of MS for a long time, as a rule, but the usual life after an ALS diagnosis was about three years. Len was three-quarters through his third.

He beamed his light on the synthesizer keys and waited for the voice. "Tired, love," it said.

"I'd hoped we could lie down and have a nap together now, darling."

He shook his head.

She said, "No? I'd like that, Len."

Again, he shook his head.

He knew her too well. She could never nap. She never had. He could nod off in an instant, and he often woke up drooling, waiting for someone to wipe his mouth.

Len would never subject her to that. He had insisted on separate rooms as soon as he couldn't count on himself for anything.

Lara asked Len, "Don't you want to watch TV together until Delroy comes for you?"

"Okay." He tried to shrug.

Lara wasn't sure whether he was doing her a favor or whether he wanted to be alone. They were slipping away from each other. The priest who had come to see Len last week told Lara to expect Len to start his moves away from Deanie and her.

The priest said, "He will begin very slowly to move on."

She resented a priest, of all people, telling her that. What did he know about love between a husband and wife? Len used to say they get paid for making up something to say to all those people thinking someone has to know the score, or we're all simply in the dark. And of course we all are, Len would say: those men rushing around in their skirts, pushing the body of Christ down people's throats know it, too. That's why so many of them drink and pull little boys' puds.

TWELVE

Before Liam went into the shower he read from *Affirmations,* the bulletin from his mind-set group concerning such subjects as Anger, Worry, Goals, and December's aptly called Proceeding.

Since Nell and he had decided to stay past summer in the Hamptons, Liam's reading material was *Affirmations* and home-repair manuals.

He had become a professional house watcher. He could fix anything broken, too, the same as he could take cars apart and put them back together. He was also good at finding things, such as the floor safes the rich often have installed for their valuables.

When time to scheme was what you wanted, and money along with it, why not find a job to give you leisure and stay right where the money was?

He advertised his services in the *East Hampton Star,* thinking he would be employed by home owners in East Hampton Village, Georgica, Wainscott, or Sagaponack, where the rich were.

He'd miscalculated. People like that had live-in servants, or caretakers somewhere on the grounds. The respondents to Liam's ad were ordinary second-home New Yorkers with houses in places like Northwest Woods or Springs.

Liam wasn't interested in taking anything from their houses. Big risk/small gain. But he did his work well.

For a long time he'd been waiting for just the kind of break Nell had provided, not even knowing what she'd stumbled on one summer evening when Liam couldn't drive her to Islip Airport. He was helping a client pump water from his cellar. Nell had been forced to call a car service.

That ride from East Hampton to the airport in Islip had started everything. All the way, Mario Rome had talked to Nell about the Lashers . . . Long after Nell's job demonstrating Star Cosmetics was finished, Nell continued to hire his van.

A new "project" was under way. Chuck floor safes and house plans, they had a scheme as beautiful as Nell herself.

In the bathroom, Liam showered, forgetting that he hadn't planned to use the shower until he replaced the caulking at the end of the tub.

Never mind! He felt wonderful. He always did after good sex. He got past all the anxieties Prozac and Affirm couldn't penetrate—most of them caused by the feeling Nell was too good to be true.

His sister used to say that how you got a woman was how you lost a woman. He had taken Nell away from a con man named Jimmy Rainbow. After that, every man Nell came near was a threat.

That very afternoon she'd fished mail out of the box which she'd tried to hide from him.

She'd said he'd make more of it than it warranted.

He made her show him the letter. Inside, a poem she claimed Mario Rome must have sent her. Who else was there?

Across the top he'd scribbled: "Something I wonder about."

It was called "The Meaning of Birds."

Liam almost blew a gasket when he read it.

> *Of the genus of birds we know nothing,*
> *save the legend they are descended*
> *from reptiles: flying, snap-jawed lizards*

that have somehow taken to air.
. . . But what does it matter,
anyway how they got up high . . .
. . . We are often far
from home in a dark town, and our griefs
are difficult to translate into a language
understood by others
. . . But still, it is morning again, this day.
In the flowering trees,
the birds take up their indifferent,
elegant cries.
Look around. Perhaps it isn't too late
to make a fool of yourself again.
Perhaps it isn't too late,
to flap your arms and cry out, to give
one more cracked rendition of your
singular, aspirant song.

"What the hell does this mean, Nell?"

"You were the one who told me to sweet-talk him. Your words exactly, Liam! 'Sweet-talk him'!"

"Perhaps it isn't too late to fucking punch his face in!"

"It's just a poem. He wants to be a writer!"

"How do I know it's from him?"

"Who would it be from? Tom Cruise?"

"Why would you try to hide it?"

"Because look at you! You go bananas!"

Liam knew she was probably telling the truth. But she always had to prove it, come through for him, give him some horizontal reassurance any-time he had the slightest doubt.

They had sex a lot. Liam had a lot of doubts.

It did no good for him to remind himself that he'd never served time and she had. He still always thought of her as being a better person than he was. She'd done four of six for grand larceny. Bad lawyer—grumpy judge—Liam would have known how to beat that rap. It was her one and only criminal venture.

She'd been assigned to the prison beauty parlor, where she'd learned to cut hair and advise inmates on skin care.

Nell Slack had gone in there frumpy and unskilled and come out this classy beautician. She'd acquired a certain cool dash, copied from a cell mate who'd once taught the tango at a Fred Astaire Dance Studio.

Liam had met Nell at Haven, a halfway house in Brooklyn Heights. In those days he was doing a lot of business with Fina Merola, a notorious jewel thief. Fina was one of the most skilled fences in the east. She could tell a fake in less time than it took to say, "You got fucked."

The first time Liam had ever seen Nell in the visiting vestibule he had asked, "Where'd she come from?"

"Cortland Correctional," Fina had said. "We call her Sweet Air because she thinks she shits roses."

After he got the courage to ask Nell out, the first few dates he couldn't order martinis. His hands trembled so much trying to hold a long-stemmed glass, he changed to Jack Daniels neat.

There was something about Nell that always made him think he'd lose her. It wouldn't last. She'd go.

It was all right now. Good sex energized things, and now (thanks to Fina) he had the final plan worked out for the project.

He felt like getting dressed, going someplace. He knew Nell would rather lie around naked and talk.

Okay, first they'd talk.

They had a lot to talk about.

Liam dried himself off with the bath towel. He reached for the caulk he'd left on the top of the toilet. He squeezed some from the tube and put it on his nose. Then, carefully, he worked it around the bridge, breaking off little pieces until it was perfect.

Naked, he strolled into the bedroom. "Look who's here!" he said.

THIRTEEN

"Look who's here!" he said.

"What'd you do to your nose?" she laughed.

"Imagine me bigger, with red hair."

"Are you supposed to be Delroy Davenport?"

"Himself."

"You could have fooled me."

Last Sunday they had gone to the Amagansett Presbyterian Church expressly to see Davenport. Mario Rome had told Nell he thought Delroy went there regularly, that it was one of the few times the Lashers lent him the Jeep. His nose and his red hair made him stand out like a clown at a convention of priests.

Liam sat down on the bed and pulled off the false nose. "I've figured everything out."

"Again?"

"This is the final plan. Delroy is our man, our courier, and he's not going to bring us cash. Our ransom demand will be the Lucky We."

Nell pulled the covers around her naked body and sat up in bed. "The ring?"

"The ring, baby. The ring. Money can be numbered or dusted and the amount we want would be heavy, too. Thanks to Fina's research, we know the Lucky We belongs to Lara Lasher. It's right there in a safe at The Highway Behind The Pond. Or it's in the safe at 825 Fifth. According to a maid who worked at Le Reve, she changes it from one safe to the other."

"Why wouldn't it be in a safety deposit box?"

"That kind of jewelry is kept in home safes. Safety deposit boxes are locked when there's a death. Whatever's in the box gets taxed as part of the estate. Rich people don't like paying big taxes. They find ways around it all the time."

"Liam, the Lucky We is like the Hope diamond."

"What do you remember about it?"

"I read a whole thing on it to you," Nell said. "The Duke of Windsor gave it to the Duchess for an engagement ring. It's an emerald with diamonds around it, and inside there's an inscription. Lucky WE. *WE* for Wallis and Edward. Lasher paid over a million for it."

"Lasher paid $3,126,000. It was his wedding gift to Lara."

"Liam, I don't understand how anyone can fence a ring like that."

"That's the fence's business. I've already inquired about it. We can get $800,000."

"Is that all, for something worth three million . . . and more by now?"

"Nell, the fence gets a cut, too."

"But who will buy it?"

"A collector. These collectors don't care where it came from, just that it's the real thing. Remember Fina Merola? She'll be our fence."

Nell grimaced. "The one from Haven?"

"You knew her a long time ago. She's a big operator now," Liam said. "She didn't stand still like Jimmy Rainbow or the other pikers from the old days."

"Why toss his name into the pot?" Nell asked.

"Why not? You used to think Rainbow was hot stuff. He couldn't move this stone across the room. But Josefina Merola can give us $400,000 cash on receipt and another $400,000 one week later, in New York City, after she's made the delivery."

"You'd trust Fina Merola?"

"I told you, love: she's not penny ante anymore. The circles she moves in don't fuck with you. You don't with them, either. That's just understood. Did I tell you what the quotation is in this month's *Affirmations?*"

"No, but I know you're going to," Nell said.

"'We are now moving forward in great and gallant company.' Winston Churchill."

"Does Fina know about me?"

"Fina doesn't want to know anything. That's how they work. The less names she knows, the less faces she sees, the better. We produce the product and she turns it into cash, after she makes sure it's authentic. She can spot a fake faster than a kike cutter from Forty-seventh Street."

"Suppose Fina says it's a copy? Don't rich people usually have copies made of major pieces?"

"Sometimes they do. But we'll warn Lasher that if he tries any tricks the child will die." Before Nell could get a word out, Liam said, "Don't worry! We're not murderers. But Lasher doesn't know that. He won't take any chances on his kid getting hurt."

"But I want a promise from you on this Christmas Eve. A solemn promise, Liam."

"About what?"

"Promise me the child will not get hurt."

"Negative thinking. If you talk trouble, you get trouble."

"Never mind that Affirm crap! I want you to say, '*She will not get hurt, I promise you.*'"

"She will not get hurt, I promise you."

But sweet Jesus, anything could go wrong. Any asshole knew that just from sitting nights watching TV cop shows. Liam knew, too, that if anything went wrong, Nell would never forgive him. She'd turn herself in. She'd want to be punished. She could not stand causing anyone injury. The reason she'd gone to prison was carelessness: going back to see if the old rich bitch whose jewels she'd just finished filching had really had a heart attack. She had not. Nell had lost just enough time returning to check on her to get herself arrested.

She never blamed Jimmy Rainbow. She said he'd told her to follow instructions exactly, and there were no instructions to stop and be certain the victim was all right.

Liam figured out the only flaw in his project was having a partner who did not believe in positive power. Nell had refused to read even one *Affirmations*. She'd called it propaganda.

"The child will never be out of your sight once I have her," he told Nell.

"Good! Thank you! And once we have the first $400,000 and Deanie is returned safely, I go to New York and stay there."

Liam said it would be better if Nell Slack came back to East Hampton and carried on as usual for a while.

"That was a mistake I made once before," she said. "I went back, and you know what happened. Once this is done, I head *for Manhattan, the Bronx and Staten Island, too,*" and then in falsetto, "*it's lovely going to . . . the zoo.*"

"I have to come back, for a while," Liam said. "Business as usual, for awhile. Then I'll dissolve Homesafe, pay a few months' extra rent, saying I'll be back, and we're off to England."

"Hey, this isn't very merry Christmas conversation."

"Just a little more, Nell. I have these clients, the Karpinskis. They leave for Naples, Florida, on the first of January. We'll use their house after we have her. The others are either closed up, water off until summer, or there are nearby neighbors. We don't want to be too far into the woods, either, in case it snows."

The Karpinskis' white brick house on Maritime Way was ideal: isolated but near the road. No year-round residents on that small street. Heat, water, and phone service was left on by the Karpinskis for a son who would stay there during his college intersession, the third week of February.

On the wall opposite the bed, photos of Mario Rome were thumbtacked to the bulletin board. The map of East Hampton was there with the

Invictus School circled, and the route from the school to the six stops before Le Reve. A little beyond the sixth stop, in Northwest Woods, there was a gold star between there and the Lashers' house.

There were xeroxed stories from magazines about the Lashers. It was impossible to print out everything Google came up with, but Liam had looked through all of it.

Liam had taped a year-old interview with Len Lasher on LTV, the local public-access station. Lasher was called to the microphone during a fundraiser, telling the reporter he admired the "wok" the "Wesowaion" committee "pwefomed." He'd sounded like Bugs Bunny.

Last week Liam and Nell had followed Mario Rome's van on its home-ward route. Nell had put on one of her old wigs from days she'd given demonstrations of Star Cosmetics to cancer victims. She'd dressed in a frumpy style she planned for a disguise, actually in pants, which she hardly ever wore.

Nell could make herself into a gorgeous woman in her thirties or transform herself into an octogenarian bag lady.

They were renting the first floor of an old house on Newtown Lane near the East Hampton Middle School. They had a year's lease, which would be up in June.

Liam said, "Let's go out, love. Right now!"

"Nothing will be open on Christmas Eve."

"Hydra is."

They usually went to roadhouses around Westhampton or Riverhead. They liked darkly lighted pubs that weren't trendy yet were busy. They chose places where they wouldn't draw attention to themselves. They weren't known very well in the Hamptons anywhere by anyone.

A cardinal rule of Liam's was not to make friends. He had once leased a warehouse when he was fencing large-scale stolen goods. He dealt with professional cargo thieves, one of them a Peruvian citizen who hijacked along the eastern seaboard. Sometimes when he brought a load in, Liam would go for drinks with him. He turned out to be an FBI plant. Liam had beat the rap thanks to the way the United States government bent over backward to keep evidence that had been obtained illegally from the court-room. But it had taught Liam not to become familiar with anyone.

Liam knew only vaguely the people whose houses he cared for. Nell had never met them. Nell knew only this horny limo driver. Under the circumstances she wasn't to blame because Mario Rome had gotten the idea she might be interested in him. Liam had told her to work him. Now she'd have to ditch him, give him the cold shoulder, act like he'd never sent that poem to her. Chill.

Nell said, "I don't think it's a good idea to be seen together in Hydra."

"Oh, most people won't be out. We'll just stop in and get a souvlaki. We need a change of scenery."

Nell was putting away her Christmas present, a Smith & Wesson Sigma pistol that was only 5.8 inches long and weighed just fourteen ounces. She didn't like heavy guns. This one could fit into her coat pocket like a small purse, or even in a small purse.

"Won't it be depressing to be out when no one's around?"

"Someone will be around," Liam said.

Someone was.

FOURTEEN

"Delroy's not Lasher's manager!" Mario's voice boomed with scorn, and it was precisely at that moment when Scotti saw Nell Slack stroll into Hydra, catch a glimpse of them, turn around quickly, and leave.

Nell Slack was with the same dark-haired man with whom she'd left East Hampton Bowl that night. Obviously she didn't want Mario to see her. What was she up to? Scotti flashed back to Nell at the bowling alley, with the cheap camera at her face, snapping Mario's picture.

Scotti didn't mention seeing her to Mario. Whatever was going on, it was between the two of them. It wasn't Scotti's business, and besides, she wanted to hear what Mario had to say about Delroy Davenport.

"Did Delroy tell everyone at the library he was Lasher's manager?" Mario was shaking his head, grinning.

"He told me that."

"Oh, he hires limos and keeps track of where Deanie is, where Mrs. Lasher is. Part of his job there is to be sort of a traffic manager, except no one in their right mind would call Delroy a manager of any kind."

"What's he like?"

"He used to be pathetic before he connected with the Lashers. He was the town joke in Sag Harbor. He worked in his aunt's knitting shop, knitted himself, and earned the nickname Needles Couch."

"Couch?"

"Davenport . . . He was the type who made you feel awful because when he was around no one ever directed any conversation his way, or made eye contact with him. I heard a rumor that he was Amish, his family banished him, and that was how he came to live with his aunt."

"How did he hook up with the Lashers?"

Mario shrugged. "It was a fluke. He used to caddy for people. Len was a great golfer. One day Len took a swing at a ball and fell on his face. It was the start of his MS. Delroy helped him home, and the Lashers began asking him to do this and that for them. He suited them because he had no life. They could count on him to be there day and night."

"Does he live with them?"

"Now he seems to. They got him a little place down the road, though."

Mario told her the help at Le Reve called Delroy Mrs. Danvers. "Remember that spooky housekeeper in the movie *Rebecca?* Judith Anderson played her. She acted as though she owned Manderly."

Then Mario told her Delroy had knitted a scarf for the Lasher child, with her pony's name misspelled on it. Pécheresse was the pony's name. Peculiar name for a little girl's pony, Scotti thought. French for "sinner."

"But Mrs. Danvers spelled it Pisheresse," Mario laughed. "And that's what the guy is: a pisher. Why are you so curious about Delroy?"

She told Mario about having to open the library for him in the morning. She said, "I'd rather you didn't tell him I mentioned him to you." Mistake, she thought. She should never have mentioned Delroy. It could lead to her being "outed" before she was ready, if she'd ever be ready. She couldn't imagine telling Mario, couldn't predict what he would think of her if he knew.

"Oh, well, Delroy's harmless," Mario said. "Don't worry."

Scotti said, "I'm not worried."

"You sound dismayed."

"I like that word. My father was a wordsmith. That was a favorite word of his."

"Was he a writer?"

"A professor of English . . . I'm really not dismayed, Mario. Where this Delroy is concerned, I guess you could say I'm wary. He's strange. I've always been inquisitive, too. My ex says the reason I'm such a good investigator is that I'm pathologically curious."

Before Scotti moved out, Jessica had even suggested that they pool their savings and start their own detective agency. That way, Scotti wouldn't have to worry about employment while she was going through the initial hormone treatment and beginning to cross-dress. To Scotti's amazement, Bolton House had left her a small inheritance. But though it seemed to be a lot at first glance, it was soon spent on the expense involved in becoming a woman.

Scotti had helped Jessica trap Edward Candle, and she had researched other investigations for Jessica, but there was really not enough work for her coming from Southgate Insurance.

Until Scotti was post-op, she had to have a low-profile job, one that did not require references and records of previous employment. That meant a low salary, too. She still did textbook editing, but sometimes she wondered if she would ever have enough saved for the final surgery.

"You said you helped your ex out sometimes," Mario said. "What kind of thing does he investigate?"

"He's an insurance investigator. He tracks down the fellow who was awarded millions for an accident that broke his back, only to find him lifting weights in a gym."

Mario signaled to the bartender for another round.

"Not for me," Scotti said. "But I'll have a coffee."

Scotti wanted to get off the subject of her ex. The hardest part of making new friends was dealing with the past. A sex change was something like being in a government witness program, only worse because besides reinventing your life, you had to change your pronouns.

"Did you ever hear from Nell Slack after that fund-raiser in the bowling alley?" Scotti asked.

"No. She's probably not taking any trips during the holidays. She's never called me for any other reason yet. All I really know about her is that she lives on Newtown Lane, up past the middle school."

"Alone?"

"I think so."

"Does she travel on business?"

"She's this floor demonstrator for Star Cosmetics. She goes to malls all over the country. That's all I really know about her. She's one of these people who makes conversation by asking you questions. And of course I'm a marathon mouth. It's a lonely job."

"Is it your only work, Mario?"

"Right now. I'm trying to get some backers and open a club out here . . . Magic C East or something like it."

"And you're writing."

"Trying to."

"The Lashers can give you some interesting material, I'll bet."

"I wish I knew more about his big deals. This Standard Broadcasting thing he just pulled off was top secret. I don't know sh—beans—about corporate politics, either."

"Neither do I. But there's a story there without the business details. Wasn't he a poor boy who made it rich? People love to read about the rich, particularly when you have inside information."

"Like the fact that after Delroy brings the mail to Le Reve he has to go through every magazine and remove all the inserts. Nothing can fall out of a magazine in the Lasher household."

"I wish I could get someone to do that for me."

"Oh, and then there's the school. Lasher bought a school for his daughter."

"You're kidding," Scotti said.

"I'm not. Deanie Lasher and six other little girls go to this very private school he owns called Invictus."

"Named after the poem?"

"How did you know? Lasher *did* get the name from a poem."

And that was where Scotti had gotten the title the Ashawagh Hall instructor didn't like. *Out of the Night.*

She said, "It was written by William Ernest Henley. He wrote it after his six-year-old daughter died. 'Out of the night that covers me / Black as the pit from pole to pole / I thank whatever gods may be / For my inconquerable soul.'"

Mario clapped. "You can quote it. I'm impressed."

She could quote it all right. It used to be a favorite of Scott's. Of Max Bernstein's, too. A lot of Metamorphs had discovered that poem when they were young and latched on to it for courage.

Mario said, "Deanie went to this Catholic school when they lived in New York City. Mrs. Lasher thought she got brainwashed there. They wanted someplace for Deanie where they could control the curriculum and also take advantage of their advantages. If the kids are studying art, Invictus flies them to Paris, to visit the Louvre."

"A little field trip," Scotti said.

"Here's a funny story. When I first began to take the kids to Invictus, I lent Deanie my copy of *The Little Prince.* When I was a kid I loved that book. So one day I asked Deanie if she'd finished reading it. She answered that she'd left the book on the plane. I was steamed! I told her that book meant a lot to me. I asked her how she could be so careless with someone else's property. Deanie said not to worry, that when she went back to the plane she'd get it. . . . They keep their own jet in Westhampton."

The waiter put the wine and coffee on the table, and Mario took a long swallow of the Roditis.

Scotti said, "I guess when you have everything, you think of everything."

"He does. He thinks of everything," Mario said.

"Start your own school. Have your own plane. Buy a half acre for your own family plot."

"What does that mean?" Mario asked. "Buy a half acre for your own family plot?"

"Mr. Lasher bought a half acre up at Green River Cemetery. I was going to ask you about it. My mother walks her bulldog there, since we live right next door. She says they've dug a grave for Len Lasher. I told her there had to be some mistake."

"Could you run that by me again?" Mario asked.

Then Scotti told him what was going on behind Jackson Pollock's tombstone.

In the parking lot where they said good night, he handed her an old book tied with a red ribbon.

"Merry Christmas, Scotti. What I do every year is recycle old favorites from my library, and give them as gifts to friends. This one's *Lord Jim* by Joseph Conrad."

He bent over and kissed her cheek.

When Scotti got home she found a FedEx package her mother had put on her bed. It was a Christmas gift from Claris Hayworth, an MTF who'd gone through the program with Scotti, moved to San Francisco after her surgery, then found work there as a cellist with a symphony orchestra.

A card said, "Here's your favorite chanteuse. I bet you never heard her sing this way. Miss you! Love, C."

It was a CD called *Barbara Streisand, Classical.*

Scotti had never heard it.

She finished a Bordeaux she'd had with dinner the night before and listened to Streisand sing lieder by Schumann and Hugo Wolf, in the original German.

While Scotti sat listening, she flipped through *Lord Jim*, and came upon an underlined passage.

> *It is when we try to grapple with another man's intimate needs that we perceive how incomprehensible, wavering and misty are the beings that share with us the sight of the stars and the warmth of the sun.*

Two gifts at the end of the day that made Christmas joyful.

FIFTEEN

He had first met Lara ten years ago, on the evening of the day Lasher Communications acquired Keystone. She had sat beside him in Guild Hall, at a revival of *South Pacific* performed by an amateur theatrical group called the Hampton Players.

He was with Jack and Delia Burlingame, and Lara was with the drama critic for the *East Hampton Star,* who was scribbling notes for her review.

One could imagine that Lara leaned in to Len to give the critic room for her note-taking, and one could also imagine that Len leaned into Lara because Jack had had several bourbons with dinner and smelled like a brewery. Or maybe no one in the audience even noticed that the only bodies touching in Row F, center aisle, were Len's and Lara's, glued together for three acts, moving against each other almost imperceptibly, like heartbeats, as the performers sang "Some Enchanted Evening" and "This Nearly Was Mine."

Len had noticed her the moment she arrived. Her coal black hair worn in a sleek chignon, her ivory skin with the light blue eyes, the regal look she had. Her parents had told her she was a young version of The Duchess of Windsor, so she bought every book about Wallis Simpson, copied her style, and by her late twenties had acquired this serene exterior, a collection of pugs, real and Meissen, and told Len that night she was nicknamed "Duchess." Len was just forty.

Right away Len thought, *She's my reward for pulling off the Keystone deal.* He was like a kid when he worked his ass off to get something, sometimes buying himself a new toy: the Bentley Azure convertible one year; Le Reve a few years later; the apartment at 825 Fifth, on and on . . . and then a reward beyond his biggest dreams: this woman.

Jack and Delia left for a smoke during the first intermission. The drama critic headed up the aisle, too.

Lara stayed beside Len.

"How do you like it?" she asked.

"I like *you* more. What's your name again?"

She told him, adding, "And you're Mr. Lasher. The woman with me says you're a real wheeler-dealer."

"Len," he said, smiling, his eyes fixed on hers. "Start by calling me Len."

"What are we starting, Len?" She laughed softly because she knew.

They had a date by the time the actors took their bows.

From then on, everything fell into place, other companies fell in his path like dominoes, and he and Lara fell for each other, basking in the kind of dream marriage his dirt-poor parents had which made them rich in cold-water Lower East Side railroad flats.

Deanie was born. Len got luckier and luckier (he never thought of it any other way) and he wallowed in it, and rejoiced, until their revels ended with a doctor telling him to brace himself, the news wasn't good.

A month before Christmas he had made his last deal, a merger that would knock the socks off the communications industry. Lara and Deanie would be set for life, and so would Deanie's kids.

Now he was a bag of bones, a baby being washed on Christmas morning after he'd dumped in his Pampers. He was so destroyed he or wanted out, so dehumanized that it had taken Delroy to remind h he should wait until after Deanie's birthday, January thirtee if he didn't allow a space of time after the holidays and he he sipped the lethal drink, his loved ones would dread brations even more.

Right after Len researched ALS on the Internet, he vowed that he would spare his family all that he could. Fortunately (and cruelly, too) the disease never affected the mind. The mind became a prisoner of the inert body until the breath was choked from it.

Before anything like that happened, Len bought the land at Green River. Lara knew nothing about it. He had thought of taking Jack Burlingame into his confidence, but Jack had only recently buried Delia there. Jack had gone through hell nursing his wife in the last stages of ovarian cancer. He could not even bear to visit the grave, which Len had chosen for him because Jack was so distraught . . . no, Len would face the end by himself. He liked to say that he cleaned his own guns.

When his illness progressed, it pained and inconvenienced everyone, adding to his own suffering as he watched Lara, Deanie, and everyone at Le Reve adjust not just to the extra work but to the sight and sound of him. Even the practical nurse, Mrs. Metcalf, showed the strain, so that Len had Delroy take over and Mrs. Metcalf only came a few hours a day.

All the while Len was planning: the inns where out-of-towners would stay, the limos that would accommodate them while they were in East Hampton, even the printing of the acknowledgment cards for those sending condolences to Lara. The poem "Invictus" was engraved on the reverse side.

Lara would have very little to do.

With Delroy's help, Len was accomplishing the final touches, before Delroy put the pulverized Valium and Nembutal into the milk shake.

It would wait until the twentieth of January.

Delroy would not be implicated in any way. Len knew the medical examiner. He had seen to it that his death would be attributed to ALS, no mention of suicide.

Once Len was dead, Delroy would give Lara the envelope with all the instructions inside.

The half acre would be for all of them: Lara, her mother, Deanie, and the grandchildren. A family plot.

Len had even thought of ordering twin headstones, one with his dates on them, the other with Lara's birth year and a dash . . . the year of her death left blank. There were several such headstones at Green River.

But then Len had thought better of the idea. Lara was too young to remain a widow. He wanted her to marry again, and to at least have the option of being buried where she chose, with whatever new name she'd have marking her grave.

His last gift to Deanie would be a trip the whole school would take, shortly after his burial. Lara would decide on the destination, depending on world affairs. Perhaps one of the islands. It would be good for Lara, too, to have time alone, to mourn and collect herself.

The one satisfaction Len Lasher felt in the dwindling days of his life was that everything about his death would proceed like clockwork, as anything and everything always had once he set something into motion.

SIXTEEN

When he was a kid, "Needles Couch" used to carry a key in his pocket that didn't belong to any lock. He called it his car key. He used it to scratch up the doors of fancy cars in the Reutershan parking lot, a bit beyond Waldbaum's, where he'd bagged groceries after Aunt Sade's fatal automobile accident.

He used to hate rich people like the Lashers. He never dreamed that one day he'd be living as part of the family, in a house with the ocean just beyond the tennis court.

While he washed Len Lasher's wasted body early that Christmas morning, he tried to remember all the good times he'd had at Le Reve. The holidays he'd celebrated with them, the picnics and sleigh rides they'd taken him on, the trips into New York City where he'd stayed in their whole-floor apartment down from the zoo on Fifth Avenue, the plays he'd seen with them, the restaurant they'd taken him to. He'd been part of everything they did for the last two years of the three he'd been at Le Reve.

The first year he'd stayed in the hall by the door, running things with the computer there, like a sentry at his post. But after the disease began taking its toll on Mr. Lasher, Delroy was needed wherever Lasher was, more and more in the upstairs.

That was when they arranged for him to live nearby, in the small, furnished farmhouse they bought for him.

He never spent much time there, but he moved his own things in: Sade's prize collection of Toulouse-Lautrec posters, and Sade's snapshots of him, the very first photos ever taken of Delroy, since cameras were taboo in the Amish community. There was a sampler his frail mother had made before her heart failed when Delroy was five, and an autograph book with his sister Eelan's imaginative drawing of their house on fire, signed "Love from Eelan Davenport."

After he began the care of Mr. Lasher he was told that he was "family." He remembered the exact moment it was said to him, last summer on Mr. Lasher's fiftieth birthday. He was helping Mrs. Lasher open champagne in the kitchen.

"You'll have some, too, Delroy," she said, but when he put a glass out for himself she shook her head and said, "No, in with us. You're family, Del."

Eelan had called him "Delly" and Sade, "Roy." The "Del" had touched him and reminded him that once he had been cherished. It had helped him forget that he was Needles Couch to some, and Mrs. Danvers to jealous household help. Mrs. Lasher might just as well have called him "dearest" or "darling," the gratuitous "Del" meant so much to him.

Before Mr. Lasher was reduced to bones and flab, waste running out of every orifice, he had invited Delroy into the library one morning and told him to close the door and sit down. He was matter-of-fact about his plans for suicide, saying, "You're a practical man, Delroy. The instructions I'm giving you now are between you and me. I'm counting on your objectivity and the responsible nature that you've demonstrated. Your loyalty, too. I'm counting on your loyalty, Delroy. Think of this the way you think of any assignment. If you see any flaws, point them out."

He'd been thankful when Delroy had reminded him of Deanie's birthday. Part of Delroy's duties before that was to keep track of important family days: to be sure there was enough help, available limos, all those details.

Mr. Lasher had said, "This illness keeps me so focused on myself I forget everyone else. Thanks, Delroy, for reminding me Deanie's birthday is coming soon. We can put off my plans temporarily, but not for long. My throat will close up eventually. I have to be able to swallow, even when the pills are diluted. The mixture can't be too thick."

He'd gone downhill rapidly after that conversation.

Now, as Delroy dried him and carried him to bed, covering him, Delroy no longer felt that lump in his throat, as though he might be unable to hold back tears. Everything was suddenly changed.

Delroy would do what he was expected to do in the days that followed, but it would no longer make him so sad, make his stomach knot.

He had even begun to think of this man as though he were a father to him. That was the ironic part. For Len Lasher had proved to be not much different than his own father had been, disappointing him in the end with his harshness.

Harrell Davenport had never seemed to his youngest son as strict as other fathers in the Amish community, though the *Ordnung* was the rule in all homes. No bicycles, telephone, electricity; no zipper clothing, no bright colors.

Harrell Davenport was an affectionate man who loved to throw his arms around his six sons and sing with them. He'd single out Delroy sometimes to sing with, in English. Hymns were sung in German, of course. English was too worldly. But Delroy's German was poor, and his father indulged him. He was simpatico, too, with Eelan. "There's a little chunk gone from her mind," he'd say, "but her heart makes up for what her head lacks."

Delroy could forgive and perhaps even understand the fact that his father abided by the excommunication and the subsequent shunning of Delroy. Delroy himself had confessed to the elders that he had always supported Eelan's whims, whether it was a doll with a face she wanted (dolls with faces were forbidden!), ice cream from the Dairyrich truck, or sneaking across the highway to the mall. Delroy had accepted blame for it all. But when Deacon Blyer had snarled that the devil had sent Delroy to ruin their poor, angelic Eelan, Delroy had run across the room to his father, crying out, "Tell him I'm from you and no devil!" His father had shaken his head sadly and told the deacon that Delroy had had a disobedient nature from the beginning. Eelan could not help herself in the face of it.

Before Delroy was sent off to Sade's, his father would not touch him, would not smile nor let Delroy speak of Eelan, not once, not even when they were alone. He was silent, like all the rest, until the very end. And then, what he had to say was enough for Delroy to know that he acknowledged what was happening could be unfair, but he could not ever forgive Delroy. "Are you to blame because my precious girl is gone?" were Harrell Davenport's last words to Delroy, and they were spoken in English.

There was Christmas music playing softly through the house speakers. But it was different now that Delroy knew he was not part of that house, or that family. He never had been. He just hadn't known it until late last night, when he had not been able to keep from going to the drawer in the upstairs study, opening it, and taking out the will.

He had found his name at the very end, after the names of the cook of ten years, and the maids of six and seven.

All who had worked at Le Reve for five years or more had received five thousand dollars.

Delroy had been closer to Len Lasher than any of them. None of them had ever sat at the table with the family, gone into New York with them, or been included in their activities. None of them had been needed as Delroy had been: heard Mr. Lasher's confidences, carried out his most personal wishes, for God's sake wiped his ass—none of them were anything more to him than backstairs servants.

Although Delroy was the same size Len Lasher had once been, all of his clothes were bequeathed to the Ladies' Village Improvement Society's thrift shop. The small farmhouse Delroy had been living in was not mentioned, nor had the deed ever been in his name.

$50,000 to the Animal Rescue Fund.

$50,000 to The Retreat.

$25,000 to the Trails Preservation Society.

The list went on and on.

The least amount of money, $1,000, was for Delroy Davenport.

"Delroy?" Mrs. Lasher stood in the doorway of the bedroom. "You said you had to go into the village for something this morning. You may take the Jeep and pick up some things for me, please." She handed him a slip of paper with her list.

He had almost forgotten his eleven o'clock date at the library.

She said, "Did you receive your Christmas envelope, Del?"

"Yes, I did, ma'am."

All of the help had received a book of passes for the local United Artists theater.

"The guests are coming at one, so be back a bit before then. Enjoy yourself, Del."

Delroy did not thank her. Thank her for what? Thank her for deciding that was all he was worth? He knew she was the authority when it came to the help. She was the one who decided what they were paid, when they could take their vacations, and now their value to Le Reve in dollars and cents. Lara Lasher had always been what was politely called "frugal." Sometimes Len Lasher teased her about it, but that never changed her mind. How could he have left it up to her to decide what he would inherit?

Delroy marched past her, down the hall, with the Bill King sculpture of the begging man, a Connie Fox abstract above it. An ominous landscape by the environmental artist Janet Culbertson. Marilyn Church Claire Romano. Margy Kerr.

Chrissy Schlesinger, Jane Martin, Sheila Isham, Carol Crassen, Ann Sager. Local artists. Mr. Lasher liked to support them.

He was fond of saying, "Support your own! Cheer for the ones you know and care about!"

Delroy felt like weeping.

SEVENTEEN

Scotti could smell coffee on his breath, see his red nose hairs.

Delroy Davenport was one of those people who stood too close when he talked to you. Take two steps back from him and he took two steps forward.

"The letter's for you," he said as they stood by the front desk in the library, the CLOSED sign on the window of the door.

"No," she said, pushing away the book he held. *Edith's Diary* with an envelope protruding from it.

"Please read it," he said. "I wrote it while the Christmas program was going on. But I didn't want to give it to someone else to hand to you. It could have gotten lost. And I couldn't find you anywhere."

Reluctantly, she took the envelope. It was used. It had LE REVE stamped in gold in the upper left-hand corner. "Delroy Davenport" was written across the front, crossed out, "Scotti House" printed under it.

"I didn't have any stationery with me," he said. "I wrote it quickly so it's not thought out. But I mean what I wrote."

She started to stick it in her coat pocket, then felt his large fingers on her sleeve.

"Please read it now," he said.

"I'm in a hurry."

"It's not long."

With a sigh of exasperation she took the paper out of the envelope. There was a note to him at the top.

"Please remember to pick up my package at Promised Land on Newtown Lane. Lara Lasher."

That had been crossed out with a pencil.

Underneath, in neat block printing, was his message.

Scotti House,

> *I don't care about things like that, although you may think I do because I was surprised. Who wouldn't be? But I don't think I deserve how you acted just now, as though you never layed eyes on me. You could have ended up in jail that night for driving drunk.*
>
> *I don't want anything from you, but it seems to me you could use a friend.*

Yours,
Delroy Davenport

She looked up at him and said, "All right. Thank you. Now we must go. The library is closed."

"I would be a good friend, too."

"I'm sure. I just don't have time. I'm sorry."

As she reached into her coat pocket for her keys she felt a crumpled pack of cigarettes. Last night when her mother was rushing out with Baba, she mistook Scotti's black parka for the navy one Scotti'd bought for her. Scott had been a chain-smoker until he'd decided on transitioning. Now Scotti was tempted. She took out a cigarette, fumbling for matches as Delroy followed her out the door.

"I don't have a light," he said. "I'm sorry."

"It's just as well." She put the cigarette back. Her black Saturn was parked in front of the white Jeep he had been driving on Thanksgiving. She hurried toward the Saturn while he skipped to keep in step with her.

He said, "Somewhere I have a Ronson lighter which belonged to my aunt. Would you like it?"

She shook her head.

"What brand of cigarettes do you smoke?" he persisted.

"I don't have one," she said, walking faster.

"I never heard of a smoker who didn't have a particular brand."

She had her car key out when he said, "I saw in the phone book there's an S. House on Tulip Path. That's near the cemetery, isn't it?"

"What do you want?" she said. She'd stopped, and she looked directly at him. He actually flinched. He made a sound somewhere between a cough and a chuckle, looking away from her eyes.

"I just thought . . . I don't know what."

"Good-bye," she said firmly. She went around to the driver's seat of the Saturn.

He stood on the curb a moment before he called out, "Until we meet again!"

She couldn't decide if he was just a poor schmuck or some dislodged personality who could become a serious menace.

She was perspiring as she drove home. She wondered if she should have made an attempt to befriend him, or at least to behave in a more friendly way.

What she hated about all of it was not knowing what had happened during that drive from Hampton Bays. What had she said to him? What had she told him about herself? Did it really matter that he knew about her? Who could he tell that she knew?

She thought of Mario. If by some chance her name did come up between them, it would be embarrassing if he was told, but Scotti sensed that Mario was a compassionate man. She thought of the underlined passage in *Lord Jim*. She had given up trying to read *The Master Key,* dropped it off in Mario's mailbox with a note saying "In the spirit of Christmas and recycling from Scotti."

Maybe Mario hadn't even done the underlining, and whether or not someone was compassionate, it didn't necessarily follow that transsexuality would be acceptable to him. He might be revolted by it. He might resent the lies she'd had to tell him, identifying her ex as a male, for example. But those were risks that went with the territory. Those were the subjects always brought up in the Metamorphs support group.

Clearly Mario was taken with Nell Slack. Scotti's friendship, such as it was with him, was just that: nothing romantic there, nothing promised or hoped for.

But if word got out about her, it would not be easy in a small town like East Hampton. It would not be easy to continue at the library, or at the Ashawagh Hall Writers' Workshop. Scotti had never planned to announce the truth about herself locally. What was the point? She had no plans to stay in the Hamptons. Her mother had made it clear that she hoped Scotti wouldn't "tell your business" to anyone here. Okay with Scotti.

When she got home Baba was not at the door to greet her, which meant he was up sleeping with her mother.

The light on the answering machine was blinking.

Scotti got out of her coat, slipped off her Merrell boots and went into the kitchen. There was a half bottle of '88 Lynch-Bages which she'd opened Christmas Eve while she'd exchanged gifts with her mother. She poured herself a glass, went in and punched the Play button for the messages.

One was from Jessica. "Merry Christmas, darling. There's good news concerning Emma. She'd like to see you. She just blurted it out last night after she'd said her prayers. No coaching from me. I couldn't be more delighted. How's New Year's Eve?"

Then Max's voice: "Can we have lunch or dinner very soon, Scotti? I have some surprising news. I'd meet you halfway. Southampton? And our tickets for *Tristan* came today for the twenty-third of January. Put it on your dance card."

EIGHTEEN

News of the merger between Lasher Communications and Standard Broadcasting had appeared in the *New York Times* two days before Christmas. Now Lara was calling close friends of Len's to tell them that he was seriously ill.

Lara was a brick until she had to get on the phone and discuss Len's prognosis. Then her voice trembled and tears flowed, so Jack Burlingame (Uncle Jack to Deanie) put the child in his Porsche and drove her up toward Northwest Woods. After his wife's death, he'd talked of moving to East Hampton. He told Deanie he was house hunting, though he still did not have back the interest in his future that Delia's cancer had taken from him.

Even though Lara had tried not to break down until her daughter left the house, Deanie knew what was up, the way Deanie always knew things.

"Will Daddy meet Jesus, Uncle Jack?"

"Sure. Absolutely."

He wanted to say, "In a pig's eye, darling," but he was already in hot water for changing the ending of *Ralph S. Mouse* so that Ralph crashed his sports car into a garbage truck.

Deanie had told him, "I know how that story ends and that's not it."

"If you knew how it ended, why did you want me to read it?"

"Because," she'd said, then she'd jumped down off his lap and run to tell Lara.

And of course Lara'd said Jack was hostile, and suggested that Jack was in denial, that he was deeply angry because Delia had left him, and now Len would, too.

Jack hated psychoanalytic gobbledygook. He refused to discuss things with people who analyzed the hell out of everything, as Lara was apt to do since becoming an analysand.

He was glad to get out of Le Reve.

He made his mind up to keep his big mouth shut about what he thought Len's chances were of running into Jesus in the hereafter.

Jack believed it was wrong to feed these myths like pablum to the young, encouraging ignorance of that sort. Len used to feel the same way, even more than Lara, in the old days. Now that he was confronted with the truest truth: you died and didn't have a clue what, if anything, came next, the tight little truths that once were his creed were no longer important. Go with the flow.

"Where?" asked Deanie.

"Where what?"

"Where will Daddy meet Jesus?"

"In heaven. Isn't that what they told you in your Sunday school?"

"Catholics don't have Sunday school . . . where in heaven will he meet Jesus?"

"At the library," Jack said. He couldn't help it. He couldn't get past the idea somehow the kid knew she was driving him up the wall and was enjoying it.

"What library?"

Then Burlingame was saved by the sight of Mario Rome waving him down near Nick and Tony's restaurant on North Main.

"It looks like Mario wants a ride," Jack said.

"There's a library in heaven?"

"Not now, Deanie." He pushed the button letting the window down as he slowed up. "Hey, Mario! What's up?"

Mario said he'd had to leave his van at the service station down the street. He was on his way to check out a club for rent on Three Mile Harbor Road.

"You could save me a hike, Mr. Burlingame."

"Hop in."

Mario's voice changed abruptly as he said to Deanie, "Sweetheart, would you get in the back? I can't squeeze myself in back there."

"You're not Barney. That's his voice, but you're Mario."

"It's not easy being green."

"And you're not Kermit, Mario! Be Mario!" She was scrambling into the backseat.

"You do impressions well," Jack told Mario.

"He can imitate anyone, Uncle Jack. Even Daddy . . . Mario? Did you know there's a library in heaven?"

"No, I didn't."

"The nuns never said it, either."

"Pretend you're a nun, Deanie," said Burlingame.

"How do I do that?"

"Nuns are very quiet. They take vows of silence. See how long you can go before you say anything. I bet you can't go long."

"Nuns can talk to themselves because their lips move when they pray."

"You can't hear them, though."

"You won't be able to hear me, either," Deanie said.

Mario asked, "How are things at Le Reve?"

"The same." Now that Lara was telling the truth about Len's illness to special friends, Jack supposed that soon everyone would know. The help at Le Reve might have already guessed. Anyone who hadn't seen Len lately only had to look at Delroy. Jack had seen him in the driveway as they were leaving. Delroy's face was grim and gray. Jack had told him he ought to get out more, exercise. Delroy'd answered that it would be nice to have a new Mercedes mountain bike like the one "the Mister" had given Jack for Christmas.

"Take mine," Jack told him. "I'll never ride it. I couldn't bear to tell Len that I just don't like bicycling."

Delroy said, "But why would you give it to me?"

"Because if you don't have any use for a possession it weighs you down."

"Well, I could use it, all right," said Delroy.

"It's yours."

It was worth it to see Delroy's face. Jack bet no one had ever made such a beau geste in Delroy's direction. It was the sort of thing Delia used to do all the time. She'd say it was the only fun she got from having money: being able to give something to someone who never got a break. She was right. Giving Delroy the bicycle was the biggest high Jack had this gloomy Sunday.

Jack had spent time on the Internet reading about Lou Gehrig's disease, the popular name for amyotrophic lateral sclerosis. Hell of a thing, too, for a great Hall of Fame ballplayer to be remembered for something that had destroyed his body, left him paralyzed and speechless before it killed him.

In the back seat of the Porsche, Deanie had picked up Radar, The Talk 'N Listen Robot, from the floor where Jack had tossed it.

"Hi! I'm Radar."

"Hi, Radar," she whispered.

"Do you want to play a guessing game?"

"Yes, please, Radar."

Deanie jiggled her knee elatedly, then held the telephone attached to the robot, to her ear, listening.

Mario looked across at Jack and said, "Mr. Burlingame? Can she hear me now?"

"She's busy with Radar."

"What's going on up at Green River Cemetery, Mr. Burlingame?"

"Call me Jack. What do you mean, Mario?"

"Why is everything ready? The half acre Mr. Lasher bought is being landscaped. They're even digging a hole."

"What half acre? What are you talking about?" Jack asked.

Mario began whispering as Deanie was doing behind him. He asked Jack, "Is Mrs. Lasher's mother sick? Is someone in the family very sick?"

"He didn't buy space up there," Jack said. "He didn't buy any at all. He wants to be c-r-e-m-a-t-e-d."

"I just drove by there before my muffler dropped off, Mr. Burlingame. Jack. You should see the place."

Jack thought that he probably should, even though he was sure Mario was mistaken. A while ago Lara had nagged Jack about never visiting Delia's grave. She'd called it "closure," as though Jack's going back to where Delia'd been buried would be like rounding off a real estate deal. Closure, for Christ's sake!

Jack supposed it was time to do it, whatever you named it. And he'd see what Mario was talking about. Later. When neither of them was with him.

NINETEEN

"It isn't because you left the front door unlocked on Christmas," Mrs. Perry said the morning of New Year's Eve. "That was very careless of you, Scotti, but we wouldn't let you go for that. We just have to cut back. We'll keep our trained help, but the new addition is costing more than we thought it would."

Scotti answered that she understood, and apologized again for not locking the library door.

It was unsettling news, but Scotti was determined not to let it ruin the evening at Jessica's. She would see Emma again for the first time in six months.

"We'll give you a good recommendation," said Mrs. Perry, "but if you're serious about working in a library you need a degree, sweetie."

"Thanks," said Scotti.

Back to business immediately.

"This shopping bag from Book Hampton is still here," Mrs. Perry said. "Someone named Nell Slack left it here. Do you know someone named that?"

"I know who she is, but I don't know her."

"Information has a listing for an N. Slack on Newtown Lane. I called there and got a machine. A woman's voice announced that I'd reached

Nell, and also Liam of Homesafe. I left a message that the books were here. I was afraid they were Christmas presents. But no one called back."

Mrs. Perry had the books on the counter. *The Girl Who Loved Wild Horses. The Black Stallion. King of the Wind.* She said, "I remember her vaguely. She came by one day to ask about children's books with stories about horses. We had some, but she isn't a member. She said she didn't want to check them out, anyway; she just wanted the names. She'd buy some. Then she left these, which she'd already bought."

"I could drop them off on my way home."

"You don't have to do that, Scotti."

"I don't mind."

"I saw an ad in the *Star* for Homesafe. They're next to the middle school. Classified doesn't list them, so they must be new."

Scotti put the books back in the bag.

"I hope they weren't Christmas presents," Mrs. Perry said.

"They aren't gift-wrapped."

"I hate to put you to this trouble."

"It's no trouble."

It wasn't. Scotti was curious about Nell Slack.

After she said her good-byes to everyone at the library, Scotti drove up Newtown Lane and stopped at the brown shingled house next to the school. A small sign in the front window announced HOMESAFE. A large, green stone cat sat on the front steps. There was no outside doorbell, but the curtained glass door opened onto a vestibule with a small table, mail-boxes, and bells above each box.

1G, apparently the ground floor apartment, listed two occupants: Nell Slack, Liam Yeats.

Scotti rang the bell, waited for an answer, then gave up and left the bag full of books on the table.

She walked back to her Saturn thinking of another Yeats: William Butler Yeats, remembering a favorite toast her father liked to make at the dinner table. Borrowed from Yeats.

> *Wine comes in at the mouth,*
> *And love comes in at the eye,*
> *That's all we shall know for truth,*
> *Before we grow old and die.*

Scotti thought of how often his references were passionate and playful, in contrast to her mother, who was frigid and stern, unlike the pretty, smiling girl in old photographs.

If Scott hadn't had such a compelling agenda all through his youth, maybe he would have discovered someone/something hidden in Bolton House's life. Some secret lover as Robert Frost had Kay Morrison—an affair Scotti's father described in loving detail for *The American Scholar.*

Sometimes Scotti felt that for all the time she'd spent with him when she was a boy, she'd hardly known Bolton House. He must have felt that way himself, once she announced she was transgendered and about to take care of it.

She'd been sure she would be omitted from his will, after the vindictive letter he'd written her, rejecting her as son or daughter. But he had left $10,000 . . . "for my son, Scott House, now in the process of becoming a female calling herself Scotti House."

As grateful as she was for the money, Scotti would rather have had some reconciling conversation with him before his death.

That night she would see Emma, and she was torn about which was the wiser way: for a child to really know a parent, or for the adult to remain distanced.

Myrna House had told Scotti, "The less your daughter sees of you from now on, the better!"

But Scotti wanted Emma in her life.

TWENTY

Late that afternoon, Myrna House thought of how much she hated the Coach bag Scotti had given her for Christmas. She should have exchanged it for one with an outside pocket. Scotti knew very well that her mother kept Baba's treats within easy reach for after one of Baba's BMs. First the little one, and then a short walk before the big one. After that, good-bye Green River Cemetery and hello, Home!

Now she had to unzip this new, fancy bag and dig around for his treat while Baba pulled on his lead impatiently. She supposed she would have to start wearing the L.L. Bean parka with all the pockets, and leave the bag home altogether.

"Wait, Baba! Wait!" and she managed to get the zipper down on the bag, find the first treat, and give it to him. Next she would have to pull out her cigarettes.

She'd never wanted a new bag or a parka! She didn't like Coach bags. They were too heavy! She would have taken it back the very next shopping day, but out of consideration to Scotti she'd kept it. Now look at the trouble she was in because of it! Baba, knowing this was not the routine, gave her an angry backward look, to which she said, "I know, Baba! But do your second BM and I'll have your second treat right away for you! . . . Where are my cigarettes? Oh, dear God, this is the difference between him and her! Scott would have seen to it that the pocketbook had a side pocket!"

Now Mrs. House dropped the bag. Everything spilled out. Next, the leash slipped from her hand and Baba ran. He looked back at her gleefully and charged ahead; never mind the second doo-doo, he was on a frolic.

"Baba! No!" And what was she to do? Leave her compact, her comb, her lipstick, cigarettes, keys all on the ground, while she ran after him? She could never catch him, anyway.

"Baba! Baba!"

Then a man's voice said, "I can get him for you."

"No, I'm afraid he won't come to you."

"I'll catch him."

Myrna House scooped up the bag and her keys, calling out futilely, "Baba! Don't run in the road!"

Baba ran the other way, up toward the newly dug grave, with the red-headed young man in pursuit, and yes, he caught him by the back leg and Baba screamed.

"Don't hurt my baby!" Mrs. House cried out.

"I won't, ma'am." He came walking toward her with an angry Baba in his arms. Baba was wiggling and nipping at the air while the big redhead told him, "No, you don't, Baba! I've got you!"

Mrs. House had managed to put everything back inside the hated Coach bag. Near to tears from all the aggravation, Mrs. House told the stranger, "Be careful of him!"

"He's all right. I have him."

"It's the fault of this wretched pocketbook! I always like an outside pocket but my daughter didn't think and for Christmas got me—"

"A very nice bag," said the young man.

"But not what I wanted."

He gave her Baba's leash.

"Put him down, please," she said. "He wants to do his second duty. His first was so scant!"

"Got everything you dropped, ma'am?"

"Yes, thank you."

Baba, on the ground and reattached to her, hobbled over to do his business near the tall, black Stuart Davis gravestone, a favorite stopping place of his.

Mrs. House sighed and put a cigarette between her lips, no matches naturally because they had always been kept in the missing outside pocket, too.

"I have a light," the young man said. "I have a Ronson. I don't smoke but I've started carrying it for those who do."

"There are less and less of us," Mrs. House grumbled. "But how thoughtful of you!" She inhaled, exhaled, and let her shoulders relax. "I remember you. You're the one making all the arrangement for the new grave. More arrangements?"

"No, ma'am. I was taking my new bike for a ride so I swung over this way. I like to walk around here. It's so peaceful."

"That's what I think, too."

"It's the only way I get to mingle with the famous," he said.

Mrs. House said, "They're all here. Most of them artists." She watched with satisfaction as Baba delivered a long, well-colored stool.

"My name is Delroy Davenport, ma'am."

"I'm Mrs. Bolton House."

"Are you any relation to Scotti? From the library?"

"I'm her mother. Do you know Scotti?"

"Not well. I knew she lived up near Tulip Path."

"We live right down there." Mrs. House pointed to the small, white brick house with the Christmas wreaths on the windows.

"It looks very cozy."

"My husband and I moved here from Brooklyn Heights in 1990. Then he died on me."

"I'm sorry. But you have your daughter, anyway."

"She wasn't around for years. She only moved here a year and a half ago."

"I lived in Sag Harbor, first," said Delroy Davenport. "Then I moved to East Hampton. Shall I carry that bag for you? You seem to be having trouble with it."

"It's too heavy."

His Mercedes bicycle was in front of Ad Reinhardt's small stone. He picked it up and put her bag on the handlebars.

"Aren't you sweet!" Mrs. House smiled at him, his hair as red as the sunset beginning in the sky.

She asked Baba, "Isn't this something, Baba? We've met someone with manners! That's a good omen for the new year. Baba, say how do you do, Mr. Davenport!"

"You can call me Delroy," said the redhead. "How do you do, Baba?"

TWENTY-ONE

There was a time, after Len's diagnosis, when Jack Burlingame let himself play with the idea of helping Lara through the grieving, and then . . . who knows? He would do anything (obviously, if he would think of such a thing where his best friend was concerned)—*anything* to pull himself out of the lonely pit left by Delia's absence.

But now Burlingame realized Lara had a whole layer he never would have suspected. This vast behind-the-scenes production—a setup for Len's suicide—was so elaborate and calculated. Lara had gone about it so carefully, playing the game to the hilt, even embellishing it with discussions of how they could move Len south if the winter was harsh—that sort of thing—when all the while she had supervised the proceedings at Green River Cemetery as efficiently as only Len himself might have done, and was probably partner to via his voice synthesizer.

Jack watched Lara that evening with new eyes and new feelings, trying to catch a glimpse of this side of her, trying to fit it in with the elegant and sexy vision in the white cashmere dress smiling at him and asking him if he wanted more shrimp and corn pie.

"This is an old recipe The Duchess of Windsor brought from Baltimore," Lara said.

"It's very good. I'd forgotten you have this thing for Wallis Windsor."

"It's not a thing. She had great style. I admire that."

A week ago, after he'd dropped off Mario Rome and Deanie, Jack had sped out to Green River to verify what Mario had told him. It was true, all right.

What was not true was that Jack would make a closure by visiting Delia's grave.

For the first time in so long the ache for Delia returned to his heart. He'd taken ten steps back to when he'd wake at night wanting her, remembering the poem Edna St. Vincent Millay had written about waking up a month, two months from the death, a year from it, two years, with your knuckles in your mouth weeping, saying "Oh, God, oh, God" . . . Jack had moved on to the grave that was waiting for Len and he'd thought what a life with Lara would be like.

Lara was able to plan large-scale things without him, not depending on him for any little part of it, looking straight into his eyes and saying, "It's good to have you here, Jack, it means a lot" . . . but never saying "I need you to help me," never even trusting him to know about it.

"Are you listening to me, Jack? Where are you tonight?" Lara asked.

"I'm sorry."

Deanie spoke up then, her mouth full of pie. "He's playing nun, Mummy. He's taken a wow of silence."

"*Vow!*" Jack suddenly snapped, "and you know how to pronounce it!"

"Jack!" Lara exclaimed. "Where did that come from?"

"Sorry," Jack muttered. "She purposely mispronounces words, though. Haven't you noticed?"

"No, I haven't. And a Happy New Year to you, too," Lara said bitterly.

He looked across at her and saw behind her eyes this busy woman phoning landscape people, gravediggers, going down the list, erect, autonomous, the kind of woman he could never imagine reading his chapters to every night, as he had with Delia, waiting for her kindness, her understanding, soft-centered candy compared to hard caramel.

Deanie said, "When my daddy wakes up, I'll tell him Uncle Jack is cruel."

"Uncle Jack didn't mean it, dearest."

"He meant it, and he gave Daddy's Christmas gift away, too. He gave the bicycle to Delroy!"

"He might have just lent it to Delroy, dear. Is that what you did, Jack?"

"He gave it to Delroy because Delroy told me so and Delroy doesn't lie," said Deanie.

"Jack?" Lara looked across at him.

"I'm not a bike rider. Delroy admired it and I thought, what the hell!"

"That was a very expensive gift to give away on a whim," said Lara. "You could have donated it to the Ladies' Village Improvement Society and taken a tax deduction."

Silence while Jack controlled the urge to say that never would have occurred to him . . . and what was wrong with giving Delroy something after all he'd done for Len?

Lara made it clear what was wrong with it. She said, "We don't indulge the help. They take advantage when you do. After I gave Delroy his Christmas gift, he began just taking off. He never did it before. He disappears for hours sometimes, just leaves. He's gone right now."

"He went on the bike late this afternoon," Deanie said.

Jack said, "Len's asleep. He's sedated. Right? Doesn't Delroy deserve some time off? He's been here day and night."

"Don't interfere with the help, Jack."

"It's our help, not yours," said Deanie.

Lara looked sternly at Jack and said, "I don't need you to tell me when Delroy should be here and when he shouldn't."

"You don't need me to tell you anything."

"Jack, what does that mean?"

"It means I'm proud of you. I really am. You know how to manage. That's all it means, Duchess."

"Don't call me Duchess."

"Doesn't Len call you that?"

"Len means it in a nice way. You always criticized the Windsors."

"Me? Criticize sybaritic anti-Semites?"

"End of discussion," Lara said angrily.

Deanie said, "Will you wake me up at the stroke of midnight to watch the ball drop on TV?"

The question was addressed to her mother, of course.

But Jack felt guilty because of his sarcasm and orneriness. Maybe the visit to Delia's grave had soured him. He said, "We'll wake you up, kiddo! Don't worry."

"I wasn't talking to you," Deanie said.

Her mother said, "We've got horns to blow and funny hats to celebrate. I'll wake you up, honey, you bet I will!"

"When is Uncle Jack going home?" she asked.

TWENTY-TWO

Scotti was celebrating New Year's Eve at Jessica's new house in Bay Shore. It was not far from their old one, but it was far enough from the neighbors who'd known Scott and admired his hedge-bordered front garden with curving grass paths swirling around islands of cherry and apple trees. Summers, they'd grown accustomed to seeing him working in his yard— blue-jeaned and bare-chested, a Gauloise hanging from his mouth, tanned and handsome.

Once he'd begun changing, and the rumors began spreading, they'd found all sorts of excuses to pass by and strike up conversations with him, or Jessica. With *her* or Jessica, as time went by and her hair became longer, tied in a ponytail, frilly blouses above tapered pants, oh, it was a change all right. They couldn't stop talking about it.

Even after Scott moved out, Jessica was never on the same footing with them. Her last attempt at reestablishing the old rapport was when she printed out an article she'd found on Google. It was from a back issue of *Harper's* magazine, called "An Economist Drops a Bomb." It was written by a distinguished professor of economics, Donald McCloskey. Quite matter-of-factly, he announced that at age fifty-three, married thirty years with two grown children, he was "cross-gendered." To remedy this situation, which he had tolerated for four decades, he was becoming a female.

Comparing the cost to the purchase of a Mercedes, he was not planning to hide his condition or change his occupation. Henceforth he would be known as Deirdre McCloskey.

Jessica sent copies to those neighbors she truly cared about. But this borrowed glory got her nowhere. She could drop all the names she wanted: McCloskey, Jan Morris, Renee Richards—nothing would change anyone's view of transsexuality.

Jessica had told Scotti that she couldn't blame their neighbors. She admitted that if it weren't happening in her own life, she'd have the same reactions: disgust, bewilderment. At worst, the idea of a middle-aged man, in McClosky's own words, turning himself into a "tall, ugly, indubitably female economist," was somehow revolting. And at best, as one old friend of Jessica's had put it, it was "a hoot!"

So Jessica had moved.

The new house was near the bay where the ferries went back and forth to Fire Island. Summers you could see them carrying their loads of renters to and from Ocean Beach.

In the old days, Scott would take the ferry that left Sayville, bound to Cherry Grove and Fire Island Pines, where the gay crowd flocked.

Now Scotti sat with Emma on the plump banquette that curved along the wall in the small living room, the windows facing the dark waters beyond. Jessica had turned on the outside lights so they could watch the snow, which had begun falling as Scotti drove there from East Hampton.

Jessica was clearing the table in the dining room, carrying dishes to the kitchen, leaving them time together before Emma went to bed.

"You've been very quiet, Em," Scotti said.

"I'm not used to you this way. It's too gross and I don't know what to call you."

"What do you want to call me?"

"You're my daddy but remember the last time I called you that? At the florist. You were mad at me. You said not to call you that!"

"What I said that day was that it would be easier for you to call me 'Daddy' when we're alone. People don't understand if you call me 'Daddy' when we're out doing things. I think we confused the lady we were buying flowers from. That was two years ago, Em!"

"I never forgot it."

"I tell you what, Em. Let's think of something else to call me. You could just call me Scotti. That's my name now."

"Mommy doesn't let me call her by her first name."

"But I don't mind."

"Then you won't be my daddy anymore."

"I'll always be your parent, Emma."

Emma frowned and jiggled one knee. "I told Janice Atwater my daddy was coming tonight for New Year's."

"All right. You don't have to take it back. Janice doesn't have to know anything you don't want to tell her."

"She might come to see me tomorrow afternoon."

"Oh, I'll be gone by then, sweetie."

"Good! . . . I don't mean good that you'll be gone."

"I know what you mean, love. You mean good that you don't have to do a lot of explaining."

"Yes. Because I don't know how to explain you."

"It's all right. I won't meet your friends until you want me to."

"Thanks, Daddy. Scotti. I bet I know what Mommy's doing in the kitchen."

"She's putting dishes in the dishwasher."

"She's going off her diet, too, I bet. She bought a box of Mallomars this morning."

Scotti put her arm around her daughter and hugged her. She felt so sorry for the child: worrying that one parent would embarrass her because he had become she, and worried that the other parent would become fat again. Jessica was beginning to gain back some of the weight she'd lost at the spa.

Until Scotti began taking hormones, she had never felt overwhelmingly maternal. She had been prepared for the physical change. As Scott that had been her whole focus: to feel herself in a new body. At first when she began experiencing the wish to nurture Emma, and protect her, she imagined it was mostly guilt at what she was putting their daughter through. But other MTFs who had no children often spoke about their wishes to adopt them, suddenly welcoming the idea of becoming stereotypical females: mothers and housewives.

Some FTMs found themselves drawn to more manly pursuits, too. Max was one. He developed an interest in automotive woodworking, restoring old "Woodies"—1940s station wagons. His backyard was filled with ones he worked on in his spare time.

Emma said, "Can we make a snowman tonight, Daddy?"

"I don't think the snow's going to stick, honey."

"Are there snowwomen, too?"

"It's funny, isn't it, Em. No one ever calls one a snowwoman."

"We could make a snowman, and then change it to a snowwoman."

"We could." Scotti felt her eyes fill. That was new, too, the sentimental reactions, the quick tears.

Emma said excitedly, "First we'll put a man's hat on it, and then we'll take it off and tie Mommy's scarf around its head!"

In the doorway, Jessica stood munching on a cookie, holding the other half in one hand. "You're not going to put one of my designer scarves on a snowman's head, I hope."

"The snowman wants to turn into a snowwoman, like Daddy did."

"Then the snowman has to buy his own scarf," Jessica said. "Bedtime, sugar."

TWENTY-THREE

While Jessica put Emma to bed, Scotti built a fire and opened her mother's gift of the '92 Vosne-Romanée burgundy.

In a few weeks she had an appointment with Ernest Leogrande to discuss her surgery. She was still $20,000 short of his fee. She remembered Jan Morris's description of herself before her own surgery, going for a swim, naked, in a small lake high in the mountains called the Glyders, in North Wales. A woman above the waist, a man below. She'd named herself a "chimera," and wrote that she was an object of wonder even to herself.

Times Scotti saw herself in the mirror, coming from the shower, she thought: how bizarre! . . . But then she would remember seeing her naked reflection when she was a pubescent boy. Young Scott had thought how odd it was to be a female and see a male in the mirror.

When Jessica came back downstairs she slipped an old Peter Allen CD on the player. *One Step over the Borderline.*

She said, "I wish he was still alive." She flopped on the couch. "I wish I wasn't fat. I wish you weren't always in a skirt. You wear a skirt more than I do."

"I like wearing them. You never did."

"It was almost like old times tonight, wasn't it? Except for the snowman/snowwoman bit. She said to tell you good-bye."

"Doesn't she know I'll be here for breakfast?"

"I think she's afraid you'll be here when her friend, Janice, drops in."

"She said Janice was coming in the afternoon."

Jessica sighed. "It weighs on her mind, I think. . . . Speaking of weighing, I don't even dare step on the scale. I've become a recidivist, I fear. The holidays always do me in."

"Don't worry about it, Jess. You can get it off again."

"I think of that poem that begins 'O fat white woman whom nobody loves . . .' Was that your Charlotte Mew?"

Scotti chuckled. "No, it wasn't. When did she become *my* Charlotte Mew?"

"I don't know anyone else who reads her. I never heard of her until you gave me a book of her poems. Remember that one from her French period that ended, 'But, oh! Ma Doue! The nights of hell!' . . . It was called 'Pécheresse.'"

"Deanie Lasher has a new pony named Pécheresse. Candle must have given it to her."

Jessica said, "You know he got thirty-three months in prison, plus a fine of $350,000. And he has to reimburse Southgate Insurance $300,000."

"Shit! That's chicken feed to him!"

"Don't say *shit*, darling. It doesn't become a lady."

"You're right. Change it to "rats"! Isn't that what Lucy says in the Snoopy cartoon?"

"Hey, speaking of rats. I just thought of something. How would you like to nail a femme fatale who's taking up residence at Annabel?"

"Annabel. She must be rich," Scotti said. It was the new, swanky inn on the ocean in Montauk, known for its spa. Rooms went for $800 a night, and cabins started at $2,000.

"Oh, Sheba is filthy rich! Her newest scam is to set herself up as a rape victim in some fancy resort, preferably one with a good spa, that draws females. She's been working on the West Coast. Sunny Shores, near Malibu, settled two million on her."

Scotti asked, "Was she raped or not?"

"Not. But they all settle, rather than have that kind of publicity . . . and she's good! She fools doctors, hospitals, police. She lets herself get roughed up by her accomplices, and get fucked so there's semen. She's head of this gang called the Samitses. Now Sheba Samitses has booked a cabin at Annabel for two weeks in May."

Scotti poured more wine, wondering how Jessica managed to find cases so handy for Scotti.

"I know what you're thinking," said Jessica.

"When didn't you?"

"But it's sheer coincidence, one case right after the other out your way. I might have planned it if I could have, but I didn't, Scott. It's strictly fortuitous. With only one catch where you're concerned."

"What's the catch?"

"You'd have to work full-time on this one. You'd have to get a leave of absence from the library."

"The library just canned me. They're downsizing."

"I'm sorry, Scott, but that makes it all the more convenient. And I have some money for you. I sold the GE stock we bought back during the Punic Wars. You get half."

"Save it for Emma."

"Take it, Scott. Lighten the load on your credit cards! The only thing Emma needs is that damn Fortune Fanny doll all the kids have. I couldn't find one for her in time for Christmas. They were sold out everywhere."

"A doll? She's nine years old! Put the money in Emma's account."

"You goose Fanny and she rattles off a prediction," Jessica said. "All the kids have her. You don't watch enough daytime TV."

"I don't watch any."

"Getting the goods on this gang could pay off big, Scott."

"The Samitses gang, hmmm? Greeks?"

"Greek Americans probably."

"I bet Gus and Zoe have heard of them. Remember my mentioning them? They own Hydra, where I hung out all summer. They seem to know every Greek who's ever hit these shores."

"The Samitses are infamous, so they probably do know them. Hey, shall I talk you up to the boss for this one? You're a minor hero around Southgate since you caught Candle. Everyone thinks my ex died."

"So he did," Scotti said. "Try to remember not to call this minor hero Scott."

TWENTY-FOUR

"I don't have happy memories of this place," Scotti said as Max jumped up to help her out of her coat.

"It's the only place around here open on New Year's Day," said Max. "I called everywhere."

Helen's family had descended on them yesterday. There would be no privacy at his house.

"That post I hit out front Thanksgiving is still askew," Scotti said.

"Let me get the lady a drink," Max said. "Bloody Mary?"

"Thanks."

When Max came back from the bar he said, "When we were last here you had a little more pizzazz."

"That's your testosterone complaining, Maxie." For the rest of his life Max Bernstein would have to inject a dose of testosterone every two weeks, just as Scotti took estrogen regularly.

Max said, "Helen's picking me up in an hour. I came in a cab. I've already had eggnogs with the family." He sat down. "How're Jessica and Emma?"

"Jessie's fine. Emma's trying but it's hard on her. She couldn't wait for me to leave today. She was worried one of her friends would come over and she wouldn't know how to handle it."

"Couldn't you be an aunt or something like that around her friends?"

"I could be. But we don't know what her friends' folks might know. Bay Shore's a small town. I don't want to make a liar out of Emma."

"The best surprise is no surprise," Max said.

"Meaning?"

"You didn't hear about the Holiday Inn ad? It was a few years ago. My phone rang off the hook that afternoon. Their old slogan was, "The best surprise is no surprise." Then they did this billion-dollar renovation and figured they'd shed their old, dowdy, family-oriented image. So they ran this ad featuring a gorgeous blond who goes to her college reunion . . . only she used to be a man. . . . You never watch sports, do you, Scotti?"

"No."

"They ran the ad once, during the Super Bowl: this sexy tran who surprises classmates at a college reunion. The best surprise is no surprise. They got so many complaints they pulled it."

"Too gross, as Emma would say."

"You're all getting along okay?"

"Jessica and I are in a good place now ever since we solved the horse killing."

"You solved it."

Scotti shrugged. "She brought me to it. It depressed the hell out of me, though."

"It depressed the hell out of everyone," Max said. Scotti wondered how long Max would look like a teenage boy.

"Why would a man like Edward Candle risk his reputation for a quarter of a million? He didn't need the money."

"Don't think need," Max said. "Think greed. You want to believe that people like that love horses. But their whole purpose is to make themselves look good. If a horse can't act in a way that brings the owners glory, their investment hasn't paid off. And you know what the rich do when they lose money. They try to recoup the loss. I don't mean all rich people are twisted. But if you're twisted and rich, too, then—then," he began to laugh. "Then you have a sex change. That's what Dad said. Dad said, 'May, if you weren't privileged this sex change would never have entered your mind. This is the sort of twisted thinking that overtakes people who don't have to scramble for a living so they join a damn cult or think they're the wrong sex or some other tomfoolery.'"

"I can hear him saying it," Scotti said. "And I can hear your mother saying if you'd only gone to Vassar instead of Smith she never would have lost her only daughter."

Max's family were oil people. In addition to his own ample income as a computer doctor, Max was heir to a fortune.

Most FTMs in the program grew beards or mustaches, a male prerogative few could resist. For a time Max had grown both, but now he was clean-shaven. His hair was in a crew cut. He loved wearing neckties, a navy-and-white-striped one that noon, with a white shirt and blue blazer. Scott doubted that anyone as well-dressed as Max had been in By The Bay since the last time Max was there with her.

"Tell me your news, Max. You said you have something important to discuss."

"What do you think of Helen and I having a baby?"

"I think science will have taken another major leap forward."

"We heard of a couple in San Francisco who can't afford the baby girl the mother will have in two months. They already have four girls, and they'll only make the financial sacrifice for a boy."

Scotti smiled. "There'd be some kind of cockeyed justice if you were to adopt a female, Max. Your female persona was sacrificed in favor of a male, too."

"We'll both have daughters, Scotti!"

"Our kids could start a support group for children of transsexuals."

"No. I never intend to tell Nola. Why should I?"

"Nola?"

"Helen chose the name."

"It's really in the works then?"

Max grinned and nodded. "Nola Bernstein."

"Congratulations."

"Thanks. Have you read *The Master Key* yet?"

"I couldn't finish it. There's that scene halfway through when the mother leaves her child? And the child's gone when she returns? All the torture she goes through? I felt as though it was happening to me. I kept thinking of Emma."

"I'm glad you're back in touch with her, Scotti."

"Then I began to wonder if the book would have bothered me when I was Scott."

"Sans estrogen as a trigger?"

"Yes. I'm beginning to understand what we hear in Consciousness Raising about emotional changes. Seeing Emma gave me all these new maternal feelings, Max. Have the hormones changed you emotionally?"

"The only change I feel is regret."

"You do, Max?"

"I regret losing my ability to sing," Max said. "I miss entertaining. I miss being a draw."

Scotti smiled. "You could have been a contender."

"I had a damn good voice!"

"Now you have your Woodies to fix up, hmm?"

"Tell Helen the testosterone is causing that, will you? She's not happy about our backyard."

On the third round Scotti switched to Virgin Marys, but Max stayed with boilermakers.

Max would probably never have passed a Breathalyzer test if he'd come in his station wagon and been stopped by the police on his way back. But he defied the idea that someone as short and thin as he was would be quick to show his drinks. He held them well. He'd been a whiny, sloppy drinker before his change, but now, of all the post-ops Scotti knew, Max Bernstein was the most composed. Scotti thought it was because he had Helen. She had seen him through everything.

Scotti wondered if he should tell Max about Delroy Davenport, and the ominous feelings she'd had since Delroy had written her the note and forced her to collect it in person. She didn't want to spoil New Year's Day, but Max was the only one she could talk to about this man. She hadn't been able to tell Jessica, give that glimpse of herself in such an unstable, vulnerable situation. Not when Jessica was finally accepting, able to tease Scotti, convinced at last that Scotti wasn't caught up in some neurotic obsession.

She was about to broach the subject when she saw a couple come into By The Bay with snow on their coats.

"I'd better go soon," she told Max. "It must be coming down hard outside." And she was relieved, too, that she wasn't going to tell Max. There wasn't time. It wasn't an easy confession no matter who was on the listening end. Untold, she kept any chaotic vision of herself safe from all eyes, just as though it hadn't happened.

Max glanced at his watch. "Helen's due any minute. Just wait to say hello. Otherwise she'll think you never forgave her for that Thanksgiving dinner."

The woman who had just entered the bar had removed her scarf and was shaking the snow off it.

Scotti knew who it was before she even turned around. She recognized the man, too, as he ran his hand through his wet, curly hair.

Some dizzy trick of fate seemed to be throwing Nell Slack in Scotti's path. Scotti didn't know the man's name, but she had seen him with Nell at the bowling alley and again, ever so briefly, at Hydra Christmas night.

The pair hung up their coats and sat on bar stools.

There was no point in mentioning her to Max, no time now, either, to fill Max in on her friendship with Mario.

"One more for the road," Max said, standing up. "Do you want something, Scotti?"

"Maybe a coffee."

Max was still standing by the booth. "You know, Scotti, you're the only person in my life I like to drink with. Helen and I always get into some kind of argument, and I can never let my guard down completely with my colleagues."

Scotti stood up. "I'm going to slip into the john before I start back. I hope Helen's on time."

"And I hope she comes alone. I'm not ready to face my mother-in-law right this minute. 'Max, you better shape up,' she'd say. 'You're about to be a father.'" He laughed, his face shining like a schoolboy's, his tie loosened, one of its tails tossed across his shoulder.

Scotti couldn't help remembering May Bernstein from summers long ago at Cherry Grove, on Fire Island.

May was this young, hook-nosed tomboy, trying to fit in to the lesbian community, her large breasts bound, her Texas-style cowboy boots stuffed with socks to make her taller. The only thing going for her was her voice, which reminded Scott of Streisand's. The testosterone had ruined that, and it was indeed regrettable.

Both Scotti and Max had worked with the program's speech therapists: Max to lower her voice, Scotti to raise hers.

"I am not a lesbian," May would insist in the old days. "I just don't have any community but the gay one. They accept me, or at least they do when I'm singing."

And Scott had argued with her, told her the nose job she was planning to have would be all the surgery she'd ever need to be happy . . . at the same time recognizing himself in things she said about being in the wrong body.

She was the first one Scott called once he heard about the institute. Max enrolled when Scotti did, and thanks to the profligate rewards of the Bernstein oil wells, finished before Scott had started the depilatory treatments. Max had wanted to lend Scott money to help him transition, but Scott could not accept it. Scott had the feeling it was the one gift to himself he really wanted to pay for.

Visits to ladies' rooms were still chancy where Scotti was concerned. In a three- or four-booth facility, she seldom had the feeling someone would discover her, but in little restaurants like this one there was often simply a toilet and sink, so that Scotti had to be sure she was alone with the door carefully locked. When she came out, Helen was sitting with Max, her coat on, her small hands wiping the snow from her glasses. Jessica had always called her "the canary" because Helen used to dress always all in yellow, to match her blond hair. She also walked like a little bird on these long, thin legs, a tiny woman Max was delighted to tower over.

Scotti reached down and hugged her.

"Hi, sweetie," said Helen. "Mother's waiting out in the car. I had too much eggnog to drive, but I wanted to wish you a happy New Year."

"Max told me the good news about Nola."

"I wish I could stay and talk about it with you."

"I have to go anyway," Scotti said.

"Sit down a second, Scotti. You have to promise me you'll be Nola's godmother."

"I promise." Scotti sat down and Max leaned forward to whisper, "We just noticed someone at the bar you may know."

"Nell Slack," Helen whispered, too. "Small world."

"How do you know her?" Scotti asked.

"From TIPS," Max said. "I never had any sessions with her, of course, but Virgil Loeper learned all her makeup tricks from her."

"Remember Virgil became Virginia Loeper, Scotti? She started it all." Helen said.

"Yes, I remember Ginny. But I never met Nell Slack because I didn't take TIPS."

It was an elective, a course for MTFs with advice on hair and makeup. The instructor even helped the new Fs shop. There wasn't any such elective for the new males. They would complain that even among transsexuals, if you were born male there were the old male priorities and privileges.

The last thing Scotti needed when she'd first begun to be a female was someone to help her shop. She'd needed someone to help her stop shopping.

"I can't believe Nell Slack is here," Helen said. "I didn't know her but Ginny adored her!"

Max said, "What I remember about Nell Slack is that she lived in Haven, a halfway house. She was on probation. When she came amongst us poor Metamorphs she was fresh out of the clink. The Allen Institute is nonprofit and under a state grant, so she was probably doing community service."

"Honey," Helen said. "Keep your voice down."

"I wasn't shouting."

"It's just that there aren't many people here. Voices carry. Do you think she'd remember you, Max?"

"I doubt it. When I entered Metamorphs there weren't that many FTMs. We were the invisible ones. The girls got all the attention. Nell Slack's cut all of her hair off. She had this big nest of rust-colored hair, and she used to wear eyeliner and false eyelashes. Rumor had it she was in love with some major con artist she took the rap for. He had this neat last name. Sunshine. Rainbow. That was his last name. Rainbow."

"Max, you're shouting. You don't realize it but you are. We have to go."

"Why don't you bring your mother in?"

"My mother? In this dump?"

"Now who's shouting?" Max said.

"Who's had too much to drink?" Helen snapped back.

Scotti stood and put her coat on while Max sulked in a corner of the booth. Before she left, Helen grabbed Scotti's hand, pulled her close, and said, "He'll settle down when he's a daddy. Now we just have to get *you* married, Scotti, honey. Happy New Year!"

There wasn't time for Scotti to tell them she knew Nell Slack, too, although Nell Slack didn't seem to know her on the first day of that new year.

TWENTY-FIVE

"I could swear he is," Nell Slack said, once the short fellow in the blazer left By The Bay with Scotti Someone and a blond. "I could swear I saw him at the Allen Institute. Now that I've seen her with him, I think all three are."

"You think everyone's a goddamn transsexual," Liam said. "Do you know how few transsexuals there are in the world?"

"Five in a hundred are homosexuals and one in fifty thousand are cross-gendered."

"Where do you get your figures from?"

"From the Erickson Educational Foundation in Baton Rouge, Louisiana. We learned all about it at the Allen Institute."

"Oh, Nell," Liam sighed and shook his head.

"I took a good look at her through the mirror. The first time I met her at the bowling alley I didn't pay any attention to her. But I just got a good look. And that kid with her—the one I've seen before—he's no kid. He's no he. At least he wasn't born a he."

"He looked like a he to me," said Liam.

"Because you were never around people like that. I spent two years helping them wear eyeliner, get fitted for bras, build a wardrobe. Not the males. The females. The half-and-halfs: pre-ops. We all had a lot of fun together."

"I wonder why whatshername didn't come over and say hello to you? Do you think she saw you?"

"Maybe. I know her first name is Scotti. Her last name is on the tip of my tongue."

"Wouldn't she have come over if she saw you?"

"She might think I'm competition, Liam. That night I showed up for the Hampton Home Benefit she fled to the little girls' room, in tears probably. But how did I know Mario'd take a date there?"

"For starters he didn't ask you to go with him. He gave you two tickets."

"Don't rub it in," Nell said.

"Are you sure he was the one who sent you that bird poem?"

"No, Johnny Depp sent it to me, Liam. John Travolta sent it to me. Whoever sent it knows good poetry."

"Like you'd know."

"I read. I always have my nose in a book. You're the one who doesn't read anything but your *Affirmations*."

The bartender brought them two burritos from the microwave in the kitchen.

They were both hungry. They had come from Liam's sister's "open house" in Copiague. Besides a too-rich eggnog, she'd only served Pepperidge Farm goldfish, potato chips, and pretzels. On the way back, when the snow started coming down again, Liam had pulled off Sunrise Highway at exit 65 to fix his windshield wipers. When they got to Hampton Bays and saw the bar with the OPEN sign on the door, Liam had said, "This looks like our kind of place."

After Nell took a bite of the burrito she said, "This better not be our kind of place after January twentieth."

"Don't bring that up here."

"The bartender's watching the game."

"Yeah," said Liam softly. "Then someday we see him in a courtroom and he says, 'I was watching the game but I just happened to hear her mention January twentieth.'"

"You're right," said Nell. But it was hard not to talk about it, and they always did, even when they agreed that they wouldn't. Liam kept changing the MO. First he was going to use his Saab for the snatch. Then he was going to get a Ford Crown Victoria, the car police always drove. He still hadn't decided how he would collect the ransom from Delroy Davenport or where he'd meet Fina once he had the Lucky We. Nell would just as soon not know those details.

She had never done anything this daring. Her brief criminal career had been masterminded by Jimmy Rainbow, a white-collar embezzler who specialized in bilking charities of their funds, until he got the idea to rob an old widow of all her jewelry. An old widow whose precarious heart condition had ultimately sent Nell off to prison.

Liam liked to blame Jimmy. Anything to bring him down in Nell's estimation. More than anyone in Nell's past Liam resented Jimmy, not only because Nell had loved him, but also because Jimmy had an education and sophistication that Liam did not have.

Liam began watching the game.

Nell didn't know if it was the Rose Bowl, the Orange Bowl, or what bowl. She didn't know one from the other. She thought about this Scotti. Nell could have been wrong about her. What Liam had said was true: Nell was always thinking this one or that one was a transsexual. If she'd never done her community service at the institute, such a thought would never have entered her head.

There had been plenty who could have fooled anyone. Plenty who did. Most of them weren't that obvious, except for the showbiz MTFs, and others who just liked to camp around.

A lot of the males who'd become female would show Nell photographs of themselves when they were men. They'd been nice-looking . . . until they became women. As women many were downright homely. It didn't matter. They thought they'd died and gone to heaven as soon as they'd sprouted breasts.

At Cortland Correctional, Nell had a cell mate you could put a suit and tie on and take anywhere. Nobody would ever know. She'd called herself

Blackie, and while she'd never wanted a different body, if she had to wear women's clothes she'd break out in hives.

She was a good lover, too. She beat having to take a vibrator to bed nights. After "lights out" in that place you could hear vibrators humming like a swarm of bees let loose. Some of the girls liked to name theirs and call out the names in the dark when they'd come.

At first, it struck Nell as hilarious. A lot about CCI made her laugh, in the beginning. But then it sank in that she was stuck there, with no relief from the noise in that place. Radios, TVs, shouts, farts, cruses, weeping. She'd wonder if she'd ever hear quiet again.

Liam ordered another Jack Daniels straight up at halftime, and a Dewar's and soda for Nell.

He said, "I just thought of New Year's resolutions for us to make."

"Like what?"

"Resolved: you never say you think someone is a tran, and I never make us spend any more time at my sister's."

"I'll drink to that," Nell said. "I don't know why you dragged us there today. You don't even like Gretchen."

"When the time comes, I want her to rent the Crown Vic for me, so it's not in my name. I want you to borrow her Pinto. So we want to stay on her good side."

"I didn't know she had one." Nell looked out the window. "Don't we have to worry about the snow?"

"The Saab has four-wheel drive." He took a gulp of his drink and went back to watching the game.

Nell thought about her life. She often thought about the strange twists and turns that had brought her to a certain point.

When she first started work at the Allen Institute she was assigned an MTF called Virgina Loeper. Ginny was a pre-op who had been a passably good-looking male biologist, specializing in mollusks. As a female she was this frump who didn't know how to dress, wear makeup, or do her hair.

Nell had spent months working with her, often paying visits to her Washington Square apartment, helping her with her wardrobe. When Nell returned to Haven, she would regale the others there with Ginny stories. Everyone collapsed with laughter.

One day at Ginny's apartment she had asked Nell to help her bring her houseplants in from the terrace. Fall was coming and they would not survive a frost.

Nell had picked up a pot and seen a zillion little armadillo-like bugs, some running, some rolling themselves into balls.

"Can you do something about these insects, Ginny?"

And Ginny, dowdy in her plaid skirt with a white bowed blouse, lipstick on crooked as always, her lashes too thick with mascara, her voice still too deep and gruff, had answered with great authority: "They are not insects, Nell. They're sow bugs. They're actually crustaceans, with eleven pairs of legs. They're distantly related to lobsters."

Once started, Ginny continued, describing mites and springtails, root aphids, bristletails and beetles. Before that they had always girl-talked their way through sessions. Nell had always poured her heart out about Jimmy Rainbow, with Ginny asking when Jimmy was going to hurt Nell more than she loved him. Ginny saying not to let Jimmy dazzle her, not to find herself back behind bars for that snake in a suit.

But once Ginny began talking about things from Ginny's world, suddenly Nell saw the seriousness in the absurd, the scientist behind the freak, the crazy way an individual struggles to bloom despite common sense and ridicule. It made Nell wonder about herself, wonder if there was any time she had ever in her life fought for herself, or for anything she wanted as much as Dr. Virgil Loeper had wanted to be Ginny Loeper.

That was when she had become friends with Ginny. It was the first time she had not only found herself sympathizing with an MTF but admiring and even envious of her.

When Ginny finally left TIPS, no less a frump despite Nell's coaching, she had presented Nell with a sampler she had sewn, a snail adorning it. The verse was from a poet named John Donne.

> *And seeing the snail, which everywhere doth roam,*
> *Carrying his own house still, still is at home,*
> *Follow (for he is easy pac'd) this snail,*
> *Be thine own palace, or the world's thy jail.*

Now, sipping her Dewar's, staring at herself in the long mirror over the bar, a wistful smile tipped Nell's lips. Ginny was still teaching at New York University, last Nell had heard. And very little had changed in Nell's life. A different man but another scam. The goal was still money, and the world was still her jail.

Carrying his own house still, still is at home.

Then suddenly Nell remembered the last name of Mario's friend. House. Scotti House.

TWENTY-SIX

"So that's my very sad story," Delroy said, sipping the peppermint tea, noting the can of Vassilaros coffee on the counter. That must be the brand Scotti drank, which her mother complained she had to go out of her way to purchase. Delroy planned to bring a can there next visit.

Indeed it had been a very sad story he'd told Myrna House, for he had left out nothing, including his Amish years and his sister's elopement with the man she'd come to call Fernando. Fernando—from some old song that went "If I had to do the same again, I would, my friend, Fernando."

But of course Delroy did not mention his first encounter with Scotti on Thanksgiving night.

Baba jumped down from his lap as Mrs. House bent over and placed her own plate on the floor. She had saved all the frosting for Baba from the carrot cake Delroy had brought. Delroy had taken it from the Lashers' kitchen. There were all sorts of cakes and cookies bought from Citarella for the stream of friends that had come to call on Mr. Lasher that New Year's Day. None of them even saw him. They were thanked for coming and served light refreshments after the announcement that Mr. Lasher was resting and could not be disturbed. The truth was, Lasher was on a feeding tube and ventilator. He ran his business through an electrode taped to his right cheek. The device converted the electrical activity in his facial muscles into signals that were transmitted to a laptop computer. . . . Lately Lasher was too tired to spend much time with it, and the real deal he'd worked out was done. . . . As for visitors of any kind, that, too, was over. Delroy had never taken anything from the house without permission, nor had he ever requested time off as he had been doing since Christmas Eve. Now he was no longer willing to be the same trusted slave they had made him.

Mrs. House sat across from Delroy at the kitchen table, still shaking her head in amazement at all Delroy'd had to say.

"Neither cast ye your pearls before swine, lest they trample them under their feet, and turn again and rend you," she said. "That's from the Bible."

"I recognized it," said Delroy, who knew the Bible all too well.

"That's the rich for you. You're right about the rich," she said.

"This is just between you and me."

"I won't even tell my daughter."

"Mrs. Lasher doesn't know what he's got up his sleeve."

"But she knows about the will?"

"Oh, yes. They've always kept the will up-to-date together. And he's richer now, with the merger. It's my hunch she decided who would get what. She's known to be a tightwad."

"He could have said something, though. He could have said, 'Why don't we give Delroy the house we bought for him to stay in?' He could have said, 'Delroy deserves more money.'"

"He could have said 'Delroy's my size, could wear my clothes.' He could have said a lot he didn't say. Yes, ma'am. He could have."

"After all you've done for him."

Delroy sighed. "I'll get along," he said. "I always have."

"Let me give you another cup of tea, dear."

"Thank you, ma'am."

She got up to do it and Delroy took the empty plate from Baba, put it on the table, and patted his knee, signaling to Baba so the little dog would jump back into his arms.

He held him close and watched the old white-haired woman fuss for him, padding about in her red booties, humming "Some Enchanted Evening" to herself.

Who would ever guess that her life was not the ordinary one it seemed to be? Who would ever fathom that the little boy she had dressed in Little Lord Fauntleroy suits and caps would grow up longing to be a female?

For Delroy that only confirmed his belief that a writer like Patricia Highsmith was trying to tell her readers people were all peculiar. Nothing is as it seems to be. No one is without a dark secret or two.

Delroy would probably not be taken as a likely candidate for *Meidung,* a form of ostracism among the Old Order Amish. But at age thirteen he *had* been excommunicated and shunned. Even his own family would not eat with him or speak to him during the days he waited to be received by Aunt Sade in Sag Harbor. He was an outcast, rejected by God and man, thrown to the English to be raised thereafter.

Aunt Sade had said, "Forget all that religious bullshit, Delly. You're safe from it now."

But it stayed stamped on his soul, so that sometimes when he slept on his stomach he felt the weight of it pressing down on him in his dreams. And in some of those dark dreams he saw his sister's laughing face, heard Eelan crying out, "Let's go to Fuck, Pennsylvania!" Her name for the nearby village of Intercourse.

When Delroy had been invited by Mrs. House to "drop in," he'd hoped Scotti would be there. But even though she was not, he was becoming a part of her world, and thoughts of her had receded as he'd begun to answer all the questions her mother had asked him.

"Tell me all about yourself," Mrs. House had said.

He knew it was not just something she had tossed out so they would have things to talk about over tea. She really wanted to know him. The Mister didn't; Delroy knew that now. All the while he had poured his heart out to the Mister about Eelan, Lasher's eyes looked simpatico, and he would say, 'Go on, go on,' but that was what he was good at, wasn't it? Seducing people. What was it they always said about him? They said he acted as though you were the only person there at a big party when he talked to you. You had his full attention, they said. He really listened, they said.

Mrs. House did not let anything Delroy told her go by without comment. She asked questions, watching Delroy with her light blue eyes, smiling at him, remarking, hands gesturing, exclaiming as he described Aunt Sade's secret love affair with Mr. Witt, who introduced her to opera and art, and left Knitwits in his will "to my loyal employee Sade A. Davenport."

Once when Delroy stopped his rambling and suggested, "You don't want to hear all this, Mrs. House," she put her hand over his and answered, "Of course I do. You just keep talking. I'm an old lady with all the time in the world to listen to you."

As she cut more carrot cake, she said, "I don't believe in suicide myself. I believe that it's a sin."

"Even if you were in the shape Mr. Lasher is?"

"The Lord has his reasons, Delroy."

"I try to believe that's so."

"It is so."

"After Mr. Witt died my aunt said if there was a God he didn't create a world without end, he created a world without any point."

"Ah ha. Your Aunt Sade was a joker."

"Not really."

"I married an atheist, Delroy. My late husband would not even call himself 'an agnostic.' He would insist that he had no uncertainty about it. There is no God, he would say. That's what I put up with. But I said my prayers every night, secretly."

"I used to pray," said Delroy, who still asked the Lord to watch over Eelan. But now he was ashamed of those prayers, and the old entreaties for Mr. Lasher, and the old, old ones for his father's forgiveness. Where had it gotten him?

Mrs. House could read his mind. She said, "You probably think your prayers were for nothing, considering what's happened in your life. Your sister's sorry end . . . your aunt's tragic accident . . . Mr. Lasher's decline and his thoughtlessness. But just remember: the Lord isn't finished with you yet."

No sooner were the words out of her mouth than a voice called, "Mother?"

She was home.

"In the kitchen, Scotti. We've got company."

Delroy had planned to leave the little Ronson pocket lighter there, with Aunt Sade's initials on it, and Mr. Witt's inscription.

Now it was a small gift for Scotti. She would remember his mentioning it at their last meeting, outside the East Hampton Library. Delroy would simply push it to the center of the table in the kitchen and say, "You ladies will get more use out of this than I ever could, so I'm giving it to you."

On the side it read "At least we had music and Toulouse."

TWENTY-SEVEN

Len Lasher had designed the school logo himself, a gold shield with I AM THE CAPTAIN OF MY SOUL printed across it in tiny black letters.

He had thought of it in the early days of his diagnosis, when he had still imagined his own "unconquerable soul" would keep him alive long enough to see Deanie enter second grade.

Invictus was located in Sandy Beach Park, two miles out of East Hampton Village. There were seven little girls enrolled that year. There were four faculty members: a history and social studies teacher, a math and science teacher, an English teacher who also taught physical education, and a Latin and French teacher. The children were bilingual. They called out in French during their soccer, tennis, and exercise classes.

On the twentieth of January a surprise announcement was posted on the bulletin board, which was the first thing the students saw as they swung past the huge oak doors and entered the small, white, one-story building.

Invictus was going on a winter field trip to Mexico, beginning the second week in February.

Deanie had already been told, and she was not as excited as the others were. Mexico was one place she had never been and always wanted to see, for she spoke a little Spanish, loved the food, and had learned about Indians in her art class. But Deanie was reluctant to leave East Hampton.

She griped about it to Mario at the end of the school day, once they'd dropped the others off.

"It's what your dad wants," Mario said. "I think it's a pretty great birthday gift."

"Something could happen to Daddy and I wouldn't be here."

"Nothing's going to happen to your father."

"You don't know that."

"I know he wouldn't send you away if he thought anything could happen to him."

"Anyway I'd rather go to Paris and save Mexico for when my mother can come with me."

"Decisions, decisions," Mario teased. "Shall it be Mexico or Paris? . . . I'm surprised he's letting all seven of you go."

"And two of the faculty."

"Right . . . You kids don't usually go places in February."

"Well, I can't go alone."

"That's true."

"I think Daddy's afraid his illness is boring me. But I'm not bored at all. I never am! I know who is."

"Who?"

"My uncle Jack. It's getting on his nerves. He picks fights with my mother and he's mean to me."

"I thought you liked him."

"I used to, but he was never around as much as he is now."

As they came from Northwest Woods, where Mario had dropped off the last child, a police car appeared and sounded its siren in three small wails.

"What's the matter with him?" Mario asked. "I was only doing thirty-five." He pulled over.

A uniformed policeman emerged: visor cap, dark glasses. He said, "Step out of the car, please, sir. Bring your license and registration back to me."

"What was I doing wrong, officer?"

"We need to examine your identification, sir. I'll explain it to you. I'm sorry, sir, for any inconvenience."

Mario thought of Mr. Lasher. Ever since he had seen the grave at Green River Cemetery he had suspected there was more wrong with Len Lasher than everyone knew. The Mexico trip that Deanie had just told him about confirmed the suspicion. Had something just happened at Le Reve that the officer did not want to announce in front of her?

"Wait here, honey," he said, getting the license and registration from the glove compartment.

He did not see the gun until he reached the white Ford sedan with a rotating cherry on its roof, blue stripes on its sides, and some kind of gold medallion on the door, a wire screen between the driver's seat and the backseat. Nowhere on the car was the word *police*.

The gun was pointed at him.

"I'll shoot you and the girl if you don't get in back fast!"

Mario got in back.

"Put on this ski mask backwards," the "officer" said, handing him a knit object. "Don't fool with me! I'll kill you both. I may kill her, anyway, depending on how you act."

"All right, whatever you say." Mario pulled the mask down over his face. There was a tiny mouth hole in the back allowing him to breathe.

"I'll say this just once more. I'll kill the girl if you try anything. Then I'll kill you. Lean forward and stick your hands out behind your back."

Mario's wrists were then handcuffed.

"No one gets hurt if you follow directions. Sit there and this will soon be over. Not a peep out of you!"

Mario could hear another car approach. He could hear the "officer" say, "Go ahead. Be quick!"

To Mario he said, "I'm right here, Mr. Rome. My gun and I are watching you."

TWENTY-EIGHT

A white-haired woman wearing dark glasses and a fur coat opened the door of the van and said, "Hello!"

"What's going on?" Deanie asked.

"I guess I'm going to take you home. Your driver has to go through a road check. He says your family will be worried if you're not home on time."

"No, thanks."

"Do you know what just happened?"

"Where's Mario?"

"What just happened is someone in a van just like this held up a bank. Your driver has to wait for another police car to come."

"I'll wait, too."

"Honey, the policeman stopped me and asked me to take you home. I think we better do what the policeman says."

"I'll wait here."

"You'll be all alone. I can't wait with you. I have to pick up my little dog from the groomer. Don't you want me to drop you off? I don't want the policeman to get mad at us."

Deanie said, "What a nuisance!"

She got out of the van. "I'll go tell Mario that you're taking me home."

"He knows that, dear. I don't have time to wait, so please just get in my car. My little dog will be frantic!"

Deanie followed the woman, a cross expression on her small face, complaining all the while that her father would fix the police for "resting" Mario.

The woman in the fur coat said, "He's not being arrested, honey. He didn't rob a bank, did he?"

"Of course he didn't. He works for my father! My father is Len Lasher."

She climbed into the Pinto and the white-haired woman shut the door.

When she was behind the wheel she said, "Where do you live? I hope it's not far."

"It isn't," said Deanie. "You probably know where Le Reve is."

"Sorry that I don't."

"I thought everybody knew where we live." She gave the woman the address. She said, "You'll get a big tip for doing this."

"I don't expect a tip. This is a favor I'm happy to do. . . . Be careful. That's a chocolate éclair in the package next to you. Don't sit on it."

"I love chocolate éclairs," Deanie said. "When I was little I used to call them chocolate affairs."

The woman started the car. "I shouldn't eat anything that rich. It'll ruin my diet. You can have it."

"Can I? Thanks!" Deanie said. "It's my favorite thing in the whole world!"

"Then enjoy!"

Deanie chomped on the éclair as they went down Three Mile Harbor Road.

Deanie said, "Where did this come from? Did you buy it at Citarella?"

"No."

"Did you buy it in East Hampton?"

"No . . . I made it myself."

"Nobody makes éclairs."

"I do."

"Then what's it doing in a bag?"

"I put some there for a friend. I saved one for myself."

Deanie was finishing it. She talked with her mouth full. "I don't usually eat this fast but I was starved. I always have my after-school treat first thing when I get home. I'd be home now if that stupid policeman hadn't stopped us."

"Never call a policeman stupid, dear. They're smarter than you think. What's your name? I'm Mrs. Brown. You can call me Rona."

"I'm Deanie Lasher. My real name is Agnes Dean Lasher but I happen to hate the name Agnes."

The woman turned onto Springy Banks Road.

"This isn't the way," said Deanie.

"I have to pick up my little dog first. Poor Derby is waiting for me."

"What kind of a dog?"

"A bichon. Do you know what a bichon is?"

"Of course! I know most breeds. Before I got my pony we had a pug, but he got run over."

"How did that happen, or would you rather not talk about it?"

"I'd rather talk about my pony. This is sort of what she looks like." She pulled off a yellow knit scarf with a chestnut-colored horse's head stitched into it. "Her name is Pécheresse, but it's misspelled there."

"What a pretty name: Pécheresse."

"My pony is named after a poem. The man who gave it to me names all his horses after poems written by this woman from England. He's related to her. His daughter goes to school with me and she's related to this poet, too, only the poet's been dead forever."

"That's very interesting, Deanie. I like poetry. Who is the poet?"

"I can't remember. But the man who gave it to me is Candace Candle's father and he's a horse killer."

"A horse killer?"

"He doesn't kill them himself. He gets someone else to do it and then he gets a lot of money."

"He gets money for killing horses? Who pays him?"

"I don't know. No one in my family talks about it."

"Are you sure, honey?"

"Everyone at my school knows it, only we don't talk about it if we see Candace anywhere. We're awfully good about that. We just talk about it to ourselves because it's not Candace's fault her father does what he does. Candace likes horses, same as me."

She put the scarf back around her neck.

They took another road and another.

"Where is this dog groomer's place?" Deanie asked.

"It's not too far now."

"I hope not! We used to take Pie Face out to Dapper Dog's near Kmart. That's where you should take Top Hat"—big yawn—"next time."

"Derby. His name is Derby."

"Derb" (yawn) "by."

"Sleepy, Deanie?"

"Not really," Deanie answered, but she was. Really.

TWENTY-NINE

That morning his wedding ring had fallen off his finger. Both Lara and Len had plain gold bands inscribed "Lucky We." Now his was somewhere under the bureau across from the bed. A little message from the Great Fly-swatter in the Sky? *Finis,* my friend.

When he did think about his death, and now he thought about it a lot, he saw his whole life, chapter by chapter, and realized in a way he never had before that while he'd always thought of it as extraordinary, it wasn't. It was just another story, shorter than some, but no more meaningful, no lasting significance in it.

Alone, he could not dwell on it, for he could not let himself cry. He could not blow his own nose or wipe his tears. As a man he had only cried on sentimental occasions, joyful tears from the eyes, not from deep inside. He had sobbed once, shortly after he heard the diagnosis, while he was taking a shower. It hit him like a punch to his insides that he could not fix this one. There was no one he could phone, no way he could reverse it, no bargaining ploys to change things.

Len looked at the clock. Every little thing he did now was special, even reading the time. He was expecting Deanie to arrive any minute. All he could do was wait, but even that was poignant, as so much was. He knew he was waiting to have the last talk of his life, alone, with his daughter.

He wanted to say something she would always remember.

Then, unannounced, Jack Burlingame walked into the room.

"How're you doing?" he called out. Realizing how asinine that sounded, he rushed on. "Len? Mario just called. He had car trouble. Lara is going to drive over to Northwest Woods and pick Deanie up. Then she'll take Deanie to the dressmaker's to have her Christmas present altered, so don't wait for her. They'll be late."

Len shook his head vigorously. "Dall Ara!"

Jack said, "Lara took my car, Len. She left her cell phone here. I'll get Delroy in here to massage you. Then maybe you'll nap before dinner."

Jack disappeared before Len could respond.

Like everything else about Len's life, the end of it was carefully planned. The talk with Deanie that very afternoon was part of the plan.

He had thought of dying in the night, but Lara checked on him several times from eleven on, to be sure he was sleeping comfortably. If she were to find him dead, she would be left with his body until a medical examiner could come to the house. Deanie would awaken to the sounds and confusion of strangers in the house as he was taken to the funeral home. He did not want that for them.

Now he had to alter his plan, irked at Lara for taking Deanie to the dressmaker instead of bringing her home. But he was good at improvisation. He shut his eyes for some seconds and opened them when he had a solution.

He would still die between ten and eleven the next morning.

Lara would be attending her Pilates class at Gurney's Inn in Montauk. Deanie would be in school.

Delroy would give him the Nembutal and Valium in a milk shake and leave him in bed, listening to the original Broadway cast sing *South Pacific*. The music was a sentimental choice Lara would appreciate. The first gift he had ever given her was a Cartier gold key ring with SOME ENCHANTED EVENING engraved on the small disc. A key to a blue Mercedes convertible was attached. He had leased the car for her use that summer.

Delroy would return and stay with him until he had no pulse. Then Delroy would make the necessary telephone calls: the ME and Yardley & Pino Funeral Home . . . he did not want any part of Campbell's in New York City.

He had deliberately chosen to die on a Wednesday evening. His close friends would be notified in ample time to attend a service for him at Guild Hall Friday morning. Thursday evening the gallery would be cleared: paintings removed, rugs, chairs, and flowers brought in. Limos would be lined up for the trip to Green River Cemetery, where his plot was ready, and where Hrens Nursery had already put in the plantings he had ordered.

If he napped now, Len could have Deanie read to him right before her bedtime. He could have the last talk with her then.

He lay there trying to sleep, trying not to cry thinking about what he would say to his daughter.

He wanted to be asleep by the time Delroy arrived. He did not want a massage. Lately, either Delroy was becoming rougher, or what was left of his frail body felt bruised by any touch.

THIRTY

When Jack Burlingame went back to Len's study, Lara was sitting at the desk, the ransom note spread out in front of her.

"He'll have a massage and then a nap," said Jack. "Did you call the police yet?"

"I'm waiting for Dr. Mannerheim to call me back."

"Your shrink?"

"Yes, my shrink. Do you mind?"

Mario was sitting behind Jack, smoking in an armchair. He had been driven in silence to Le Reve by the kidnapper, the threat to Deanie keeping him under control. The ransom note had been presented to him as he got out of the white Ford sedan.

Jack said to Lara Lasher, "The only ones to discuss this with are the police! You're taking a huge chance telling anyone but them."

"Anything I say to Dr. Mannerheim is privileged information. Jack? Please. Listen to this again." She read the last lines from the piece of paper left with Mario. "'If you call the police or the FBI you will never see your child alive again. This we promise you . . .' They scare me, Jack! Whoever they are, I believe them!"

"Lara, we have to call the police. They know how to handle this sort of thing. They're trained."

"Trained!" Lara repeated in a disgusted tone. "How many kidnappings do you think these local yokels have ever handled? Word would travel so fast I might just as well call the *East Hampton Star*. It would be like setting a match to a long line of spilled kerosene."

Mario spoke up then. "You can't call the FBI anyway, can you? A state line has to be crossed to bring them in on it."

Jack shook his head. "Wrong. They give assistance to local police all the time while an investigation is ongoing."

"But Mrs. Lasher is right about the locals," Mario said. "They botch everything they do."

"Mario," Burlingame said. "We'll handle this. Thanks for trying to help, but we'll make the decisions."

"I was just—" his voice trailed off. With the kidnapping had come news of Mr. Lasher's ALS. The household help had been told on New Year's Day, but Mario guessed he was not considered part of the household. Jack Burlingame had just told him.

Mario felt chagrined and out of place in the Italian ebonized and parcel-gilt armchair, his grubby plaid wool jacket slung over one of the flower-head finials. He was dressed in jeans and a worn T-shirt proclaiming BE A BACKSEAT DRIVER IN A SOUTH FORK VAN.

"How many kidnappers did you actually see, Mario?" Lara Lasher asked.

"I saw one. A man dressed like a cop. The other one was in a second car. I didn't see him."

"What kind of a car?" Burlingame asked.

"I don't know. I had the ski mask over my head by then. I heard it but I didn't see it."

"There could be two more, three more. Someone could be watching the house," Lara said.

"That's why we have to call the police," Burlingame said.

Lara ignored that and swiveled her chair around to face Mario. "Can you do your imitation of my husband, Mario? They'll want to talk to Len. They won't know he can't talk."

"Would it work, ma'am?"

"Why not? You can fool me. Will you do that for us?"

"Of course. I'll have to break my date. We were going out after our writing workshop tonight."

"Call her now," Lara said.

"She's on the jitney. She doesn't have a cell phone. . . . I'll call her mother."

"Do something," said Lara. "And please don't smoke, Mario."

"I'm sorry."

Burlingame passed across an ashtray.

"Imitate Len now," Lara said. "Jack, I want you to hear this."

Mario sat up straight. He said, "We agwee to the wansom demands. What is the next step?"

"Perfect," Jack said.

Mario said, "Someone should be on the extension. I don't want to get their instructions wrong."

"I'll be on the extension," Jack said.

"Do you mind if I call my date's mother now?" said Mario.

"Dr. Mannerheim will be trying to reach me," said Lara.

"You can use my cell, Mario," Jack said. "It's in my coat, in the hall."

"Is Delroy with Len?" asked Lara.

"Probably."

"Probably?" Lara said angrily.

"He wasn't there when I left Len, but he's always there. He was probably in the bathroom for a minute."

"Lately, he's not always there," Lara said. "He thought Deanie was reading to Len after school, that they were going to have some private time. He could have gone out. Where? Who knows? He never says where he's going lately."

"I'll go back and check on Len while you cancel your date, Mario."

Jack was surprised at himself for the sense of exhilaration he felt. He vowed to captain this crisis for Len's sake, and for the sake of Len's only child. But who would ever have imagined this astounding turn of events? For the first time in so long he thought of buying a new notebook and jotting down ideas that had been coming to him.

THIRTY-ONE

Scotti had a habit of reading two or three books at the same time, one upstairs in her room, one in the downstairs, one at work. Away from them, she forgot their plots and characters, but immediately when she picked one up again, all of it flooded back. It was the same with the Allen Institute in Manhattan, and the Metamorphs. As soon as she walked inside the faces became familiar. Their stories did, too.

Every post-op was given a Full Circle party. That day the box luncheon was in Elliot Kidd's honor. Scotti had come in from East Hampton expressly to talk with Elliot's surgeon, Ernest Leogrande. He was to have flown in from Denver before a snowstorm in the Midwest grounded his plane. Leogrande never referred to the operations as "surgical changes." Instead, he called them "surgical confirmations."

Scotti decided to attend Kidd's party, anyway.

Two huge, blown-up photographs dominated the decor: one of a frowning seven-year-old girl dressed as a cowboy, her hands grabbing play guns in holsters at her hips, ELEANOR KIDD printed underneath. The other a picture of the new Elliot Kidd, after male-hormone injections, two mastectomies, a hysterectomy, and surgical creation of male genitalia. He was photographed on the job, a carpenter with rolled-up sleeves and muscular arms, long legs in jeans and boots, holding a hammer, grinning.

Elliot's fiancée was there with Dr. Virginia Loeper, who had sponsored him. She hadn't changed much since Scott had first seen her on campus. She dressed in the same conservative, tailored way, wore bright red lipstick, her gray curly hair short and thinning, her name tag announcing her PhD, her connection with NYU and Lanier Labs.

Loeper grabbed Scotti's arm with one of her large, square hands and said, "I heard you're a friend of the Bernsteins. How are they?" Neither the hormones nor the speech therapy had made a dent in the professor's tone. Her voice was still unmistakably masculine. With some, that was the case.

"Max is my best friend," Scotti said.

"Before he came here he was working at the Regis School."

"Yes, we both were." Scotti knew that Loeper was famous at the prep school—or infamous, depending on the viewpoint. She watched while a group of pre-ops called out to Elliot's fiancée.

"Remember when Max had his Full Circle?" Ginny Loeper asked Scotti. "Dr. Leogrande was his surgeon."

"I hope to have him, too," Scotti said. "I didn't know you were friends with Max and Helen. Do you remember Nell Slack?"

"I adore Nell," said Dr. Loeper.

"She came into this bar where Max and Helen and I were—this joint, really it was a joint, in Hampton Bays, and there we all were together."

"What fun!"

"We didn't even speak. I don't know Nell that well, and neither do Max and Helen. We weren't sure we should speak. I don't know if she read us or not. She was with a man we didn't know."

"I wonder what she's doing now," Dr. Loeper said. "I hope she's not back with Jimmy Rainbow."

"That's not his name. He has the same last name as my favorite poet. Yeats."

Ginny Loeper smiled at Scotti. "I love Yeats, too. . . . Nell's taste in men was always atrocious! I used to tell her that even in heaven she'd find

Mr. Wrong. And she was such a caring person, always doing good works, with cancer patients, with us. Her jobs always benefited the community in some way."

"Was it community service?" Scotti asked.

"Who told you that?"

"No one. I heard she'd come from a halfway house, and that's often part of the deal."

"I don't care if it *was* community service. She was good at it. Ask anyone here."

"I'm curious because we both live in East Hampton," Scotti said.

"Oh, how grand!"

"That's the reputation we have but it doesn't apply to most of us. I'm still saving for my surgery."

"What do you do in East Hampton?"

"I'm a part-time insurance investigator," Scotti said. "A part-time text-book editor, and I was a librarian until I became a victim of downsizing."

"I thought I'd lost all track of Nell Slack. Is she married to this Yeats?"

"Liam Yeats. I don't think so. I never took TIPS so I never knew her."

Elliot Kidd walked to the podium, ready to address the gathering. Male ops called it "the Bar Mitzvah speech."

"Today," Elliot began with a small smile tipping his lips. "I am a man." Applause. "Thanks to Dr. Leogrande, who can't be with us because of inclement weather somewhere near St. Louis." Groans. "And thanks to all of you, for your support."

Ginny Loeper whispered to Scotti, "Only a laborer can afford Leogrande. At least you're trying, Scotti, not like the pair in front of us."

She meant two flashy MTFs in front of them. They were old friends of Elliot's who had gone through every stage but the final one. They had no intention of having their penises removed, priding themselves on belonging to the group called Chicks With Dicks. They were heavily made-up and perfumed, in dresses and expensive Manolo Blahniks; a lot of the Metamorphs resented them.

Scotti didn't give a damn. She was always glad to be back among the Metamorphs. Whatever one was: a pre-op, a post-op, a Chick With a Dick, she was herself there.

Going home on the jitney, she finally gave up trying to read the Rose Tremain book recommended by the Ashawagh Hall Writers' Workshop leader. It was one of the most intelligent novels she had ever read about a male becoming a female. But it was growing dark, making it impossible to see by the dim overhead light.

That night Mario was reading at the workshop. Afterward, Scotti was going for drinks with him. He was good company, probably as lonely as she often was. Already she felt protective of him, and wary of Nell Slack after the frosty response from Dr. Loeper when Scotti tried to find out more about her. It was an unspoken Metamorph rule that you didn't pry, didn't ask leading questions about anyone's personal life. You were discreet about what was offered and you let it end there. Too many had too much to lose.

In any other circumstance, Scotti might have told Mario the little she knew about Nell Slack, but there was no way she could tell him how she knew. If she were to pass it off as gossip she'd heard at the library, it might be interpreted by Mario the wrong way: vicious hearsay she was eager to spread. And for what reason? A bitchy delight in tearing down a woman he was attracted to? Or a jealous reaction because Scotti was interested in him, too? She was better off not mentioning anything about Nell to him. But aside from wishing she'd found out more for Mario's sake, there was her own curiosity about Nell Slack.

Why had Nell Slack been so interested in photographing Mario? Why was she so careful about not letting Mario see her with Liam Yeats?

Maybe she was as fascinated with Mario as he believed. Maybe Yeats was another Mr. Wrong—the jealous type, perhaps, and Nell Slack didn't want him to know how she felt about Mario. But that didn't explain why she would bring him to the bowling alley, where she knew Mario would be, and why Yeats would wait in the bar while she talked with Mario . . . why they would leave together, his arm around her so possessively?

Did she have a child? Who were the horse books for?

Scotti wondered, if Jessica ran Nell Slack's name through her computer, would there be a record of her? Jessica could locate anyone who had ever been involved in an insurance scam, and sometimes she could bring up names of embezzlers, larcenists, criminals who had done time for offenses that had nothing to do with insurance.

As the jitney approached East Hampton, Scotti put the package from FAO Schwarz on her lap so she wouldn't forget it. She had found Fortune Fanny there, and bought the bizarre little doll for Emma. She had not had time for them to gift-wrap it. The doll was white-faced, with dark purple hair and bright red eyes. When you pinched its bottom, its mouth popped open and a robotic voice said, "You are in for a big surprise!"

That was all Emma needed to hear! She'd had her fill of surprises. But the clerk had assured Scotti there were thirteen other "fortunes" programmed into Fanny. That particular one would not come up again right away.

Scotti decided to take the doll along on her date, amuse Mario, see what his fortune was, and get some kind of take on the tone of the other forecasts, before she gave it to her daughter.

Scotti was relieved to have someplace to go after the workshop. Sometimes Delroy Davenport dropped by evenings. Whatever compelled him to spend so much time with her mother, Scotti was not able to figure out, but she had lost some of the anxiety he had caused her to feel in the beginning.

He just appeared, unannounced, taking a break from his duties at Le Reve. He brought along a brown paper bag that contained his knitting, prompting her mother to comment that the mark of a "real man" was the courage to indulge in unmanly behavior. Mrs. House was oblivious to the memory of once scolding Scott for surprising her with an Easter hat he had made for her. "You made it, Scott? What a strange, unattractive thing for a boy to do! You should have just bought me a corsage!"

If it bothered Delroy that Scotti always excused herself soon after he arrived, he didn't show it.

The first time she had found him there, sitting in the kitchen with Baba on his lap, Scotti had been rude, cutting him off in mid-sentence to announce she had work to do. Later, her mother had complained about it, whining that there was no one as thoughtful as Delroy. She had raved over the small Ronson pocket lighter he'd left behind, saying it had belonged to his Aunt Sade, "and he knows you don't smoke, but he pretended it was for us, because I think he was embarrassed to give me such a valuable present. Ronson lighters are from another time! They're worth money!"

Scotti did not mention her conversation with him in front of the library, when she had almost given in and smoked a cigarette, and he had promised that next time he'd have a lighter.

Perversely, Myrna House had decided to give up smoking shortly after he left the lighter with them, but she took it to her room to put with her valuables.

Although Delroy had switched his attention to Scotti's mother, there was something annoying about hearing the two of them downstairs jabbering away. Occasionally Myrna House would let out a hoot, as though he had said something terribly funny, or terribly shocking—it was hard to know which—and the rapport they had obviously achieved sometimes made Scotti think they talked about her. One thing was certain: he had not told Myrna House about his first meeting with Scotti on Thanksgiving night.

Scotti knew her mother well enough to know there was no way her mother could have kept that to herself. She would have had to chide Scotti, make some sarcastic reference to it.

The whole situation did not set well with Scotti, but she told herself she was selfish, or paranoid or controlling, and maybe all three . . . Why wouldn't she just be relieved to have them both off her hands for that small amount of time?

When the jitney finally stopped in front of The Palm, in East Hampton, it was twenty minutes to seven. Her Saturn was parked across the street. She was ten minutes away from Ashawagh Hall, where her writing workshop met in the attic.

THIRTY-TWO

The Lashers' safe was not in the floor, or hidden behind a picture on the wall. It was a small room off Len's study, much like a miniature bank vault. Nothing inside was insured.

The IRS would not collect on anything there when Len's estate was being settled.

On one side of the room were tiers of steel boxes of various sizes, each one numbered. The Lucky We was the only jewelry in No. 27, which was the date of the day in May when Lara and Len had married. It was enclosed in a teak box inlaid with onyx.

Jack had not seen the ring since Len had put it on Lara's finger, in the latticed pavilion at the end of their garden, nearly eleven years ago.

The flawless emerald was cut from a stone the size of a bird's egg, once owned by a Mogul emperor, reset by Cartier in yellow gold with diamonds.

Inside was the inscription: LUCKY WE. 1937.

"I wear it only on very special occasions," Lara said. "Last summer on our anniversary was the last time. This year, of course, we didn't have our usual New Year's Eve Day party."

"At least it's here, and not in New York," Jack said.

"Len wanted me to have a copy made, but I said no. I'd no more want a replica of it than I'd want a stand-in for Len. Times he couldn't get away to go somewhere, I wouldn't call a walker. I wouldn't go at all."

She put back the ring, closed the lid, and shoved the box into its slot. "If I have to lose it, now is the time."

"I don't think it'll be a permanent loss," said Jack. "But why is now the time?"

Lara shrugged. "Because nothing I lose matters once I lose Len. And with Deanie's life in the balance, I couldn't care less about it."

They left the safe, Lara dabbing at her eyes with a Kleenex.

It was six o'clock.

Jack went into the kitchen for sandwiches the cook had prepared for them. Mario was upstairs with Len.

There was no sign of Delroy; no word from him.

Jack had slipped Valium into Len's soup. He was asleep now, after an angry reaction to news they invented: Deanie had been allowed to have a sleepover that night.

Lara had told Len that it had come about unexpectedly, while she picked Deanie up at Invictus. She told him they had run into Elaine Candle in the parking lot. Elaine said she had been trying to call Lara, but Lara had not had a chance to get back to her.

All the Invictus students were gathering at the Candles' to watch a DVD on Mexico, have dinner on trays, and stay over. Mario would pick them up the next morning and take them to school.

Len believed Lara. Why wouldn't he? But he made it clear that he didn't like it, even though Lara had imagined he'd feel glad that Deanie was going there. It had been a bone of contention between them. Len had always felt bad that Lara made Elaine and little Candace pay for something Edward Candle had done. But Lara had remained adamant. At the time she felt lawyers and money would get Edward off, that ultimately the whole business would be forgotten. Lara wanted to show Candle that she and Len were not going to forget it, or forgive it, ever.

Until the Valium began working, Len's face was a cloud. He gave Lara dirty looks and waved her out of the room.

Lara knew that since he had so little autonomy, what he could control he did not like relinquishing. He did not like giving up the planned story time, when Deanie read to him. It was one of the few "traditions" they could continue to enjoy.

Another thing that bothered Len was Delroy's absence. Where was he? Why was Mario there in his place?

We will contact you this evening, Mr. Lasher. After eight. Please be available.

Nothing was written about how Len would be contacted. Lara had presumed it would be by telephone. So that Mario could attempt his imitation of Len, Lara had arranged for Mrs. Metcalf to come. A practical nurse, she had cared for Len often, mostly overnight.

While Jack and Lara ate tuna-fish sandwiches in the library, Jack said he had something to tell her.

For a few weeks Jack had been loaning Delroy the keys to the estate Jeep, which the gardener used or the cook did, to do errands. Now it seemed Delroy had met some woman in Springs he was seeing, using the bicycle Jack had given him. When the snow made it impossible for Delroy to bike there, Jack had felt pity for him and let him take the Jeep there, too.

At first Lara took it calmly, but by the time they had scarfed down the sandwiches she was red-faced with anger.

"What woman in Springs?"

Jack shrugged.

"What does it matter?" he said. "He'll be back."

"You don't know the woman's name?"

"Why would I know her name?"

"Or where she lives?" Lara's voice rose.

"Lara, cool it! There's enough aggravation without worrying about Delroy's love life. And you've let him take that Jeep before."

"I'm not worrying about his love life, or the Jeep! I'm worrying about the fact that he's not here at the same time Deanie's not here! Do you get it?"

Jack was holding half a Fig Newton. He said, "Oh, come on, Lara," but he didn't eat the other half of the cookie. He stood there with it in one hand, staring at Lara, letting what she'd just said register.

The possibility of Delroy having something to do with the kidnapping had just popped into Lara's head, but as soon as it did, both Jack and Lara were shocked at the thought.

Jack said, "Delroy's not smart enough to pull off something like this."

"Maybe the woman in Springs is, Jack."

He finished the Fig Newton and stood there shaking his head, mumbling to himself, "Jesus H. Christ!"

"Delroy knows everything, too," said Lara. "He knows about the Lucky We. I don't know why, but Len told him where the safe was, how to get into it, everything."

Jack said, "If there was a fire here, or anything like that, Len didn't want a family member risking his life for something in the safe. . . . And Len has always, always trusted Delroy. I trust him, too, Lara."

"Why?"

"What?"

"Why do you trust him? What do we know about him? What did we ever know about him?"

Silence.

Then, "Zilch!" Jack admitted.

THIRTY-THREE

When Delroy heard the seven cuckoos from the clock in Myrna House's kitchen, he slapped his hand to his mouth. He had already missed Mr. Lasher's evening bath time.

Mrs. House said, "You're not worried about the time, are you?" not waiting for his answer. "Maybe they should worry about you for a change. They just take you for granted down at Le Reve, if you ask me."

"Yes, they do," he agreed.

It had been a comforting afternoon, with Delroy knitting away on a sweater he had not told her was for Baba. There was something enormously cheerful about knitting in a warm kitchen, a little dog snoozing at the foot of this white-haired woman's rocker.

Mrs. House had told him more about her husband, Bolton S. House, PhD. The trouble with him, she had declared, was that he had no interest in anyone he couldn't teach.

"When we were first married, he taught me everything. He taught me more than I wanted to learn. Serve champagne in a fluted glass, but not wine. Don't bother opening wine so it can breathe because it can't breathe unless you decant it. Wine, wine, wine, and then he got after my bracelets. I shouldn't wear so many bracelets, so much jewelry, just one piece at a time, and just one ring besides my wedding ring! The walls in our house had to be all white! No blue rooms, no pink ones, and no shag rugs or recliners of any kind. Never say "consensus of opinion." It dismayed him. What didn't dismay him? That was his favorite word. . . . He ruined my son's life with his set ways!"

Then she stopped her harangue abruptly, after blurting that out.

"I didn't know you had a son," said Delroy.

"He went away. . . . That was what killed Bolton. It hit him in the heart, that loss. But if you don't mind, I prefer not to speak of my son."

"All right." Knit one, purl two. Delroy was calm. His new friend could do as she liked. Friends let friends do as they liked.

But obviously Mrs. Myrna House did want to speak of her boy, and Delroy very much wanted to hear what Scotti had been like.

"My poor little son wanted to be just like Bolton, wanted to know everything Bolton knew. But he was just a child. He should have been out with the other little boys playing ball, not holed up in his room reading books Bolton gave him. On every subject. The poor little tyke learned too much too fast, and I believe that it affected his mind. He had all this information twisted in his head, three years old and he would say to me, 'Mama, did you know that a piano is a percussion instrument?' Or 'Mama, Papa is a noctiphile!' Can you imagine?"

"A noctiphile?" Delroy looked up from his knitting surprised. "Someone who fancies corpses?"

"Oh, no, no, no. Someone who's a night owl. . . . But do you see what I mean? What is one and one, Bolton would ask him, and when the poor boy chirped up 'Two!' Bolton would say 'It's also eleven.' . . . Education gives you too many choices, Delroy, too many options and answers. Take the weather. Before all these meteorologists got on the television, we had a simple weather report. Rain tomorrow. Sunshine tomorrow. Now they give us all these possibilities and they take five minutes to do it. When they're done, we still don't know if we need our umbrellas the next day."

"I never had one," said Delroy.

"You never had an umbrella?"

"I never had an education."

"Sometimes I think my poor son would have been better off without one. Bolton taught him and taught him. They were like a pair of scissors. Inseparable. I think my son was afraid to be without him. When he was just a tot he even asked Bolton once if he could marry him when he grew up. You see, he had everything mixed up in his little brain."

A few seconds of silence as Mrs. House must have perceived that suddenly their talk had taken a very odd turn. Delroy's knitting needles clicked faster.

He said, "It is hard to talk about missing members of the family, I know that . . . I don't even know if Eelan is alive."

"Your dear sister . . . I think she is alive."

"Mr. Lasher once said that someday that mystery will be solved."

"No thanks to him! A man with his connections could have found that out for you, Delroy."

By now, Scotti House was at her writing workshop. Delroy had started a second letter to her after she'd snubbed him on New Year's Day, but he doubted that he would ever finish it. He was no longer sure that she had snubbed him. She really was working on a novel. Mrs. House complained again and again that her daughter spent very little time with her. She said she was often awakened early mornings when her daughter got up to write. That very day Mrs. House had told Delroy that the coming weekend Scotti was off to the opera, to *Tristan und Isolde*.

"Of course," she added, "I'm not invited. I never am."

It was the only opera Aunt Sade had ever taken Delroy to, one night when Mr. Witt could not attend. Delroy still remembered how moved he'd been by it. Afterward, Sade had bought the tape and played and played it.

Delroy said, "I should have asked Mr. Lasher to help me find Eelan. I don't know why I didn't."

"You didn't because you knew instinctively that people like that just don't care."

"Maybe . . . maybe . . . well, tomorrow it will be all over."

"Really? Is tomorrow the day, Delroy?"

"I shouldn't say."

"Then it is! I don't envy you, dear."

"Mr. Lasher has taken care of everything. The doctor provided the pills. He'll sign the death certificate. I won't be blamed. Don't worry about that."

"I still wouldn't want it on my conscience," said Mrs. House, bending over to pick up Baba. "It's not for us to decide such things, is it, Baba? It's not for Mr. Lasher or the doctor to decide such things."

"I've thought of that."

Baba licked her face as she continued. "Of course you've thought of that. With your religious background, how could you not? Say all you want about growing up and changing, but the early years are stamped on your soul, aren't they, Baba?"

"I know they are, ma'am. Eelan could never escape the Amish, even though she ran from them."

"Eelan haunts you, doesn't she?"

"Well, I have no one else."

Mrs. House shook her head, pet Baba with eyes closed, rocking slowly. "Oh Delroy, the things you say sometimes."

"What about the things I say, ma'am?"

"You are such a lonely young man." She looked down at the bulldog on her lap. "Baba? Tell Delroy he has us. Tell him we're his family. We even gave up smoking for him."

"You did, ma'am? For me?"

"Tell him, Baba. Tell Delroy we decided never to have another cigarette because God put a new friend in our lives."

Baba looked up, drool on his hairy chin, a tooth missing.

"Baba wants to go back to sleep," Delroy said in a fresh, peppy tone, which belied the thick emotion flooding through him. Tears burning behind his eyes, Delroy popped his knitting into the brown paper bag, jumped to his feet, and called out in a voice too light and gay, "And I have to run along, that's what I have to do. Toodle-loo, toodle-loo!"

He climbed into the Jeep and blew his nose, overwhelmed by what Mrs. House had said to him. He had the new can of Vassilaros coffee he had found for Scotti at Citarella, but he had not taken it inside when he arrived because her car was not in the driveway. He wanted to give it to her personally. Another time.

Driving away he thought of Scotti at the opera, wondering what she would wear, if she would sit where everyone dressed up, if she would be with the young man she was with on Thanksgiving Day.

The night he went to that opera with Sade, Sade said she was almost glad Mr. Witt could not attend with her, for if he had been beside her when they played the love music, she would surely have passed out. . . . "From drinking?" Delroy had asked. Sade had replied, "From desire. Sometimes you swoon from it."

THIRTY-FOUR

Nell Slack had placed the gold Cartier locket which Deanie Lasher had worn in a small black Sportsac. She had put it in the mailbox on Maritime Way, where Liam had picked it up.

There was this note inside the Sportsac, printed out from a computer.

Your daughter could be wearing this locket again tomorrow if you follow our instructions. REMEMBER IF THE POLICE BECOME INVOLVED, OR IF YOU FAIL TO DO EXACTLY AS YOU'RE TOLD, SHE WILL NEVER WEAR IT AGAIN. We are not amateurs and we expect The Lucky We to be the one and only. If it is then the girl is safe. Our next communication will be this evening after ten.

Then Liam had Scotch-taped a twenty-dollar bill to the Sportsac, put the Lashers' address on the tag, and left it on the doorstep of the East Hampton Library, inside a white Gap shopping bag. En route to the library he had called Joe's Taxi in Amagansett.

"I'm on the jitney," he said, "and I did not have a chance to drop off a shopping bag at the Lashers' on The Highway Behind The Pond. Can you pick it up now at the East Hampton Library and take it there? I've left money with it."

They could.

They did.

Liam watched them do it from the Ford, across the street in front of Guild Hall. He had placed the rotating cherry and the wire screen that separated the front seat from the back in the trunk. He had peeled off the gold medallion and the blue stripes from the sides of their Ford and burned them in the trash.

When he returned to the house, he called Nell.

"Everything okay there?"

"She's waking up. Very groggy."

"Tied?"

"Yes."

"Keep her in that one room."

"Don't forget to bring the books I bought to read to her."

"They're in my car. Anything else?"

"When will you be here?"

"As soon as I call them from the pay phone at ten o'clock."

"I don't like it here alone, Liam."

"I'll be there by ten-fifteen at the latest."

"Okay."

"I love you."

"Yeah."

"What kind of an answer is 'yeah'?"

"I'm nervous."

"Relax, love."

"All right. Good-bye."

He had parked the Ford behind the house on Newtown Lane. Their landlady, who occupied the upstairs apartment, was in Florida.

The police clothes and visor cap were stored in Liam's closet behind his pants, shirts, and shoes.

He looked in Nell's closet.

True to her word, she'd packed up. Everything was gone but the hangers and an empty shoe bag. She'd put it all into the trunk of her Buick, determined never to return to East Hampton once the child was delivered to her parents.

Okay, let her have her way. Liam intended to come back without her. They would sublet a place for a few months in Soho. She could stay there while he took care of any Homesafe obligations. She wouldn't be missed locally. Mario Rome could eat his heart out, but she had no other connection with anyone in the Hamptons.

Liam showered and shaved. He put his toilet kit and some underwear and shirts in a bag.

The phone rang while he was urinating and he let the machine take the call. Nell would never call him. The only calls he ever got were from the few clients he still had. Sometimes they wanted him to ready their houses. Sometimes they asked him to send something they needed from the house. In bad weather they wanted to know things were all right at the house, but there had not been any big storms so far that year.

He zipped up his trousers and walked into the living room while Nell's recorded voice announced: "You've reached Homesafe. Please leave a message and a number and we'll get back to you."

A male voice that Liam did not recognize said, "Nell? This is Ginny. Same number when you get to New York. *Be thine own palace or the world's thy jail*. Remember? Can't wait to see you."

What the hell was that about?

Liam went across to the machine and played back the message.

He could not believe what he heard.

Jimmy . . . jail . . . It took a few seconds for that crooked grin to come to Liam's mind, the dark laughing eyes, and one of those spiffy little bow ties Jimmy Rainbow always wore.

THIRTY-FIVE

On Main Street Delroy heard the wail of the police siren and pulled over.

He knew the officer. Sergeant Sam Bratski. He'd gone to school with him, in Sag Harbor.

"Where you headed, Delroy?"

"I'm going to the Lashers' and I'm late, Sam."

"I know. They've been worried about you."

"So what's the problem?"

"I think they wondered if you were planning to return the Jeep?"

"No, Sam, I'm going to steal it."

"I guess you forgot to tell Mr. Lasher you were borrowing it."

"Jack Burlingame gave me permission to take it. He's their houseguest."

"Where have you been, Delroy?"

"What are you asking me all these questions for?"

"Because Mrs. Lasher asked me to find you, find out where you took her car, and to be sure you return it."

"Did she think I stole it?"

"She used the word *borrow*, Delroy."

"And she called the police?"

"She was worried, I guess. Where were you?"

"I was at Myrna House's, up on Tulip Path."

"Don't get excited, Delroy. I'm just doing my job."

"Don't get excited? I work for them and she calls the police because I'm late returning one of their half-dozen cars?"

"Maybe she was worried about you, Delroy."

"That would be news."

"What's in the bag on the seat?"

"Something of mine."

"May I see it, please, Delroy?"

"Why?"

"Because it might be important."

With an exasperated sigh Delroy handed him the paper bag.

"Aha! You're still knitting. I'd forgotten about that, Needles. And some coffee, hmmm? Vassilaros."

"What are you doing, Sam?"

"Just my job. If I get called to investigate anything, I investigate it." Bratski handed the bag back to Delroy, who was blushing angrily.

Bratski said, "You just head down to the Lashers' and I'll follow you as far as the gate. Okay?"

"What *is* this?"

"I just want to be sure you and the Jeep get home safely."

"It's not my home, it's their home."

"Don't take this personally, Delroy," said Sam Bratski with a two-fingered salute.

But Delroy did take it personally.

There wasn't any other way to take it.

THIRTY-SIX

Lara was using Len's private phone to talk with Dr. Mannerheim.

She had not asked Jack to leave the room, but he finally did after ten minutes of listening to a one-sided conversation that went like this:

"Isn't it also a form of denial if I disobey this kidnapper and put Deanie in even greater jeopardy?

"Because I don't trust the police!

"How can you call it denial?

"Yes, I remember we talked about that.

"I called you because I want some input, but that doesn't mean I'm going to do as you say, Dr. Mannerheim. She's not *your* daughter."

On and on while she clutched Deanie's gold locket and watched the clock.

Mario was in the kitchen warming up a chicken casserole the cook had left for them.

Mrs. Metcalf was upstairs sitting with Len, watching an old Gary Cooper movie on AMC. Len was asleep.

Jack went from there to the enormous closet just outside Len's door, which Lara had converted into a nook for Delroy. There Delroy could be within seeing and hearing distance of Len.

There was a large leather chair with a footstool, a bookcase with a TV built into it, and a small refrigerator filled with Stewart's root beer. Delroy used the Queen Anne cherry dressing table as a desk.

There was a pile of the latest magazines stacked on top.

One of Delroy's duties was to remove all the blow-in advertising cards before he put the magazines downstairs on the living room table. If he missed one and it fell out while Lara was looking through them, she went ballistic.

There were a few mystery books with yellow Post-it flags marking the places Delroy had stopped reading. There was a well-thumbed Bible. At the back of the Bible was a withered rose and a photograph of a young girl with "Eelan" printed on the back. There was an envelope with "Scotti House" printed across the front.

Jack opened it, took out the paper inside, and read an unfinished letter that said at the top right-hand corner: "New Year's Day Evening."

Dear Scotti House,

Why did you act so nervous this afternoon? I have not told your mother our little secret, if that's what you think. Rest assured no one knows.

I have been thinking, Ms. House, and I

That was all.

Jack returned the envelope to the Bible and put the letter in his back pocket.

Mrs. Metcalf poked her head around the corner and said, "Where's Delroy tonight, Mr. Burlingame?"

"We just found him. He'll be along any minute."

"Because I can't stay over tonight."

"We know that. Don't worry."

Then Jack went back downstairs and opened the study door.

"The police located Delroy and he's on his way back here but I didn't tell him a thing. I shouldn't, should I? I can trust him for sure, and perhaps it's best if I—"

She was still on Len's phone with her shrink. It was agreed that after ten, when the house phone rang, Mario would take the call. Jack would be on the extension in the kitchen.

Jack went into the kitchen.

"What's up?" Mario had finished his dinner and was sitting smoking, reading a paperback.

"Who did you say you had a date with tonight?" Jack asked him.

"Her name is Scotti House."

"That's what I thought you said. House."

"Scotti House. She's in my class."

Jack reached in his back pocket for Delroy's letter. "Read this," he said.

THIRTY-SEVEN

"Where were you?" she said.

"I couldn't make class, Scotti."

"I know that, but what happened?"

"I left a message with your mother."

"I haven't been home since early this morning. I was in New York."

"Leave your car here and we'll take my van," Mario said.

"Okay."

In the headlights he watched her lock the Saturn, which was parked in front of Ashawagh Hall.

Eating in the Lasher kitchen that night, Mario had glanced through the book Scotti had put in his mailbox, a belated Christmas remembrance. It was used, as Mario's gift to her had been. It was a Penguin edition of *The Master Key*. He had put it in the glove compartment of his van, reading a little at a time, mostly at airports while he waited for a client. He had almost forgotten it until he flipped through it at the kitchen table.

His heart began thumping as he read a description of a four-year-old boy being kidnapped.

It was right at that point when Jack Burlingame appeared with the unfinished letter from Delroy to Scotti.

Scotti was smiling as she walked toward the van, pushing her hair back from her face, looking glad to see him.

He could not help thinking of how many times he had been wrong about women. He didn't know them at all, did he? He was not a good judge of them, not even when all he wanted was a friendship.

She got into the van and said, "You didn't miss much tonight." She was carrying her bag and a small package.

"Who read?"

"Cheryl Lewis."

"Uh-oh. The Civil War epic."

"It's your fault. Someone had to fill in for you at the last minute and Cheryl's the only one who drags her novel around with her at all times."

"*Back with the Wind*. That's what she should call it."

Scotti laughed and put the package by her feet, on the floor.

"Were you shopping in New York?"

"I just bought one thing."

"You're not like most women. A whole day in New York and you only bought one thing?"

"I didn't go there to shop."

"What did you go in for?"

She glanced across at him with an annoyed frown, which disappeared almost as quickly as it had appeared. It was not like Mario to ask her a personal question and he appreciated that that was the reason for the look.

"I went there to see old friends," she told him.

"I started that book you recycled to me."

"And?"

"And I wonder why you chose that one?"

"How come *you* chose *Lord Jim?*"

"I was getting rid of fiction. I never reread fiction."

"Well, I was doing the same thing. . . . Did you do the underlining in *Lord Jim?*"

"Yes."

"I like that quote. . . . I passed on *The Master Key* because I just couldn't get into it."

"Why not?"

"Mysteries don't interest me that much. I like writers like Mona Simpson, Thea Astley. I love her. Do you know her? She's Australian. You must read *The Acolyte*. . . . Where are we going, Mario?"

"I have a treat for you. We're going to have a drink with Jack Burlingame."

"You said he was staying with the Lashers, but I didn't know *you* were friendly with him."

"He was the reason I missed class. He wanted me to help him with something. When I told him we had a date he said to go to Ashawagh Hall and bring you back."

"I'm not dressed to meet someone like Burlingame."

"Oh? But what you're wearing is good enough for me?"

"Mario, I don't really feel like conversation with a stranger, an important writer, at that. . . . Let's skip it." She looked at her watch. "It's almost nine-thirty."

"All right, Scotti. This is about Delroy."

"What about him?"

"He may be in some trouble. He's been coming and going without telling us his whereabouts. It turns out he visits your mother, too, or so he claims."

"He isn't claiming it. He does."

"So he said."

"You called my mother about Delroy?"

"Not about Delroy yet. I called her to see if I could catch you before you went off to the workshop. . . . Later on we learned that Delroy visits your mother. It seems so unlikely."

"It is. They met at Green River Cemetery, near our house. My mother walks her bulldog there. I told you: Delroy's been over at the cemetery in connection with this half-acre gravesite. . . . My mother's a very lonely woman. They seem to have hit it off."

"Okay," Mario said. "Just tell Mr. Burlingame that."

Mario could not bring himself to ask her what he knew Burlingame would: what was "the secret"? But he had a disturbing feeling that somehow this woman wasn't at all what he had thought she was. He had never really believed her when she'd talked about frequenting the discos, covering the same territory he had so many years ago. She wasn't the type. She was too refined, too hidden. She was the only member of the workshop who was not eager to read her work . . . if there even *was* any. She had never once talked about her book to Mario, though he had told her all about his.

She said, "Is Delroy in serious trouble?"

"I don't know," Mario said.

"Well, how did *I* get involved?"

"After the police verified the fact he visits your place, Mr. Burlingame wondered about it. He knew we had a date after class, so he suggested that I bring you by for a talk."

"The police?" Mario could hear the panic in her voice.

"Delroy took the estate Jeep," said Mario. "Actually he had permission, but Mrs. Lasher didn't know that."

"Does he still have it?"

"It was in the driveway when I left."

"I just don't understand this, Mario. What is really going on?"

"Wait and let Burlingame talk to you. It's nothing dire."

But she knew better.

Mario didn't know what she knew, but he could feel she knew something, smelled trouble of some kind. She was not reacting like someone who wasn't part of the trouble.

"How did you get involved?" she asked Mario again.

"I told you: I drive for them. I brought Deanie home from school and I walked in on all this: Delroy missing, the Jeep missing." He had glanced at her as he said Deanie's name and she'd met his glance with no change of expression.

She said, "You're not telling me everything."

"You said Delroy had this 'connection' with your mother. Does that go for you and Delroy, too?"

"You know better than that, Mario! I hardly know him. I don't even like him."

Her gloves were in her lap. She was wringing her hands.

"Anyway, you'll get to meet a famous author," Mario tried to humor her with a chuckle.

"I won't be able to tell the famous author much about Delroy Davenport," she said angrily.

"I'm sorry." He was. Sorry, disappointed, mistrustful. It was familiar, wasn't it? Another woman he'd misjudged. The past repeats itself.

"Mario?"

"What?"

"Can we skip this meeting and just have a drink someplace?"

"We can't."

"Why not?" Besides anger in her tone there seemed to be fear, too.

"Scotti," he said, "would you mind going along with this as a favor to me? We're almost there. It won't take long."

"Are you giving me a choice?"

"No. I work for them, Scotti. I'm sorry."

He could feel her rage.

He went faster, fearing she might even try to jump from the van.

THIRTY-EIGHT

"He's been waking up and he's very agitated," Mrs. Metcalf told Delroy. "He keeps asking for Deanie, and he's thrashing around and making those noises of his. But I think he's asleep now. . . . Where were you?"

Delroy said, "The Missus sent the police after me. Can you believe that?"

"She said you ran off with the Jeep."

"I had permission from Mr. Burlingame."

"That's not permission from her. You know *her*."

"Mr. Lasher was planning to spend special time with Deanie, so I didn't hurry back here."

"Deanie's not even here, Delroy. She's sleeping over at the Candles'."

"You must have heard wrong. Deanie can't go to the Candles'."

"She's there right now," said Mrs. Metcalf, putting on her coat.

"She couldn't be."

"She is. I'm leaving now."

"You might be needed here tomorrow, too, Mrs. Metcalf."

"Where are you going to be?"

"Don't worry about me."

"What do you have, a girlfriend, Delroy?"

"I have a conscience."

"Oh my my my. A conscience. Who doesn't?"

"Some people don't."

"What does having a conscience have to do with your not being here tomorrow? . . . Now, as far as I know Mr. Lasher hasn't had a sedative, though he may not need it."

She was putting on her gloves, not at all interested in what Delroy had to say about what having a conscience had to do with his not being there the next day. Not that he would have told her the Mister was planning suicide. It was just as well she wasn't curious about why he had mentioned his conscience. That had just slipped out.

She said, "I have to know tonight if I'm needed tomorrow, and when. I've been having car trouble and tomorrow I have to take it in."

"You're needed all day. I won't be around."

"I can't come for the whole day. What does having a conscience have to do with your not being here?" She reached for her bag from the table and slung it over her shoulder. She looked at him. "Well?"

"Never mind," Delroy said.

"And never you mind about planning on me being here all day tomorrow. I'll come in the morning and stay no later than noon."

"Tell Mr. Burlingame that," Delroy said.

"Mr. Burlingame doesn't want to be disturbed. He's in the kitchen with guests. You tell him."

"Tell Mrs. Lasher then."

"She's in the study and she doesn't want to be disturbed. I didn't want to be disturbed tonight myself, but you had your new sweetie to see, so you handle it."

She started out the door, turned, and said, "If your conscience permits you to do so. Good night, Delroy."

"Good night," he said.

Then he sat down beside Mr. Lasher's bed.

"Mister? Sir? Mister?" He sat there for a moment. Then he said, "I know sometimes you wait until Mrs. Metcalf's gone, so you don't have to deal with her. If you're awake, please listen carefully to me. I can't go through with it, sir. Living and dying are in the hands of God, Mr. Lasher. It's not something you or me should decide. You or I. It's not for us to decide. . . . Mister?"

Delroy reached out and shook him gently.

He turned him over, face up.

Len Lasher's eyes reminded Delroy of the eyes of a fish at the end of a hook.

Dead eyes and the mouth slack.

"Oh, no, Mister. Oh, no."

The chair fell over as Delroy sprang from it and ran, down the hall, to the stairs, taking them by two, calling out, "Missus! Missus! Missus!"

THIRTY-NINE

The moment Mario had mentioned that the police were involved, Scotti had automatically thought of the letter the institute issued pre-ops explaining their situation. Hers from Dr. Rush was in a file in her desk. She never carried it with her, anymore, not even on her brief visits to Manhattan.

Although she couldn't imagine needing it that evening, anything to do with authority brought back all the What If Exercises the institute drilled into its members.

Whether you were pre-op or post-op, they devised every imaginable situation you might find yourself in and provided answers to help you cope.

What if you're to blame in a traffic accident and you find yourself at a police station? What if they hold you there? The letter from Rush would probably allow you to be put in a cell by yourself, but it might not keep you from a cavity search.

The institute dealt with a variety of confrontational situations, and Scotti had only half listened much of the time, for she could not believe anything of that sort would happen.

It could easily have happened on Thanksgiving night, and ever since she'd thanked God for her luck, if she could call that murky interlude with Delroy "luck."

Since her arrival that night at Le Reve, Scotti began to entertain the possibility that her luck could be running out.

It was bad enough that Mario had brought her there under protest. It was worse when Burlingame did not invite them into the rest of the house. He kept looking at the clock above the stove and then checking it against the time on his wristwatch. He did not offer her or Mario a drink, and did not even sit down.

Thankfully, there was no sign of police.

". . . and that's all there is to it," Scotti wound up her brief statement regarding Delroy. Of course it was minus the bladder emergency at the side of the road.

She sat at the table across from Mario. His light blue eyes could not look at her, and he kept running a hand through his straight brown hair.

Neither Scotti nor Mario had removed their coats, nor had Burlingame suggested they do so. Scotti was holding her bag and the package from FAO Schwarz.

"That is not all there is to it, Miss House," said Burlingame. "There's this."

He held out a piece of paper.

As Scotti leaned forward, her hand trembling, her elbow pressed against Fanny Fortune, the mechanical voice sounded.

"What the hell was that?" Burlingame said.

"It's nothing."

"What's in that bag?"

"Something I bought in New York this morning."

She was about to take the paper from Burlingame's hand when he held it back. "But what is it in that bag?" he asked.

"A doll."

"A talking doll?"

"It's the Fanny Fortune doll," she said, but he would not have any idea what the Fanny Fortune doll was.

He grabbed the bag, rude son of a bitch.

Mario spoke up. Finally. "I saw those advertised on television."

"I got it for a friend's daughter. May I have it back, please?"

Burlingame had the doll out of the bag. He squeezed it. The doll's mouth opened and the voice said, "You're going on a trip. Good-bye."

Scotti held out her hand. "May I please have it back?"

"Sure," said Burlingame. "Any little girl would love that . . . You want to read this now, Miss House?"

She put the doll back in the bag. She heard Mario's agonized sigh. Then she read the letter addressed to her, which Delroy had begun and left unfinished.

"What's the big secret?" Jack Burlingame asked her.

She could feel her face get red.

"I have no idea," she said. "And if I did, Mr. Burlingame, I wouldn't feel obligated to tell you."

"Why not?" When he tried to smile, amiably, the effort twisted his face to a nearly feral expression that reminded Scotti of a fox.

"Why would I?" Scotti said. "You're not up-front with me about everything that's going on here. I don't know what *is* going on, but something is."

Jack Burlingame said, "A secret your mother doesn't even know?"

"Does your mother know everything about you?" Scotti asked.

"Then there is a secret?"

"Is this about the Jeep Delroy borrowed to visit my mother? Or is this about something else?"

Burlingame gave her the fox grin again. "I ask the questions."

"So do I," Scotti said. "And I'm not getting anywhere. Shall we go, Mario?"

She looked across at him, and his answer was a helpless shrug. She was disappointed in him, sorry for him that she was a witness to his servility, but no longer angry at him. He was too pathetic, too weak for her to feel anything but pity for him. Her father used to call Scott an "infra-caninophile": an underdog lover.

Before Bolton House had ever heard the word *transsexual,* he would ask his young son why he was so taken with underdogs, say, "It takes one to love one, but you're no underdog!"

"Please call me a taxi," Scotti said to Burlingame.

"Why is it so hard for you to cooperate?"

"Cooperation is a joint venture."

"There are reasons we can't tell you everything," Mario finally spoke up, and quickly Burlingame put him back in his place, saying, "I'll handle this, Rome."

Burlingame looked at the clock above the stove again, at his watch again, a far cry from the soft-spoken author who had come to the East Hampton Library a month ago, his deep, sea green eyes making contact with the audience as he read in gentle tones about a corpse beneath a Christmas tree.

"What are you hiding, Miss House?"

"What are you hiding, Mr. Burlingame?"

"My hands don't shake. My face isn't red. I'm not hiding anything."

It was right at that point when they heard the wailing. "MISSUS! MISSUS! MISSUS!"

FORTY

Liam stopped in at Rowdy Hall for a few fingers of bourbon, to get a grip on himself. He wanted to be calm when he called the Lashers. He had to get Jimmy Rainbow out of his mind, get past that message on the answering machine and get back his control. He would put off dealing with Nell, put off thinking about her insistence that she stay in New York City once this was past.

Rainbow was back in their lives; in hers, anyway. He didn't know that for sure, but how much proof did he need?

It was just the sort of thing that happened when you worked with a partner. He had known men who botched perfectly plotted jobs because they misjudged situations. Men who ran when they didn't have to, screwed up in some irreversible way when they didn't have to. Nell herself had done that, going back to check on the old lady she'd robbed, getting caught, serving time.

He had already broken one of his own rules by stopping for a few fast ones. The Jack Daniels hadn't calmed him down; it never did. You got from booze what you took to it, and he'd taken Rainbow to it. Whatever was going on with Nell and Rainbow, Liam had to deal with it later, or he would lose everything, serve time like all the others who lost control.

He left Rowdy Hall and walked down Newtown Lane, went behind the Village Hardware to the parking lot.

It was a clear, cold night. He went toward the phone booth. The sky was filled with stars. Liam worked his jaw, doing an Affirm exercise for teeth grinding, loosening himself up.

He shook his shoulders and spread his fingers, telling himself to let go of everything but what he had to do.

He took the phone off the hook, heard no dial tone, then lost two quarters trying to summon one. The phone was out of order.

Just as he hung up the phone, Liam saw him.

He was getting into a car down where it was not well lighted, but it was Jimmy Rainbow, no mistake.

Jimmy Fucking Rainbow with his tailor-made suits and his college education, sweet-talking his way into banks and churches and charity balls. Big-time con who let women do his time.

Liam watched the car pull away.

He couldn't see the make (a Lexus?) or read the license plate.

Then how the hell could he be so sure it was Rainbow?

It wasn't Rainbow.

It was nerves and it was panic. He was doing what Nell always said he did: making wall-to-wall carpeting out of a throw rug.

There was no way he would hear a phone message from Jimmy Rainbow in New York, then see him right there in East Hampton.

He thought of the *Affirmation* sheet on panic. Instead of imagining the worst, you turned it around. You wrote a new ending.

The phone message was from some other Jimmy, someone Nell knew from one of her old jobs. Maybe someone from the halfway house, someone who'd mention jail casually, or as a joke.

The man in the parking lot was just a local heading home after a movie. Tomorrow at this time Nell and Liam would be $400,000 richer, a day away from $400,000 more . . . and the kid was home safe.

To keep the new ending, Liam had to eliminate any negative thoughts.

If you talked trouble, you got trouble. Keep your fears to yourself and share your courage. I affirm because I am firm. I deserve what I want.

As he got into his car behind Devlin Realty, he looked at his watch. He thought of the pay phone up on Old Stone Highway, outside the Springs General Store, not far from Maritime Way. That was perfect.

FORTY-ONE

"Where did you come from? You frightened me!"

"I'm sorry," Scotti said. "I was going to call a taxi but there's so much commotion going on inside I thought I'd just get out of everyone's way. May I hitch a ride with you? I'm Scotti House."

"Lorna Metcalf. Get in! I wasn't sure I'd get this old buggy going," said the woman as Scotti got in the Chevrolet. "I've been having battery trouble."

Scotti was breathless. She'd run out of the house while Burlingame rushed to see what Delroy was shouting about, Mario calling after her, "Wait! You'll need a ride!"

Scotti didn't know what Burlingame was after, and she no longer trusted Mario.

Lorna Metcalf said, "I heard Delroy calling for Mrs. Lasher once I started this thing, but I'm already late getting home. I can't go back in there or I might never get away."

"I'm in a hurry, too," Scotti said.

"Some people think you don't have a life of your own."

"I know what you mean."

The car rolled down the driveway, went along The Highway Behind The Pond, and turned right on Egypt Lane.

"Mrs. Lasher's in a state tonight," Mrs. Metcalf said. "And I don't mean New York State. She's off the wall over something. It's always some little thing. She's been through too much."

"I can imagine."

"What were you doing there tonight?"

"I came with Mario Rome. But he seems to be in a state, too."

"What's Mario doing there at this hour? He always leaves after he's dropped off Deanie."

"I don't know," Scotti said.

"He didn't even drop her off today."

"I thought he said he did."

"He didn't. Mr. Lasher was real upset, too. 'All Andle, All Andle' he says to me. That's how he sounds, at best. I was lucky I could make out that much he's gotten so bad lately. 'All Andle' means 'Call the Candles,' where Deanie is supposed to be. So I picked up the phone by his bedside and I called them. I was going to say maybe we should send a car for her, her father wanted her home, when Mrs. Candle herself said, 'Deanie Lasher is not here and has not been here in ages.'"

"Mr. Lasher must have misunderstood."

"Somebody did. . . . Where do you live, Mrs. House?"

"Miss House. I live in Springs, on Tulip Lane, but I left my car at Ashawagh Hall."

"I live in Springs, too, so it's easy for me to take you to your car."

"Do you work full-time for the Lashers?"

"No, no. I'm a practical nurse. I'm not part of the household."

"Is Mr. Lasher dying?"

"I'm not privileged to talk about it."

"Oh, I'm sorry. I didn't mean to pry."

"I often fill in when Delroy takes off, which wasn't that often these past two years, until now. Now he's got himself a sweetie. I didn't think I'd live to see the day he'd have a girlfriend. He took the Jeep to see her earlier tonight and that got everyone going. Mrs. Lasher thought he'd stolen the Jeep, I think. She even called the police."

"I heard something about that." Good God! Did they imagine Scotti's mother was Delroy's girlfriend? And then suddenly Scotti thought of another possibility. They thought Scotti was the girlfriend. Delroy's letter to her. His mention of the "secret." Only Delroy and Scotti would know what that meant. . . . Was that what it had all been about? Mrs. Metcalf glanced at Scotti and said, "Are you Mario's girlfriend, dear?"

"No. We take a writing class together."

"Little Deanie loves Mario. . . . Delroy's always trying to win her affection, but children know the strange ones in life same as dogs do. Both stand back from them."

They rode in silence a while, Scotti trying to figure out Mario's behavior. Even if, God forbid, Mario actually did believe Scotti was capable of having any interest in Delroy, why would it have upset him so? He might have felt disappointment in her, but his actions all evening were too harsh for it to be that.

And what was Jack Burlingame in such a snit about?

"Do you know Mario well?" Scotti ventured.

"Some. He's too good for what he does there, chauffeuring their luggage back and forth, driving the girls to school. There's too much up here," she tapped her head with her fingers, "for him to be doing that. They treat him like a servant, same as we all get treated in that house."

"I can imagine." But Scotti couldn't imagine very much at all about that house and what was going on there. Why all the clock-watching? Why was Delroy wailing like a banshee in the hall?

Mrs. Metcalf turned right on North Main and headed up Springs Fireplace Road.

"They don't know what they're doing anymore at Le Reve. Calling the police on Delroy that way. Calling me to sit with Mr. Lasher, actually thinking Delroy stole their Jeep. Now, normally, they have everything under control. But I could see tonight they're cracking under the strain."

"Perhaps that's why they sent Deanie away someplace," Scotti said.

"That little girl's been there through thick and thin! And I've never, ever seen Mrs. Lasher red-eyed from crying the way she was tonight. Something's going on, if you ask me. It's not my business."

Yes, something was going on. The moment Scotti'd gotten into Mario's van she'd felt the chill, felt him completely changed. It was almost as though he knew about her, knew and detested her for her deception. Yet why would it bother Burlingame?

The rest of the way up Springs Fireplace Road Mrs. Metcalf complained about things she said were not her business: Mrs. Lasher's habit of having fresh flowers brought in from Whitmore's every two days, only white ones: lilies, orchids, tulips, peonies. The fact that Mr. Lasher wore his white terry-cloth robes only once, put on a brand-new one every day. The air-conditioned room in the basement just for wine. On and on, while Scotti half listened, staring out the window, dreading going home, imagining her mother's state of mind after the police had questioned her about Delroy.

There was no way to get a handle on the situation, no way to make sense of any of it. By the time they reached Ashawagh Hall, Scotti had almost bought Lorna Metcalf's version: that all of them connected with Le Reve were just coming apart at the seams, from the strain of Mr. Lasher's long illness.

At Ashawagh Hall she thanked Mrs. Metcalf.

It was a bright, moonlit night. There was also a streetlight by the pay phone near the road, outside Springs General Store.

It was easy for Scotti to recognize the man leaning far out of his car, holding the phone. She had never seen him anywhere without Nell Slack.

Scotti slowed down, pulled over, and turned off the motor so she could watch him. Now what was *he* up to? And did Liam Yeats have anything to do with all that was going on at Le Reve?

FORTY-TWO

"Mr. Lasher?"

"Speaking."

"Is everything ready?"

"Yes."

"Please tell me what's ready."

"I am weddy to meet the wansom demands. The Lucky We in exchange for my daughter. Awive."

"She's alive and anxious to get back to Le Reve. Who did we tell you must deliver the Lucky We to us when we're ready?"

"Delwoy Davenport."

"Right."

"Have the police been told?"

"No! The powice will not be told, either. That is a pwamiss."

Liam said, "Be ready for the exchange tomorrow. Have local maps ready for when I call tomorrow. Hamptons maps and a Montauk one, too. All the streets must be clearly marked. Got that?"

"Yes."

"Have the Jeep ready and the Range Rover . . . and that fancy convertible. What kind of car is it?"

"A Bentley Azure."

"Yes. Have all the tanks full and ready to go."

"What time?'

"We'll tell you tomorrow, Mr. Lasher."

Liam put the phone's arm back on the receiver and started the Ford toward Maritime Way. *Okay,* he thought, *concentrate on the project. Ask no questions of Nell, act no differently.* The Lucky We was the target. He could see it in his mind's eye, an eye now set on seeing only the new ending.

FORTY-THREE

After the funeral Delroy would go to Mr. Lasher's bureau, where a gold lorgnette was kept in the top drawer under a stack of white linen handkerchiefs. The lorgnette was in a light blue box with a note in an envelope. Delroy was to choose a quiet moment to give it to the Missus.

Now was not the time, that was for sure. Le Reve was in an uproar with Mario there for some reason, Jack Burlingame short-tempered suddenly, and the Missus in a state Delroy had never seen her in before.

No one had thought to cover Mr. Lasher's face with the top bedsheet, as Delroy had seen nurses do in movies. When Delroy tried to do it, the sheet was not long enough.

He sat by the bed and waited. Burlingame had told him to stay with the body.

He had heard the soul did not leave the body immediately, and he spoke softly to the Mister, telling him everything has worked out for the best, for Delroy had come very close to breaking his promise because of his conscience. Thou shall not kill. Helping someone die was killing.

Delroy was not sorry that he had lied to Mario and Burlingame about the "secret." People who went through other people's private papers were not entitled to the truth. Here was Mr. Lasher dead, and there they were downstairs still trying to make something of the fact Delroy had borrowed the Jeep to visit Mrs. House! At a time like this, how could they keep at it? Him dead in his bed, and still they nagged Delroy about the "secret" until he made up an answer to appease them.

He had finally told Mario how he had come upon Scotti House in Hampton Bays and realized she shouldn't drive. She was so drunk! He had brought her back to East Hampton and left her car there. That was the secret!

Mario had exclaimed, "Christ, Delroy! Why didn't she just say so!"

"A lady like her doesn't want to admit she was intoxicated," Delroy had said. "That's why I kept it secret, even from her mother."

Mario had said, "She beat it out of here the moment you came down the stairs calling for Mrs. Lasher. Where would she go at this time of night?"

"She must have gone with Mrs. Metcalf," Lara'd said. "She was leaving then, too. She didn't even know Len had died."

"No one acts like they know it," Delroy had said.

"Go upstairs and stay with him!" Jack had ordered Delroy.

Which had been fine with Delroy.

But before he had left the den, he had said, "Shouldn't I go to the Candles' and bring Deanie back?"

For some reason that had started Mrs. Lasher sobbing into her hands, and Burlingame had given Delroy a look as though Delroy were to blame for everything.

FORTY-FOUR

The area Liam had picked out for Deanie Lasher was a carpeted, wood-paneled cellar suite complete with a pool table, a Dolby sound system, a bunk bed, and a small bathroom. The walls and bookcases had celebrated the years from childhood to college of the son of the house: Chip Karpinski.

His photographs and his golf, soccer, and wrestling trophies had been removed, along with family photos, school banners, rock star posters and skis, skates, a bowling ball, a toboggan. All of that was moved into the adjoining room. After the project was a fait accompli, Liam would reassemble it.

The windows were small, square ones, up high, unable to be opened without the long pole attached to one wall. Soundproofing prevented any noise from intruding, except for the occasional rumble of the water heater or the furnace, in the room where Chip Karpinski's belongings were stored.

Even if Nell had remembered to bring the books about horses, Deanie Lasher was not in any mood to be read to. Neither was she crying—she hadn't cried once, not even when Nell explained that she could not go home yet. Her father, Nell had told the child, owed some money, and until he paid it, Deanie would have to stay with Rona and Al. The child had answered that her father never owed money, that people owed her father money, and that it was her suspicion that Rona and Al were "kidtrappers."

When Nell told her they were calling her father to arrange for him to pay the money he really did owe (no matter what Deanie thought!) Deanie announced that they had better get her home because her father was dying of "Lugerick disease."

"You mean MS, dear, and he's not dying. I have a sister with MS and she's lived a long time." A lie. She had no sister, but it was a time to lie.

"He only pretends it's MS," said Deanie. "He had deals to make. He's so sick he can't even speak without a 'synthesizer.'"

"I never heard of a 'synthesizer,' Deanie."

"It's a machine that speaks for him. It sounds like the voice in airports when you take trains from one gate to another. It announces whether to get off at Gate A or B or C. . . . His grave's dug, too."

"Where is his grave dug?"

"I'm not supposed to know about it, Rona. One day I was driving along with Jack and Mario, and they thought I was playing with Radar, The Talk 'N Listen Robot, but I was really listening to them. I hate that robot! I know all the answers to his questions."

"People don't dig their graves ahead of time," said Lara.

"Daddy does. His is in Springs, in Green River Cemetery, behind this very famous painter's grave."

"Oh, Deanie, you're fibbing."

"I don't fib. I know the painter, too. It's Jack Pollock. Our whole school went to his house which is a museum now. My daddy's grave is right behind his at the cemetery, a whole half acre!"

Nell knew the cemetery. It had been written about in *Newsday*. Famous people were buried there, not just artists. It wasn't far from Maritime Way. Nell had wanted to stop and look around one afternoon when Liam was showing her the Karpinski house. Liam would not stop. He had complained that it was too negative, and that a visit there could materialize unlucky spirits.

Nell asked Deanie, "Did you tell your mommy you knew about the grave?"

"I don't call her 'Mommy.' That's childish."

"But did you tell your mommy about the grave?"

"No, because I wasn't *supposed* to hear about it! There's a lot of things I don't get to hear about because I'm only seven."

"Some seven," said Nell.

"I was just seven, the thirteenth of January. . . . How old are you, Rona?"

"Very old."

"You look old because your hair's white but you don't talk old and you don't move old."

"I'm old. I'm getting older by the minute."

"I felt old when I first woke up from the sleeping pill but I don't feel groggy anymore. . . . Was that a lie about the bichon?"

"Yes. I don't have a bichon."

"I knew it was a lie! I didn't think so at the time, but at the time I didn't know you were a 'kidtrapper.'"

"Remember something, honey. I have to tie you up again when Al comes home. Don't you ever tell him I loosened the ropes."

"Is he cruel?"

"No, but he wants you tied up. He's bringing some books for you to read, books about horses."

"Which ones?"

Nell told her the few titles she could remember.

"They're too young for me. I read those kinds of books when I was little."

"Well, we'll pretend you haven't. Then he'll think I'm reading to you and we can have some alone time to talk. Would you like that?"

"Did you know there's a library in heaven?"

"I never heard that."

"I'm not sure I believe it but Jack Burlingame told me there was and he's an author of books, so he ought to know."

"Well, maybe there is."

"Do you know Jack Burlingame?"

"No. I don't know anyone you know."

"Because nobody I know would 'kidtrap' me."

That was when Liam burst through the door, ski mask on, the books under his arm. Nell had refused to wear a mask. She said she could do miracles with makeup, but not for a male.

"Hello, little lady," Liam said. "Why aren't you tied up?"

"I was."

"Why aren't you still tied up?" He dumped the books on the upper bunk.

Deanie stretched out on the lower bunk, flinging her hands behind her, straightening out her legs and spreading them so Nell could fasten the ropes to the bed posts.

"You cooperate very nicely, young lady."

"I don't want to be murdered is why."

"Why wasn't she tied up?" he asked Nell.

"It's not good for her circulation. I wanted to let her move around a little."

"The hell with her circulation!"

"All right. It won't happen again."

He waited until the ropes were knotted. "That's better. How are you, Rona?" Nell didn't answer him and Liam wondered if she'd already forgotten the name she thought up to call herself.

"How are you, Rona?" he asked again.

"Oh. I'm fine, Al."

"It's a lovely evening, isn't it?"

"I guess it is," Nell said.

"The stars are out and there's a little slipper moon. Is that what you call it, a slipper moon?"

"Yes, a slipper moon," Nell said.

He said, "And the street is absolutely still . . . except for one lone car that followed me."

FORTY-FIVE

With the help of Nytol and one glass of Shiraz, Scotti had succeeded in getting her mother to bed, just as the police arrived.

Their visit to Tulip Path came near midnight, one policeman ringing the front doorbell, another pounding on the back door.

They asked for permission to search the house, which Scotti granted, admittedly out of fear they would take her in for questioning. Whatever it was they were after seemed to be too crucial for Scotti to win any arguments over correct police procedure. She was wary of these uniformed officers, as well as convinced nothing about their mission was routine. She thought of Delroy, his wailing as she'd run out of the Lashers', as though he'd stumbled on something horrific and come running for help.

They took statements from both Houses concerning their relationship to Delroy, all contacts that either one might have had with the Lashers, and their whereabouts in the last twenty-four hours.

When Scotti identified the Allen Institute as "an educational organization involved in funding" they didn't question it, although they noted the time of the jitneys she took, and the time she spent at the Ashawagh Hall Writers' Workshop.

There were no questions about Delroy's unfinished letter to her, nothing said about the "secret." But they had asked to see Fortune Fanny, curious to know why Scotti had bought a doll?

"It's for my grandchild," her mother had spoken up. "She lives in Bay Shore."

Whatever they were looking for they had not troubled to say. They'd left as abruptly as they'd arrived, ignoring Myrna House's weepy inquiries about Delroy, as well as her declarations that the "poor boy" was guilty of nothing!

Nytol would not do the trick once the police had left, so Scotti talked her mother out of "just one cigarette" and gave her a Halcion, then spent a restless night herself, falling asleep and waking up several times before the gray light of early morning came through the blinds.

For the first time in many years she'd dreamed she was Scott, looking in his school locker for his clothes and finding only Scotti's, fearing to put them on in front of the other boys in the gym. Bolton House had figured in the dream somehow, as well, but she could not remember that part of it.

While her mother slept, Scotti made toast and coffee, then called Jessica. She told her everything, to see what Jessica could make of it. She also gave Jessica the license numbers she had impulsively jotted down the night before, of the only two cars visible on Maritime Way. A Pinto and the Ford that Liam Yeats drove there.

"Do you think there's a connection between this Yeats and what's going on at the Lashers'?" Jessica had asked.

"I don't know. When I followed Liam Yeats, I was just curious about what he was doing in Springs so late at night. Ginny Loeper had said Nell Slack took up with bad guys. And I have a hunch Nell Slack is involved in whatever's going on. But it's just a hunch."

"Your hunches are not to be ignored," Jessica said. "Why didn't you tell me about this Delroy before?"

"I was too embarrassed, Jess."

"Did he make a pass?"

"Oh, no. I'd have remembered that. But I had to pee, and he saw me, so he knows. That's the 'secret' he was referring to in the letter they found."

"The police don't know, though?"

"No. I don't think I have anything to do with what they're after."

"Could this Delroy be involved with drugs?"

"Jessie, I don't have a clue."

"A house search at that hour, out there, is major."

"That I realize."

"Are you okay, Scott? Scotti? It's not every night Bolton House shows up in your dreams."

"Thank God for that. I'm fine. Thanks."

While she waited for Jessica to call her back after she checked the license plates, Scotti sat watching a scant snow flurry outside and listened to some more of the Streisand CD, Barbra singing in French, Debussy's "Beau Soir."

She thought again of the dream, knew that it was prompted by her fear when the police arrived, even though common sense told her they were not about to do a strip search.

She thought of how she had tried to explain, in the book she was writing, her deep affection for Jessica. The Ashawagh Hall instructor had commented that it was "more tell than show" and asked for a few examples of their "interaction."

The dream was a good example. Jessica had groaned when Scotti told her how she'd felt her father's presence. No one but Jessica understood the hold Bolton House had once had over her, over both of them, for that matter. When Scott had first introduced them, Dr. House had said later, "Someday choose a girl you're not sorry for. You are not the Salvation Army, Scott."

At subsequent meetings he would not glance in Jessica's direction: he refused to acknowledge her presence.

Appearances were everything to Bolton House, a major factor in his unhappy marriage as time went on. He had several nicknames for Jessica: "Miss Five By Five," "Orca," and "The Waddler." All Scott had been able to surmise from his taunting remarks concerning Jessica was that she was not winsome enough for a son of his to hang out with, and then marry.

Only after Dr. Rush's probing during the institute's psychological examination had it dawned on Scott that his father was jealous of Jessica, that he could not bear their easy, exclusive rapport.

If Scotti were ever to lose Jessica, she would lose that part of her history, the same way Myrna House complained that with so many of her contemporaries dead, she was losing her identity. Winters, what was left of it went to Florida with her friends.

Scotti had gotten bogged down at the point in her book when she'd begun to deal with Emma. She'd been unable to finish a scene in which she had first tried to explain to Emma why she was letting her hair grow long, and why she was wearing a skirt.

Emma was just five. For a moment she had listened with a beatific expression on her face, anticipating some game they must be playing together, until what Scotti was telling her began to sink in.

Suddenly, Emma had punched her, hard. Then her small hand had tried to cover Scotti's mouth, and the tears began, the hollering: "Take that off!" pulling at Scotti's skirt.

New Year's Eve flashed in Scotti's mind, and the quiet talk on the couch. Even though Emma explained how much it would embarrass her if her schoolmate met Scotti, it was a solemn admission—not one hurled at her angrily, but a sincere attempt at adjusting to a new way of life. Scotti was encouraged by the thought of a rapport with her daughter.

Baba suddenly came downstairs with his leash in his mouth.

He began to whine and dance about with that certain urgency which meant only one thing.

The Halcion had probably knocked her mother out, for she never failed to wake up if Baba sent out one of his distress signals.

Scotti hurried into her boots and coat.

She attached Baba's leash to his collar, and Baba pulled her out the door.

A creature of habit, even in an emergency, Baba only did his business in one place: the Green River Cemetery.

They ran in that direction.

Up a slight incline in a small grove was the grave of the famous musician Stefan Wolpe, with the remains of Bolton House next to it.

The last time Scotti'd been there was the day of his funeral.

She remembered being intrigued by the inscription on Wolpe's headstone:

When I die, out of my mouth, a hundred birds will fly.

FORTY-SIX

Something had happened between them that Nell could not fathom. She knew Liam had not liked it when he'd walked through the door last night and found the child untied. He had lectured her often enough about following procedure to the letter. He had reminded her too many times that the reason she had spent those years at CCI was that she had ignored Jimmy Rainbow's instructions and gone back to see if the old lady was all right.

But Liam had not seemed peeved at her over an infraction of his rules. It went deeper than that.

The only thing he had told her was that he had seen a car follow him, go to the end of Maritime, turn around, and then head back slowly toward the cross street: Deep Six Drive.

"Was it a man or woman driving?" she asked him later that evening when they could talk.

"I've already cancelled it." Affirm was rearing its ugly head. Its devotees "cancelled" any negative possibilities when the course was set.

"Then why even tell me you saw a car following you?" Nell asked him.

"I said it's cancelled."

"But it *is* strange. A car on the street at this hour, going by the house slowly."

"Probably an old boyfriend looking for you."

"Why don't you cancel your mouth?"

They shot each other dirty looks. It was so very strange. They had never had this kind of fight. They had never disrespected each other with harsh words and snide expressions on their faces.

"I thought you were going to read to the kid?" he said.

"It can wait. Tell me about your telephone call."

She had the feeling that what Deanie told her was true, that Liam hadn't been able to talk to Len Lasher, that the project was flawed from the start and Liam could not face it. Affirm followers never admitted defeat.

Liam said, "I'm going to take a nap."

"Have you been drinking?"

"Oh, sure. I'm that dumb."

"You smell of peppermint and you never nap unless you've had a few."

"Thank you, Sherlock Slack."

"Liam? What's going on?"

"Al," he corrected her. "I told you: in this house, Al."

"Al, I think I know what's wrong. Deanie says her father can't speak. He's too ill."

"Really?"

"She said he uses a synthesizer, a machine to help him talk."

"Interesting," he said, yawning and making a point of it with an exaggerated stretch.

"That's what she told me. He has something called "Lugerig disease," and not MS. She says he's dying."

"When I talk to him again, I'll ask him."

"You did talk to him then?"

Liam said, "Yes, I talked to him. I know that man's voice as well as I know yours, sweetheart. He's paying the wansum. The kid's pulling your leg."

"She's just a child," Nell said. "She's not smart enough to—"

"Not smart enough to what? Not smart enough to get you to untie her?"

Nell had no answer to that. Deanie had told her that the ropes really hurt, even though Nell hadn't pulled them as tightly as she could have.

Liam said, "What's happening here is you're not keeping faith with the project, and I wonder why."

"Because you're not telling me what's going on, Al!"

"There's a kidnapping in progress. Okay?"

"You seem different suddenly, even since we talked on the phone earlier."

"Why would I be different?"

"I don't know."

"Why would I be different? If you can think of any reason why I would be different, let's hear it."

It had been a terrible night.

The child became angry with Nell for not keeping her promise to untie her when "Al" was asleep.

Nell could not bring herself to chance it with Liam in that strange, distanced mood.

Nell made Deanie hot Ovaltine, which she refused to drink. The egg salad sandwich Nell made for Deanie the child called "*drek.*"

"What does *drek* mean?"

"It's Yiddish for 'filth.' My grandmother calls Edward Candle *drek*. If she ever met you and Al, that's what she'd call you two."

"That's not very nice, Deanie."

"Are you very nice?"

When Nell went back upstairs, Liam was not napping, but peering through the blind slats in the darkened front room.

"Are you worried about that car?" she asked him.

He gave her this sinister look and didn't answer.

She was sure that he'd had a few drinks. That kind of paranoia in him was straight from the bottle.

She knew the one way to jolly him, a way she did not like at all, but anything to bring him around.

"I know what you need," she said when he flopped down in the armchair. But as soon as she was on her knees before him, he grabbed her hands in a painful grip.

He said between his teeth, "All I want is to get this done. What do you want?"

"The same thing."

He shoved her away and she stood up. Usually Liam appreciated her sexual playfulness, but now he snapped, "Save it for New York!"

"Maybe by then I won't be in the mood."

"Oh, you'll be in the mood," he answered sarcastically, as though she was guilty of some wrongdoing he could not forgive.

She went across to the couch, stretched out, shoes off, and pulled the afghan over her.

She pretended to sleep, watching him chain-smoke and brood until she could not bear to go without a cigarette herself.

When she sat up and went to her bag to find one, Liam marched down the hall into a bedroom and shut the door.

She woke up, the television she'd been watching into the early morning hours still on. She could hear Liam stamping around the kitchen.

She went there and without turning to look at her he snapped, "Where are the fucking eggs? I bought a half dozen."

"I hard-boiled them last night for egg salad. They're in the refrigerator."

"Shit! I want hot eggs!"

"You shouldn't eat them anyway, with your cholesterol so high."

He turned to show her a face she had never seen before: hard, hateful eyes and mean, tight-lipped mouth. He snarled, "I want fucking eggs over easy and bacon!"

"Cancel it, since you're into canceling. We're out of eggs."

He walked across to the hooks hanging on the wall, just beyond the kitchen in the mudroom. He grabbed her coat and scarf and walked back with them, thrusting them into her arms.

"Get us some breakfast."

"Where?"

"The Springs General Store is down the street. It opens at six. It's six."

She put on the coat and scarf without his help. "I'll check on Deanie first."

"She's fine. I just came up from there."

"Why don't you get the eggs?"

"I'm working on the hookup with this Delroy Davenport. I can't be distracted in any way."

She said, "When I come back, you'd better be in a different mood."

"Or what?"

"Or you're going to mess this up."

He came across to her and for a moment she thought he was going to reach out and hold her, give her some reassurance that things were okay with them.

He did reach out, with both hands, only to yank her wig down on her head. "If you're going to wear it, get it right!" he barked.

When she went out into the cold a mild flurry was blowing. She was furious with Liam. She hated the cold! He should be the one going for the eggs! What was he pulling? She had never joined him in a venture of any kind. Maybe this was what Jimmy Rainbow used to call "the eleventh hour jitters." Jimmy used to get the runs.

Maybe the whole reason Liam had suddenly glommed onto Affirm last spring was that he panicked before a job. He had been out of action ever since he'd beat the rap on the hijacking scam.

For the first time she thought: what have I gotten into? What if I just didn't come back? What if I got out right now, got into my car and went, with everything I own right there in the trunk? What if I headed for New York without a backward glance?

Even if she could summon up the nerve to ditch Liam and this project, she could never leave so long as Deanie Lasher was tied up in the basement.

Liam knew that. That was probably why Liam had let her go.

FORTY-SEVEN

Myrna House made up her mind to get a prescription for Halcion. She had been awake for over an hour, but she had no desire to get out of bed. She did not even have to go to the bathroom. She did not even crave a cigarette. When Baba sat on the rug by her bed, on his hind legs with his leash in his mouth, she did not feel like letting the bulldog run her life that morning.

Eventually he went downstairs, where Scotti was. Rather than call up to tell her Baba was waiting for his walk, Myrna House bet Scotti would break her rule about leaving his care to her mother and take him herself.

Scotti would not want to discuss last night. She hated what she called "rehashing" things. That was why she had given Myrna House the Halcion, because last night Myrna House did want to talk about it, couldn't stop talking about it, until Scotti told her she needed something to help her quiet down. . . . That was like Scotti: to pretend that she was helping her mother, when what she was doing was relieving herself of the burden of listening.

Scott would have barked, "Cork it!"

Scott had not had Scotti's patience.

It had been only about six hours since Myrna House had swallowed the magical pill, so she was still under its spell, basking in this new sensation of peaceful languor.

She rarely took any drug, including aspirin. Nytol if she absolutely could not sleep, but never the prescription drugs Bolton was so dependent on. Painkillers for his migraines, Celebrex for his arthritis, Valium for his nerves.

Strange that this pill was called Halcion, for that was a word she knew very well, with a different spelling. That was a word which Bolton had used some six years into their marriage, announcing that he'd bought a bed for his study, and there he would sleep henceforth.

"Our halcyon days are over!" said he.

She had gone to the dictionary to learn that their supposed time of "happiness and prosperity" was at an end, puzzling at the idea of prosperity on a professor's salary, but not surprised that he was unhappy sharing a bed with her.

Relieved that Bolton didn't want a divorce, and that she no longer bore the burden of the bimonthly, obligatory jackrabbit attacks on her person under the sheets, she acquiesced. Along with other faculty wives, she looked the other way while he suffered through crushes on various graduate students and young, untenured teachers. There was possibly one realized affair with a pint-sized instructor who taught a course called Melville and Whitman, wore peasant skirts and huaraches year-round, and played the harp at college concerts with her wild, wheat-colored hair flowing to her waist.

Myrna House had heard Bolton singing, "How are things in Glacamorra?" in the shower, and remembered Miss Butler's fingers miraculously coaxing the same tune from the string of the huge instrument she hugged between her stubby legs.

Scott was beginning his teens then, effeminate (she realized in retrospect) and bossy. Remember Bolton House's harangues about his wife's shortcomings? Apples don't fall far from trees. Scott was always making suggestions: not to do with social graces as Bolton did, but more to do with Myrna House's hair, her clothes, her shoes . . . and yes, one year Scott actually made an Easter hat for her.

Scotti was easier than Scott, Mrs. House mused as she heard the front door slam and knew Baba had won out. Guilty people were always easy. Scotti probably believed that her mother missed Scott, but she didn't. Aside from the embarrassment his sex change had caused (and now thanks to *Oprah* and other daytime talk shows it was not all that rare), life was more pleasant with Scotti.

Fat Jessica was out of the picture at last. Little Emma was available for outings with Grandma and holiday visits. And praise the Lord, or the hormones, or the scare the police had put into Scotti last night, this morning Scotti was actually headed for the cemetery—a place she had always avoided like the plague. Baba would not do his duty anywhere else. Scotti knew that. She would just have to ignore the fact that there was a headstone there with her father's name on it.

When the telephone rang, Myrna House answered with a peppy "Good morning!" and was rewarded with the one voice she wanted to hear: Delroy's.

"I've been so worried about you, dear, and I almost lit a ciggie poo."

The Halcion had left her in this peculiar state where she noted all that was going on without reacting to it, as though she was floating on some puffy cloud above it all.

Delroy brought her back to earth.

What he had to say not only shocked her, but also sent a delicious shiver down her spine. The Lasher child had been kidnapped!

Of course she wouldn't tell. Cross her heart and hope to die.

She wouldn't even tell Scotti!

Incredulous, elated to think she was privy to such momentous news, Myrna House could hardly contain herself.

But she remembered to counsel Delroy, "Be careful. Be very careful! Don't let those people use you! You know how people use you, dear."

FORTY-EIGHT

Baba did his second BM in front of Stefan Wolpe's grave.

Scotti remembered the exotic inscription about birds flying out of a dead mouth from the horribly hot afternoon of her father's funeral. She had stood by herself, away from the other mourners, as her mother had suggested.

No need to call attention to herself at such a time. It was hard enough on her mother to have to fend off the question "Where's Scott?" from those who didn't know Scott was right there, in high heels and pearls.

Beside Scotti that day, the dwarflike Dr. Betti B. Butler suddenly leaned against Scotti sobbing as Scotti would have liked to be able to do. There were no tears from the eyes of Bolton House's widow, either. Besides Betti B., there were no tears at all.

As Baba finished his business, Scotti pulled him along, ignoring her father's grave. What point was there in moving down to stand and look at the slab of black stone?

"No point?" her mother would cry out times she'd tried to persuade Scotti to walk there with her. (On his birthday, at Christmas.) "There's something very wrong with you if you can't face your own father's tombstone. Look at what you put him through!"

Baba loved the snow and zigzagged past the graves gaily, after Scotti let him off the leash.

Then, a few inches before Jackson Pollock's enormous stone, Baba stopped by the oblong piece of marble jutting up toward the gray sky. He looked back at Scotti as though to ask, "Didn't you forget something?" Obviously he visited there often.

Scotti knew the Swinburne quote by heart.

Sleep, shall we sleep after all? For the world is not sweet in the end.

Scotti remembered hearing wee Dr. Butler recite a fuller version, perspiration mingling with tears on her face, her strange, high voice choking on the words:

Laurel is green for a season, and love is sweet for a day;
But love grows bitter with treason, and laurel outlives not May.
Sleep, shall we sleep after all? for the world is not sweet in the end;
For the old faiths loosen and fall, the new years ruin and rend.

Dr. Butler did not recognize Scotti at the funeral, though Scotti remembered meeting her after harp concerts that Myrna House would not suffer. Scott went with his father in her place.

"Did you know him well?" Butler had asked Scotti.

"I think not well," Scotti had answered.

"He was really not a cynical man despite that inscription. He had such élan!"

Scotti had been thankful someone there had respect for him, though she imagined this diminutive colleague of her father's probably always cried at faculty funerals and spoke in hyperbole. All Scott had known about her was that she lived alone and dressed like an ersatz hippie.

Bolton House had never been well liked. He was always at the thick of faculty infighting, insisting on the traditional over the innovative, balking at change of any kind. It should not have come as a surprise to her that her own dramatic change would do him in.

Scotti was right. There was no point in visiting a grave. Perhaps Myrna House had been right, too: what you could not face you lent significance.

Baba was barking somewhere beyond Pollock's grave. Trudging in that direction, Scotti saw Baba jumping up on a woman wearing dark glasses, down in a clearing where a lone grave was dug and covered with a tarpaulin.

Len Lasher's grave? She bet it was.

But who was the woman standing there alone?

"Baba! Baba!" She called the bulldog and walked down to the half acre she had heard described by her mother. There were the elaborate plantings, too.

As she approached the woman, she saw only a wisp of white hair falling across her forehead; a scarf covered the rest.

Scotti bent down to reattach Baba's leash.

She straightened up again and said to the woman, "I'm sorry he jumped on you."

The woman shrugged and pulled the scarf around her face.

Scotti saw only the large sunglasses as she walked away without uttering a word.

But there was something else Scotti saw: the horse's head on the scarf, and the single word: "Pisheresse."

Some random piece of information tried to make its way into Scotti's consciousness . . . something about that scarf and that name.

The woman kept going.

So did Scotti's mind, gnawing away at whatever it was she'd heard someone say: beginning to get it, slowly, starting with Charlotte Mew, then Edward Candle . . . wait a minute, wait a minute, it was coming.

FORTY-NINE

In the front seat of Liam's sister's Pinto there were two grocery bags: one with eggs and a cash receipt from the Springs General Store, the other with bacon and a cash receipt from the One Stop market on Springs Fireplace Road.

Nell had called Liam from One Stop, lied about the Springs store being out of bacon, informed him in a deliberately cool tone that there was a line of tradesmen paying for their breakfasts, so she would be just a little late.

His voice sounded calm, almost back to normal.

"Don't worry about it. Sorry I blew up."

"See you soon," she told him with the same crisp delivery.

After that she had gone directly to the Green River Cemetery.

Now Nell Slack hurried down the path from the unfilled grave and got into the Pinto she had parked in the circular drive.

Deanie Lasher had told her the truth, but that fact was overshadowed by the sudden appearance of Scotti House.

Nell was sure there was no way Scotti would have recognized her. How could she? Nell checked her reflection in the mirror as she started the car. The wig was in place. The eyeglasses were huge. Around her neck was the child's scarf, which Liam had flung at her angrily an hour ago.

This House woman bothered Nell. She had a habit of turning up places she was least likely to be: Hydra on Christmas Eve, the bar in Hampton Bays on New Year's Day. Now, the Green River Cemetery.

Coincidence perhaps. Yet Nell remembered the first time she'd encountered Ms. House, at the bowling alley. After Scotti had gone into the ladies' room there, Mario had said something about her working as an investigator.

Nell had laughed and answered, "What does she investigate at the library?"

"No," Mario had said, "She's part-time at the library. She works for her ex, too. He's an insurance investigator. And she's also in my writing workshop."

"Multitalented," Nell had sniffed, and Mario had rushed to add, "We're just writing buddies, that's all."

Nell hadn't quite believed that then. The way Scotti took off for the bathroom after Nell arrived, a distraught expression on her face, made Nell believe she was just plain pissed because Nell had shown up.

And what about the way she'd sashayed out of the bar with that little he/she and the other woman on New Year's Day, not a glance in Nell's direction when Nell knew damn well she'd seen her? Nell had thought she was just a jealous bitch. But now she wondered if something far more lethal and intricate was going on.

Common sense told her Scotti House could not have followed Liam and her New Year's Day. She was in that bar when they got there.

Still, it tied knots inside Nell. It didn't sit right with her. This freezing, snowy morning and Scotti House just happened to show up at the cemetery with her bulldog! She just happened to find her way down to the newly dug grave of Len Lasher!

Where was her car? And was it the same car Liam said followed him from the Springs General Store last night?

Nell drove slowly up Springs Fireplace Road trying to figure out any connection between an insurance agency and the Lashers. It did not take her long to theorize that somehow word had gotten out that the Lucky We was in jeopardy. Liam had said it was not insured, but how could he be certain of that?

It did not take Nell long, either, to place blame on Fina Merola. No matter how Liam had raved about her, Nell could not forget what she'd been like back in their days at Haven. "Two-time" was her middle name. She'd plea-bargained herself out of so many jams, every lawyer in New York City knew how she took her coffee.

Nell told herself to just jump ship. Get out while the getting was good. Go directly across Old Stone Highway to Route 27, keep driving past all the goddamn Hamptons, then a left onto 495 and into New York City.

Instead, when she reached Old Stone Highway she turned onto Deep Six Drive and drove down to Maritime Way.

Since the grave was dug, chances were all the rest that Deanie had told her was true. Len Lasher was dying. Len Lasher could not talk. A policeman must have posed as Lasher, imitated his way of talking: *wansom* for *ransom*, just make the *r*'s into *w*'s. If the police and FBI were alerted this early in the game (thanks to Fina?) there was little likelihood the project would work as planned.

Nell had already thought of letting Deanie go. She could do it when Liam went to claim the Lucky We. She did not think she could depend on Liam anymore. If anything needed to be canceled, it was him.

Now, after the encounter with Scotti House, it was not Deanie Lasher's safety alone that made Nell determined to quit. It was also the hunch that the only way she could save herself was to free the child.

A sudden ball of yellow, foggy sun broke through the clouds as she arrived on Maritime Way.

She wondered if Liam's unfathomable mood swing the night before was due to his own suspicion that the police were involved. He could no longer promise the child would not be harmed.

Ready for whatever it was waiting for her inside the house, she drove up the driveway with the sun aimed at her determined eyes and set mouth.

It took her a moment to see clearly, to realize that the rental Ford was missing . . . and only a few moments more to discover no one was waiting for her inside.

Liam and Deanie were gone.

FIFTY

While she stripped Len's bed of Porthault sheets that cost $2,000 each and put them inside a $600 pillowcase, she argued with Burlingame over his idea to give Delroy another $1,000 besides what Len had left him.

"He's complaining about how little he got before we've even had the will read?" she asked. "How does he know what Len left him?"

"Len probably told him. Delroy is very, very disappointed. He thought at least he'd get the little house he lives in."

"The so-called little house is worth about $700,000. Has he gone crazy?"

"It could easily be passed to him to live in, rent free, for four or five years."

"For what reason, Jack? Because he does this errand?"

"Delivering the Lucky We to those kidnappers is hardly an errand. He could be in jeopardy."

She muttered, "After all we've done for Delroy, I can't believe he'd hold us up at a time like this."

"It's not his idea. It's my idea, Lara. Give the guy a break."

"An extra $1,000 and the little house rent free for several years? That's some break."

"It's not much considering all he did for Len."

"He was paid to do it."

"I'd feel better, Lara, if we could guarantee that he could live there rent free for a few years. Skip the extra thousand if it's breaking your heart."

"Is he to live there rent free while he works here?"

"Why not?" Jack Burlingame shrugged.

"For one thing, I won't need him to work here, because I won't be here. Do you think I'd stay here, with all these memories of Len?"

"I did think you would, *because* of the memories of Len."

She gave him a look. "Are you living in the house you lived in with Delia? Have you even gone to Delia's grave?"

"I don't think Delroy should have anything troubling his mind while he follows the kidnappers' instructions. Let's not have any unconscious feelings on his part that he's being used. That's how he says he feels. Let's have him calm, at peace, satisfied."

"We're not reading the will right away, Jack."

"He knows about it, Lara!"

"I wonder if he knows how much I could get for that little house in the summer?"

She took the pillowcase filled with the dirty laundry across the hall to the chute and dropped it down. She was saying, "If Delroy's already said he feels he's being used, he won't have any unconscious feelings that way."

"Don't get psychosemantic, Lara. Ask your Dr. Mannerheim if I'm not right about putting Delroy's mind to rest. . . . And for God's sake, sit down! Take it easy! Why are you doing things you hire people to do?"

"Because the alternative is sitting downstairs with the police we have here, thanks to Delroy and his stupid 'secret'! Only Delroy would get his underwear in a twist over the idea a woman was skunk-drunk."

She got a fresh sheet out of the bureau. "I have to keep busy. I can't think about Deanie. I can't stop thinking about Deanie. I've never felt so threatened or so helpless. I've never fully realized before this how protected I was by my husband."

"I can understand that," said Burlingame. "But I feel Len would approve of the police presence."

"I don't trust the funeral home to keep Len's death quiet, either. People walk in and out of there. It's a public place."

"Not where Len is."

"Don't! You make it sound like Len is hanging from some meat hook in the funeral parlor basement!"

At that, Jack gave up. His shoulders caved in, his patience gave out, he drew a deep breath and said, "Would you like a Bloody Mary?"

"It's nine in the morning."

"I need something."

"How do you know Delroy hasn't told everybody?"

"Who would he tell?"

"Everybody. That old lady. Her daughter. Random people around East Hampton."

"Lara, he promised he wouldn't."

"Oh, he promised," Lara said sarcastically. "A man of his word. Dependable, honorable, and into me for more money and a house and God knows what else he'll come up with! I thought he really cared about Deanie, too."

"He does. But there is such a thing as fair play. You could be a little fairer with him."

"Maybe if we can hang on to it, I should give him the Lucky We."

"You're not going to make the bed?"

She was. Jack grabbed an end of the bottom sheet and helped her. He said, "Porthault. Delia used to love these sheets."

"Deanie calls them pothole sheets."

"Not that we had but one set of them. Just one."

"We only have Porthault. Here and in New York. Len loved them, too."

"You two were well matched."

"We were, weren't we? Pull that side tighter, please."

Jack did. He said, "Nine A.M. and I'm getting tired."

No one had slept but Delroy, who had taken a sedative after the police finished talking with him early that morning. Jack had gone into one of the guest rooms to nap for a while, emerging in time for breakfast prepared by Mario. Lara had called the cook and the other servants, advising them they had a day off.

Both Jack and Lara had swallowed several cups of coffee, but neither one could eat.

Jack was ruling out the drink he wanted so badly because his stomach was empty; he'd get a headache.

He was helping Lara with the top sheet when she suddenly said, "You're right, Jack."

"About what?"

"If Delroy can get Deanie back to us safely, I'll let him live in the little house rent free from now until Memorial Day. That doesn't include utilities or upkeep!"

Jack went downstairs, headed for the bar, ready for that drink anyway—the hell with his head!

FIFTY-ONE

When Scotti got back to the house she heard the upstairs shower running. She saw the message light blinking on the answering machine.

"Scotti?" Jessica said. "The Pinto is registered to Gretchen Yeats from Copiague, and the Ford she rented from U-Drive in Copiague three days ago. . . . Emma says thanks for getting her Fortune Fanny and to send it on. I'll be in the office about two this afternoon."

After scribbling a note saying she would be back soon, Scotti grabbed her keys, got into her Saturn, and drove toward Maritime Way.

It had been Nell Slack at the cemetery, Scotti was sure. She'd seen the woman drive off in a Pinto, just as it flashed in her memory that Pécheresse was Deanie Lasher's pony. *Pisheresse* was the way Delroy had spelled it on the scarf he'd made for Deanie, which Nell Slack had worn over the white wig. Scotti remembered Mario telling her about the scarf Christmas night at Hydra.

Scotti was sure that was who she was, and that was why the woman turned her face away, and wouldn't answer.

Other things were flashing through her thoughts now: Mario's question about why she had chosen that particular book to "recycle"—a book about a child being kidnapped. Jack Burlingame's crack about Fortune Fanny being a perfect gift for a child. His clock-watching. Mrs. Metcalf's confusion about where Deanie was last night. The horse books Nell Slack left at the library. Mario's mention of Nell Slack's curiosity about the Invictus School.

And then, finally, something Jack Burlingame had said during the question period when he spoke at the library.

"Nothing sells books like the endangered child theme, and nothing sets the police into action like a kidnapping."

Scotti had no idea why Nell Slack would disguise herself and appear at Len Lasher's grave, but she was on to something, she knew it as surely as she knew how to get to Maritime Way.

She had no idea, either, what she would do when she got there, but her wheels squealed around the twists and turns of Old Stone Highway, Deep Six Drive, and finally the left turn that took her directly to her destination.

FIFTY-TWO

Detective Abrahams sat at the desk in the library, recounting local incidents of kidnapping to Burlingame, who'd made himself a Bloody Mary.

Mario sat on the couch. Thoughts that had nagged at him all the while he'd tried sleeping on that couch last evening were becoming more insistent.

Most local kidnappings had to do with parental custody cases, "which is why," Abrahams said, "we tried to convince the Invictus School to cooperate with us in making videos of individual students. In a case like this, we could use one. The parents put them in a file with dental records and addresses the child is known to frequent. They help us greatly."

"Why did Invictus object?" Burlingame asked.

"They said it would frighten the children unnecessarily. The other schools welcomed it. We use these videos for runners, too. The most common runaway is a Caucasian white female, age twelve."

Mario couldn't concentrate on what Abrahams was saying. He was remembering the way Cynthia always told him not to talk about business—"it upsets you"—after she'd instigated the talk, all the while noting everything concerning the club's business, right down to the payroll, the payday, the bank deposits—all of it. And what was it Nell so often said after she'd question him during those trips to and from the airport? "Don't talk about the Lashers. It upsets you."

The phone interrupted Mario's train of thought. Lara Lasher slipped into the room then, too.

Abrahams had his hand on the extension he'd assembled, with a speaker, a recorder, and caller identification. He pointed at Mario, who picked up.

"Len Lasher speaking."

"Well, hello, Mr. Lasher. I hope you have a map of all the streets in Southampton, Bridgehampton, East Hampton, and Amagansett."

"Yes. There are maps like that in the cars you asked to be weady to go. I am pwepared to folwo your instwuckions to the letter, and there are no pweese inwolved."

"There better not be if you want to see your little girl. She's all right, and eager to get home. Meanwhile, Mr. Lasher, be sure Delroy Davenport is standing by with the Lucky We."

Click.

Lara Lasher said, "I wonder if he's someone who worked for us? A yard man. A kitchen man. They come and go."

She looked askance at the shape the library was in. Overflowing ashtrays, empty Coke cans, plates with sandwich crusts. She was making her way toward the door, asking the room, "Where is Delroy?"

"He walked down to his house for a change of clothes," Burlingame said.

"I don't like that, Jack." She paused in the doorway.

Abrahams said, "I don't like it, either. He should be here. These people could call back any minute and tell us they have a new plan of action and are ready to go."

Burlingame put his drink down and followed Mrs. Lasher out of the library, saying he'd walk down and get Delroy.

Once he was alone with the detective, Mario finally said, "There's something I probably ought to mention."

Someone, he should have said.

He almost called Nell "Cynthia."

FIFTY-THREE

Although there were fresh tire tracks in the driveway, by the time Scotti reached the house on Maritime Way, both the Pinto and the Ford were gone. Karpinski was the name on a small square sign near the road. Whoever that was, he did not live there year-round. Two wooden braces protected the picture window in front against storms. Months-old telephone directories in plastic wraps were tossed into the yard, decaying with the leaves under the snow.

Scotti figured Karpinski could be a Homesafe client, giving Yeats access there.

She rang the bell, knowing in her heart that what she was doing was futile or dangerous. Nell Slack had probably already fled with Deanie Lasher. If she hadn't, and the child was inside, she was likely bound and gagged.

Scotti did not dare break in, for fear a hidden alarm system would alert a protection agency whose guards would descend on the house. Whether the child was there or not, such an invasion could jeopardize Deanie Lasher's life. What kidnappers did not warn that if the police or the public became involved it would cost the child's life? For the same reason, Scotti could not chance going to the police. Judging from the midnight visit to Tulip Path, the police already were involved, but Scotti was aware that in such cases there was an elaborate "need to know" procedure, a careful blanketing of information.

She could not simply march into the police station and take the risk that the right person would hear what she had to say.

When no one answered the door, Scotti decided to drive down to Newtown Lane where Nell Slack lived with Yeats. She did not expect that Nell Slack would be there, nor would the child be there. She didn't expect to run into Liam Yeats, either. But she wanted a look. It was her only option, under the circumstances.

She was not unaware that there was a remote chance that she was completely wrong about what was going on. But she felt that it was very remote.

East Hampton Village was typically quiet on this winter morning in late January.

There were few cars in the driveways of the house near the middle school. She could not see behind the house. She made a U-turn and parked across the street near Wittendale Florist.

This time she did not go to the front door where the vestibule inside had the nameplates Nell Slack, Liam Yeats.

She went past the green stone cat around to the back door.

Incredibly, it was unlocked.

Very carefully she turned the knob and tiptoed inside, entering a kitchen.

The first thing she spotted were the three books on the counter. The children's books about horses. Next, she saw the scarf. Pisheresse.

Someone was in the front room. She could hear sounds from there.

But she had not heard the feet that went with the large hand which suddenly reached from behind to cover her mouth.

FIFTY-FOUR

In her panic, Nell had brought the horse books with her, but she doubted that she'd find Deanie or Liam in the house. Desperate for any clue to their whereabouts, she played the messages on the answering machine.

"Liam? This is Gretchen. When are you returning the cars? Do you want me to meet you at U-Drive? Then we can have a bite somewhere and I'll bring you back to get your Saab."

"Nell? This is Ginny. Same number when you get to New York. *Be thine own palace or the world's thy jail*. Remember? Can't wait to see you."

"Liam, this is Ryan. I'm at Kennedy, about to fly off to Greece again, but last night my neighbor called to say the gutter at the back of my house is hanging down. Would you check on it and repair it if it is? I'll be out in a few weeks. Thanks!"

That was all.

Nell could not believe that suddenly, out of the blue, Dr. Loeper had called! How had she known where Nell was? What kind of eerie intuition had told her to recite that poem at the end of her message?

Nell had no answer to those questions, only the suspicion that Liam had probably taken the child with him to Copiague to reclaim his Saab. If a car truly had followed him down Maritime Way last night, he would want to get rid of the Ford.

He could be anywhere with the child by now. Nell couldn't bring herself to call Gurney's Inn, where Fina Merola was. Fina had never wished her well, siding with Liam always. She would side with Liam, anyway, for it was Liam who was in charge of procuring the Lucky We.

Having heard Ginny Loeper's deep, welcome voice from the past, Nell know what she would do.

Without bothering to remove her makeup or the wig, without bothering to lock the back door, Nell went out the front.

She had parked the Pinto around the corner from Newtown Lane, on Osborne. Her own car was just outside the door. That was the car she would drive to Manhattan.

FIFTY-FIVE

Delroy leaned back in the leather chair and stared at the small television in his nook.

Dick Tracy was playing, with Warren Beatty and Madonna, sound off. When he had first come to Sag Harbor to live with Aunt Sade, that was how he had watched television, without hearing it. The Amish had no television, and he had not been sure for a while that he should hear the worldly words of the English, as the Amish called the others. He had kept it on mute, for company, when poor Sade was down at the corner bar.

Sometimes he reverted to that old way of TV-watching when he was anxious.

Another thing he did was reread the letter from Patricia Highsmith, to remind himself that a famous person whom he had admired had answered a letter he had written her.

He had found the fragile rose on the floor, which he had put in his Bible to mark her death. Apparently it had fallen out when Jack Burlingame snooped around the nook and found the unfinished letter to Scotti.

Burlingame had not even apologized for going through his things, which had disappointed Delroy, for he had always behaved decently before all this.

Without even showing Delroy the ransom note, Burlingame had informed Delroy that he was the chosen courier, that the kidnappers wanted Delroy and only Delroy to pass the Lucky We to them.

"I guess the kidnappers realize how important you were to Mr. Lasher. Since they don't know he's dead, you still are his main man, from their viewpoint. So we're all depending on you, Delroy, to save Deanie."

But he was not invited into the library, where Mrs. Lasher and Burlingame (and even Mario!) were sequestered with Detective Abrahams.

He was told to wait upstairs until the time came. The Missus had even suggested that he might use the time to remove the blow-ins from the assortment of new magazines delivered in the morning mail.

It was odd that it reminded him of another wait a long time ago. He had been upstairs then, too, in his family's house in Pennsylvania. Downstairs, the bishop was laying down the rules for *Meidung*. When he was finished, Delroy would be shunned. He would be cast off from the fellowship of the church, committed to the devils and his angels. (*"Dem Teufel und allen seinen Engeln übergeben."*) Thirteen years old, hanging to the banister, Delroy heard his fate pronounced in the bishop's solemn tone. From then on, no faithful member of the community, not even a relative, would talk with him, eat with him, have anything to do with him until he was taken by horse and buggy to the bus depot, an aunt he had never met waiting for him on Long Island.

But it isn't like that now, he told himself. He was not being cast out. And if he was being used, as Mrs. House might believe, they were using him for a noble cause: to save Deanie! To undo, in fact, what Mario had let happen!

Delroy got his knitting from the top of the cherry dressing table.

In the Mister's room, in the top drawer of the bureau where he kept his handkerchiefs, was the gift for the Missus.

Delroy had been thinking about that lorgnette ever since the Mister had passed on. The Missus, of course, knew nothing about it, just as she knew nothing about any of the rest of it: the letter detailing the plans for the funeral, everything prearranged: rooms at the inns, for instance, which Delroy was to have reserved the moment the Mister's body was taken to the funeral home.

Instead of thanking him for his remarkable presence of mind in calling the ME immediately, the Missus had lashed out at him.

At first he imagined it was because for the briefest time he had called out for her hysterically, before he pulled himself together and almost mechanically took charge as he had been told to do by Mr. Lasher. He was amazed and deeply insulted by Mrs. Lasher's reprimand. How was he to know Deanie had been kidnapped, or that Mrs. Lasher had hoped to keep the Mister's death a secret?

Delroy was certain he would have been fired on the spot had he not been the chosen courier.

All of Mr. Lasher's elaborate planning was now brought to a halt.

Delroy had not told anyone at Le Reve about it.

When he had made his secret, hurried call to Myrna House, she had agreed that it was no longer appropriate for him to follow those instructions. He had not had time to mention the lorgnette to her. There had barely been enough time for her to admonish him, "Don't let them use you!"

He had not known then that he had been singled out by the kidnappers to hand over the ring.

Delroy mulled all of this over as he knitted Baba's sweater.

If he was able to save Deanie, even Scotti House would finally take notice of him.

That thought was enough to bring a bitter smile to his countenance. If she had never trusted him before, and never warmed to his presence in her house, wouldn't matters be different once it became known that everything had depended on Delroy Davenport, and he had not let them down?

Burlingame had said something about speaking to the Missus concerning the house Delroy had thought would be left him in the Mister's will.

Delroy's hands were still a moment, and he closed his eyes. His brow furrowed as he prayed earnestly for Deanie's safe return. Lately, every time he said a prayer he added something on Scotti House's behalf, this noon a very generous request to the Almighty that she would enjoy her evening at the opera. It was the kind of gratuitous gesture he admired himself for making, considering the fact he did not approve of Max Bernstein, who had let her get behind the wheel drunk. He imagined Scotti, dressed to the nines, sitting in the sumptuous setting of the Metropolitan Opera House, caught in the spell of *Tristan und Isolde*—Delroy could hear the swooning, orgasmic love songs in his head. And a moment before his amen, he had an inspiration.

Amen.

Of all the Toulouse-Lautrec posters, Sade's favorite was "L'OPÉRA." It was a picture of a redheaded woman wearing long black gloves, holding a lorgnette in one hand, peering down at a stage. He had not thought of it until that moment, for it hung with the other two in the small house down the road, where he seldom spent any time.

Delroy left his knitting on the chair while he went into the master bedroom, where he opened the top drawer of the bureau. There, under the handkerchiefs, was the light blue box with the lorgnette inside.

Carefully, Delroy freed the envelope from the Scotch tape and with his first finger eased the back of it open. He pulled out one of Lasher's small cards, not a business card, but the simpler ones engraved with just his name.

There in the old, bold handwriting were just five words:

I LOVE YOU! GOOD-BYE, BABY.

Delroy pocketed the card and the envelope.

He closed the bureau door and carried the box back to his nook.

FIFTY-SIX

"Hush, Scotti!" he had whispered, his large hand clamped across her mouth. "It's Mario."

Held tightly in that strange embrace, she had heard the end of a message on an answering machine in the other room.

". . . Nell? This is Ginny. Same number when you get to New York. *Be thine own palace or the world's thy jail.* Remember? Can't wait to see you."

That was followed by a request from a man named Ryan, bound for Greece, worried about the gutter on his roof.

Scotti had recognized the verse the first male voice had quoted. It was from a letter John Donne had written to Sir Henry Wotton, obviously intended for Nell Slack.

Sir, more than kisses, letters mingle souls—that was how it began . . . an unlikely, incongruous bit of poetry to be recorded for someone like Nell Slack.

Immediately after the messages played, footsteps crossed to the front door, and it slammed.

That was the moment Mario let go of Scotti.

Scotti said, "If that's Nell Slack leaving, don't let her get away!"

"There are two plainclothesmen in front of the middle school. They'll follow her. How do you fit into his picture, Scotti?"

"Never mind the cross-examination, Mario! I had enough of that last night! The Lasher child has been kidnapped, hasn't she? That's what this is all about."

"Yes, she was kidnapped."

"You have to tell the police to go to the Karpinski house on Maritime Way. There's a possibility the child is there."

Immediately, Mario used his cell phone to call Detective Abrahams. He handed it to Scotti and said, "Tell him."

When she hung up she said, "We'll meet an Officer Chayka on Maritime Way. First, I want to call my mother. I want to see if word is out about this."

"My van is low on gas," Mario said. "We'll take your car."

"Always write down whether or not Baba has done his duty!" her mother said when she phoned her. "Do you imagine that he can tell me 'yes, I made big my two times'?"

"I wouldn't be surprised if he could."

"Where on earth are you, Scotti? I even called Jessica."

"I'm in the village, Mother, but I can't talk now."

"Emma wants Fortune Fanny."

"You talked to Emma?"

"I just told you that I called Jessica. Emma wants Fortune Fanny and she wants you to send it. She doesn't want you to bring it."

"All right. I just wanted you to know I'll pick up something for dinner tonight."

"The poor little tyke. She's afraid you'll surprise her when her playmates are there."

"I'll see you later," Scotti said.

"I know what all the fuss was about last night, too, in case you're interested."

"Of course I am, Mother."

"It's top secret and I promised Delroy that I wouldn't breathe a word. The Lasher child has been kidnapped, and her father had a heart attack and died."

"You don't miss a trick, do you, Mother?"

Her mother said, "And you never react. You always act as though you already know anything I have to tell you."

"I have to go now, Mother," Scotti said.

FIFTY-SEVEN

On their way to the Karpinskis' Mario said to tell the police that her mother had told her about the kidnapping. "Otherwise they'll think I told you." He chuckled. "I think at one point Detective Abrahams even suspected you," he said.

"Did *you*, Mario?"

"It crossed my mind, particularly when you showed up at Nell and Liam's apartment on Newtown Lane. By that time I had a few plainclothesmen keeping an eye on me."

"I wonder about you myself."

"Truly?"

"Truly. Anyone could be involved in this, couldn't they? How did you get in Nell and Liam's place?"

"When no one answered the bell there, I remembered there was an extra key to the back door. Nell kept it under the stone cat on the front steps. Once when I chauffered her from Islip Airport, she'd let herself in with that key. She'd lost hers."

"What were you looking for? Not the child."

"I was worried. Nell's car was there in the driveway, but there was no one inside. I looked around to see what I could find there when suddenly I saw a figure getting out of a Pinto out front. She was wearing the disguise she'd worn the day before in Northwest Woods, only then I never dreamed it was Nell under that white wig."

"What did you say to her?"

"Say to her?" he said with a surprised tone. "I hid from her. I slipped into the pantry. I didn't want a confrontation with her. I wanted her to leave, maybe lead the plainclothesmen outside to Deanie."

"So what happened?"

"She was bent on retrieving the messages from the answering machine. Then she was in a hurry to go. That was the moment you suddenly came sneaking through the kitchen door and I grabbed you."

Silence for a moment, and then he said, "You're still mad at me because of last night, hmm?"

"Did you really think I could be involved in something so despicable?"

"I'm having trouble believing Nell could be."

"But you could believe it about me?"

"That damn book. *The Master Key.* Then the doll. I thought: *Why would she have a doll?* And finally the fucking, excuse me, the secret!"

"My secret love, Delroy," Scotti said.

Mario laughed weakly. He said, "Delroy told us you were smashed one night and he drove you home. I thought someone who hung out in discos when she was a kid would know how to handle her liquor."

"When she was a kid, she did."

"That's some nowhere secret! Why didn't you just tell us you were drunk and he drove you from Hampton Bays?"

"Mario, I didn't like the way the famous author interrogated me. I could not believe his arrogance."

"Now you know what was going on."

"What's still going on," she said. "When I told Abrahams about the calls on the answering machine, I don't think he even wrote down the information."

"I wouldn't play detective anymore, Scotti. This isn't like one of your ex's insurance frauds . . . although . . ."

"Although what?"

"The ransom they want—and this is between you and me, okay?"

"Okay."

"The ransom is a ring worth millions. Jewelry instead of money. So I suppose an insurance investigator *could* be called in."

They were turning onto Old Stone Highway.

Scotti said, "Even if the ring is insured, it's not covered once it's turned over for ransom."

"How come? Isn't that a form of robbery?"

"Not if it's handed over in exchange for something or someone. That's barter, not robbery."

"But it's like being held up, isn't it?"

"There's no weapon, no confrontation. It amounts to bargaining."

"All the more reason for you to stay out of it," said Mario. "Let the police do their thing. And they've liaised with the FBI. Liaised. I don't even think that's a real word."

"The police have their own vocabulary."

"Yeah." He sighed. "Do you mind if I smoke in your car?"

"Go ahead."

"I feel to blame for the whole damn thing," he said, shaking up a cigarette from his pack. He went through it all again: how Nell had used him to get information about the Lashers, how quickly the abduction had been accomplished, how he hadn't suspected anything until he was pulled over by one of the kidnappers disguised as a cop. Then Deanie was in another car and the crime was in progress.

"Mea culpa, mea culpa," he said.

"Don't blame yourself, Mario."

"I made Delroy breakfast this morning, but *I* couldn't swallow anything besides coffee. And speaking of coffee, we ran out at the Lashers, but Delroy had a can hidden away up in his nook. A kind your mother likes, he claimed. Some Spanish or Italian brand he says is hard to find out here."

"Vassilaros."

"Right! What's his big attachment to your mother?"

"Maybe he likes older women."

"Seriously. He wasn't going to part with the coffee. We had to beg him!"

"Really?" She tried to sound surprised. She didn't tell him that Myrna House only drank tea, or that Delroy's fascination was with her and not her mother. Scotti didn't want Mario wondering why driving a drunken woman home would cause Delroy to get fixated on her. No need for Mario to explore that one.

She said, "Why would anyone choose Delroy as the go-between?"

"My fault again. I told Nell how he did everything for Mr. Lasher—what a reliable gofer he is. Yet I didn't play down his nerd aspects. He's the perfect combination of obedience and gullibility. He follows orders without question. He was Len Lasher's faithful dog."

Mario exhaled a cloud of smoke and said woefully, "Yeah, I shot my mouth off big-time! They couldn't have done this without me."

"But if it wasn't for you telling me about Pisheresse, I might never have picked up on the fact it was Nell in the cemetery," Scotti said. "That started *my* mind working. So there's a good side to your mouth."

"What do you think Nell was doing at Green River Cemetery?"

"I know what I saw her doing. She was staring down at Len Lasher's grave. Did you know Detective Abrahams thought that's where the kidnappers might have put Deanie? He went over there to look at it."

"So Nell was just standing there in the snow, alone?"

"Yes. I never would have made a connection without that scarf. She looked very different. She'd done something to her face. It was incredible."

"Well that's the business she's in: makeup, cosmetics."

As miffed as she was with him for his behavior the night before, Scotti heard the dejection in his voice and she felt pity for him. "I'm sorry, Mario. I know how you feel about her."

"Felt," he said.

FIFTY-EIGHT

Deanie Lasher was wearing a ski mask backward when he pushed her up the attic stairs. She had no notion where she was. He was too tall to stand. Crouching, he whisked off her ski mask. She had lost her scarf. Probably it was back in the house where she had spent the night.

"You better eat," he said. "This might be your last hot meal for a while."

Deanie didn't tell him she hated tomato soup. She didn't say things to Al she would have said to Rona. She didn't even ask Al where they were.

Al sat at the head of the stairs near the lightbulb he had to twist once to turn on.

Deanie sat on the blanket he put on the floor for her.

There were no windows.

He sipped a cup of the soup and ate a roast beef sandwich on a roll.

She tried to make it look like she was eating because she was afraid of his temper. She forced herself to swallow a spoonful of the soup. She knew it was out of a can. She had had canned soup once before, at a summer camp her mother regretted ever sending her to. And last night she had tasted bread sold in wrappers, the cottony kind Camp Kwapa also served.

But she didn't hold that sandwich against Rona. She almost liked Rona, who had tried to be kind to her. She wanted to ask Al when Rona would come to wherever they were, but he did not like questions. He had told her questions made him nervous, that they made him want to take his knife out of his pocket and cut off things: ears, noses, toes—anything goes, he said, and then he had said, "I like to rhyme things, do you?"

"Sometimes," she had answered, trying hard not to cry, thinking of her father and how he never cried, no matter what happened to him.

"You know what rhymes with *run?*" Al had asked.

"Nun?"

"I was thinking of *gun.* If you run, I shoot my gun. Get it?"

She got it.

After he finished the soup and sandwich he said, "I have some work to do before I leave to meet your pal, Delroy. You'll hear me hammering. If you're good and promise to eat your lunch, I'll think about keeping the light on when I leave here. But if you don't feel like obeying, I'll take the lightbulb with me."

"I'll be good." Why was he meeting Delroy, of all people? Delroy didn't always know how to do things. He had spelled Pécheresse wrong on the scarf he'd knitted for her. You couldn't count on him.

"No crying. No hollering. No one can hear you anyway but me. But I don't like sounds when I'm working. I don't like to be distracted. So shut up, kid!"

He crouched over to go down the wooden stairs. Then the stairs sprang back and lay flat, as the trapdoor swung shut with a heavy thud.

FIFTY-NINE

Dr. Virginia Loeper spent every noon hour online exchanging information with other scientists interested in polymorphism.

It was a very agreeable work situation, for she could enjoy her view of Washington Square Park and lounge about in one of her various robes, this morning's a zip-front turquoise chenille robe with patch pockets containing her notes on the driver ant, Eciton.

Most of her clothes came from catalogues; the robe was from a favorite source, Chico's.

As soon as she had found the data she needed, she treated herself to a few minutes in her favorite talk room: "Tranny Treats," for transsexuals and transgendered.

Someone had just asked the question: "How do you say *transsexual* in Ebonics?"

Ginny waited for the answer. A lot of times there was boring vulgarity in the chat room, but that was usually at night.

"Susan B. Anthony" came the answer, and it took Ginny a moment to get it. Then she laughed aloud, just as the downstairs buzzer sounded.

She went across to the wall receiver and asked who it was.

"A Ms. Nell Slack to see you, Dr. Loeper."

"Well, hooray! Send her up, Donald."

But Dr. Loeper's excitement was decimated by the look of her old friend the moment she emerged from the elevator. What had she done to herself? She could have been some off-off-Broadway actress who had come directly from the stage, in full makeup, playing the role of Hecuba or Medea. Her countenance was wrinkled with tear-stained powder. No wig. Just this fringe of red hair: the kind of cut female collaborators were given in wartime.

Ginny put her arm around her. "It's all right, dear. It's all right."

"No, it isn't."

Once they were inside they hugged, a cigarette burned down to the filter threatening Ginny's graying, chin-length hair. She rushed to the coffee table and took the saucer from under her African violet.

"Here, dear. It's been so long since I've had a visitor who still smokes."

Nell ground out the butt and said, "May I wash up in your bathroom? I'm a wreck."

"Of course. You know the way."

In the kitchenette, Ginny turned on the kettle and took two Twinings Darjeeling tea bags from their violet package. She got down a blue china plate and cut a blueberry muffin in half.

Telicare was playing softly on the small television in the bookcase near her desk. She favored that channel for whatever succor it offered— at the moment the sight of a monk in a yellow robe talking to Father Ted. She could not hear the conversation. It never mattered, though sometimes she did turn up the sound when the nuns were featured, singing and playing the violin.

She thought that whatever this visit from Nell was all about, it would probably be some no-account taking advantage of her again, a Jimmy Rainbow type dragging Nell down to his level.

She carried the tea and muffin into the living area, set it down by the violet, and sat on the couch waiting for the bad news.

Soon Nell appeared, her face washed, her eyes bloodshot, reaching into her pants pocket for one of those long, brown cigarettes she smoked. "I may have to stay with you for a while, Ginny? Could you put me up?"

Ginny pushed the saucer toward her, thinking, *How can I live with a smoker?* saying, "Of course I'll put you up. What's going on, Nell?"

"Ginny, did something tell you to get in touch with me, some feeling that I was in trouble? You don't know what a godsend it was to hear your voice on the answering machine!"

"I met your friend from East Hampton at Elliot's Full Circle."

"My friend? What friend?"

"Scotti."

"Scotti House? She's not a friend."

"All right, an acquaintance then."

"Is that how you got my number?"

"I called Information."

"Did she know Liam's name?"

"Yes. Liam Yeats."

"Oh damn! Damn! I knew she was one of you!"

"What does that mean, Nell?"

"She transitioned. I could tell because of the FTM I saw her with last New Year's Day. That boyish face they all have."

"I think you'd better tell me what's going on."

Then Ginny heard the sordid story from the beginning.

At the end, Ginny said, "What are we going to do immediately about this little girl? Where is she now?"

"Probably in one of the houses Liam watches. I never knew his clients. When I went to our house, hoping he'd be there, I played back messages on our machine. There was a man named Ryan with a falling gutter, but no last name, no address. I don't know *where* the child is. When I heard your message, it seemed like fate offering me a way out. I got in my car and drove straight here. I should have called first but I didn't remember your number, so I finally just rang your bell." She began to sob again.

Ginny stood and marched across to her desk, bringing back her white Princess phone, setting it before Nell.

"Don't waste another minute! Call the police! The child is in danger!"

"Liam swore to me he'd never hurt her."

"And you believe that?" A flicker of anger flashed in the doctor's light blue eyes. "Call the police, Nell! Now!"

"How can I tell them what I know without saying where I am?"

"Just call them or I will!"

Nell Slack had no sooner finished saying, "I won't go back to prison!" when the downstairs buzzer proved her wrong.

SIXTY

The view from Ryan Simon's roof on Cranberry Road was breathtaking. The early afternoon sun lent the bay waters a deep blue color, not a ripple on this almost windless, cold day.

Liam could see the ocean lapping the shore in the distance, and just ahead of him Napeague, then Montauk.

He had his cell phone with him as he went over and over the project revisions (now with Nell gone), deciding on the tone of two more calls he would make to the Lashers. They would have the cars and the maps ready, waiting for his instructions. He wanted them to imagine there was some elaborate plan, instead of the simple one he'd devised for a rendezvous with Davenport on a lonely trail near another Homesafe house. He wanted them to think others were working with him. If there were police involved, which he doubted, they would be spread out and ready with cars all over the South Fork.

The child would be all right in the attic. She was not strong enough to push the stairs down, and before he left he would wedge a piece of lumber between the floor and the trapdoor to make sure of that.

Whatever minimal heat there was in the house rose to the top. She would not freeze up there.

Simon's neighbor had given Liam the perfect excuse to be at the house by reporting the fallen gutter to him. There was no way anyone could have seen Liam enter the house from the back with the child. There were too many trees and there was the twelve-foot deer fence surrounding the property.

Thanks to Ryan Simon, he would leave the rented Ford at this house, too, and take Simon's Kawasaki. Ever since the car had followed him to Maritime (if it was following him and not coincidentally going down Maritime for some other reason), he'd been wary of driving the Ford.

Liam did not believe that Nell would go to the police, for all her concern about the child. She would be charged as an accessory, and with a record already she would have little chance of plea-bargaining her way out of a prison sentence. She was terrified of being locked up again, and anyone who had ever been in a women's prison knew what inmates thought of other inmates who had let harm come to a child.

Liam admitted to himself he could not figure Nell out. Either she had planned to take her share (or all) of the money and run off with Rainbow, or, in a more diabolical scheme, work with Rainbow to hijack the project. That damn car on Maritime still puzzled him . . . angered him, as much as the message on the machine did—"Jimmy"—working him into such a state he'd even imagined he'd seen Rainbow in the parking lot. If Rainbow was involved, it would not be like him to show up here. He always worked the strings behind the curtain, let the others take the risks. That was his fucking style.

Cancel.

Cancel.

Without the child, Nell had no power, and nothing to offer Rainbow. That did little to assuage Liam's feeling of betrayal. It was hard enough to accept Nell's desertion, but it was devastating that she would leave him for his old nemesis.

He had always suspected Nell Slack would never settle for him if there was a way she could have Rainbow.

Still, he would not emerge the loser in this contest with Rainbow. All he had really lost was Nell, who would be of no use to Rainbow now. Neither one of them would win this game, thanks to Liam's quick thinking that morning, when he had grabbed the child and run.

Liam hammered a loose shingle almost joyfully, buoyed by the thought that Nell wasn't the only one who didn't have to settle.

He looked at his watch.

2:10.

In Affirm it was suggested that when you overcame a major hurdle, you thought of it as a rebirth and you marked its occurrence.

He was going to remember the time and the date and the beautiful winter afternoon when he first perceived that after he had the Lucky We in his possession, neither would he have to settle for a woman who had learned how to be one in the slammer.

SIXTY-ONE

Lara Lasher said, "If this works out, Del, I'm going to reward you. Right now I'm going to give you $300." She had in her hand one of the personal stationery envelopes with LE REVE engraved in gold in the upper left corner. "This is not money left by Mr. Lasher, either. This is money from Deanie and me, to thank you."

Delroy put out his hand to take it, but she placed the envelope on the cherry dresser top and said, "Leave it here until you return."

The three cars were parked in front of the house, their tanks full. The maps of the Hamptons' streets were on the library desk.

"There'll be something else waiting for you if all goes well, Del."

"What is that, Missus?" He knew she'd make him ask, that she wouldn't just tell him outright. It was her way, to make a production out of giving anything to someone. With Deanie she'd do something like put her hands behind her back and say, "Guess where a new bracelet is, sweetheart. You have to guess to get."

Lara Lasher smiled coyly at Delroy. "It's what you want. It's the house."

"My house?" he said. He hadn't meant to say "my." That had slipped out, propelled by his astonishment.

"Yours from now until Memorial Day," she said. "I'll write a letter promising it to you, rent free. All you'll be responsible for is maintenance and utilities. The kitchen needs a new coat of paint and so does the out-side trim, but we won't worry about that now."

OK, he thought. *I know you, Missus. You can't help it.*

That was him now, too. He couldn't help it, either.

Over the chair in his nook was the leather jacket Mr. Burlingame had given him. "A peace offering, Delroy, because I had no business going through your things."

Delroy had always admired that jacket. It had the smell of good leather and there were inside and outside pockets with silver zippers.

Delroy had put the velvet bag containing the lorgnette in an inside pocket. He had tossed out the blue box; it was too cumbersome. He had a scenario for how he would present the lorgnette to Scotti, but for now it was enough to have it where it would be next to his heart, as she was, in his thoughts. As he wished he were, in her thoughts, at the opera.

The Missus gave him a pat on the back. "We're all depending on you, Del."

"Yes," he said. "I know that."

"Something else. Detective Abrahams plans to have an unmarked car following you. They'll keep a good distance and they won't interfere unless they feel you're in danger."

"That's good, Missus."

"Abrahams will brief you when the time comes. There's nothing to fear." Her voice broke.

She had been doing that ever since Deanie had been taken, acting just like her old self until suddenly she'd weep. Then she'd get past it in sec-onds and carry on.

Len Lasher's death could only be a relief to her. He had overheard a phone call to Dr. Mannerheim way last October when she had said, "Why can't he die? This is not my Lennie!"

Everyone at Le Reve was nervous but Delroy, who could not help thinking that maybe when this was all over, when Deanie was home safe and sound, word would get out that he was the one who took the ring to the kidnappers.

Then Scotti would have two reasons for seeing him in a new light.

He was a trustworthy man, yes, but he was also a generous man. He could hear himself saying, "What would *I* do with a lorgnette?"

"Sell it," she'd say. "It must be worth a lot."

"I'd never sell something given me as a gift, Ms. House. That wouldn't be right. It was his way of thanking me for all I've done for him. He's heard me say often how I love opera, even though I so rarely get the chance to attend."

He knew she'd probably say, "I can't accept something so valuable."

And then he'd say, "One thing the Mister taught me: possessions are anchors if you have no use for them." It was really Burlingame who had said that. It was not something the Mister was liable to say, but Scotti House wouldn't know that.

Delroy would tell Scotti how he had always loved the looks of it, too! A black panther with emerald eyes; it was so rare! Delroy had not even seen it until he had removed it from the blue box that very day. The sight of it had not overwhelmed him, either. It resembled one of the gimcrack ornaments Sade kept on her "Shelf of Souvenirs" from every state she'd visited.

Just to look at it was a thrill, he'd tell Scotti, but to know someone who could use it, the Mister would have approved of him passing it on to such a person.

It had also crossed Delroy's mind that Scotti would be impressed by the idea that Len Lasher thought enough of Delroy to give him something so costly. It made him feel slightly sick to his stomach to imagine what she'd say if she knew the truth about the will . . . and then a while ago the measly $300 for risking his life (why not think of it that way, even though he did not think of it that way at all?) to save Deanie.

"Delroy?" Lara Lasher said, "I want you to help me pick out some clothes to take to Yardley and Pino—" but she could not manage "Funeral Home." She just waved her hand as though she'd waved away the whole idea the Mister was there. The morticians had been instructed to keep his presence top secret.

Delroy said, "I know the suit he wants to wear."

That was all written down in Mr. Lasher's instructions, with "Be sure I have on underwear" underlined.

"Then let's get everything ready while we wait, until it's time for you to go."

"Yes, Missus."

The Armani suit was hanging in the back of the Mister's closet, with the light blue Turnbull and Asser shirt, the striped tie, and of course his favorite shoes: the reversed, waxe-calf John Lobbs.

Delroy had not attended his father's funeral, shunned even on that occasion. But he had an autograph book from his childhood with a first-page entry in his father's tiny, perpendicular writing. It was the only remembrance Delroy had of anything to do with his father.

The leaves are green
The roses are read
And here is my name
When I am dead.
 Harrell A. Davenport.

Ha, Eelan liked to call him sometimes. Ha! Ha!

Afternoons in the old days, Delroy would sneak across the highway near their farm to visit the forbidden mall with her. She would chant: "Ha! Ha! Ha! Ha! If you could see us now! Ha! Ha! Ha!"

Delroy would be her lookout while she'd stop in Music Music to hear Bernado play the accordian. He'd play his favorite old song for her, "Fernando," and she'd sing along, changing the words to, "There was something in the air that night, the stars were bright, Bernado. They were shining there for you and me, for liberty, Bernado."

Bernado would have been incredibly handsome save for acne that spotted his cheeks. Thick black hair and bright blue eyes, he wore tight satin pants and a ruffled silk shirt with a bolo tie. He rode to the mall on a red and black Bandit 1200S with a red Bieffe helmet and goggles over his head. He was a demonstrator of the accordion, the harmonica, and the flute, and he had other fans besides Eelan, most of them teenage girls with acne, too, but it was Eelan he favored. His eyes shone and looked all over her face as he played, and Eelan would hug herself and whisper to Delroy, "Look! I can see his thing!"

"Don't talk that way, Eelan."

"You and Ha think your things are shameful, but Bernado's proud of his and I like to hold it in my hand."

Delroy would blush and look away

Eelan ran off with Bernado on an early summer night with a red sun easing down into the dark blue clouds. Delroy had crept away from a community songfest with her when she heard the ice cream truck signaling its arrival down by the fence where the English would shout and run toward it, just as he had with Eelan.

Behind the truck was the motorcycle.

"I'm not taking anything, Delroy!" she'd grinned and hopped on behind Bernado. "I don't want one damn thing from them! But I'll miss you, darling brother!"

Delroy watched them go, then turned and saw Deacon Blyer standing on the top of the hill Eelan and Delroy had just run down.

Blyer looked like an enormous, predatory hawk in the setting sun, getting ready to flap his wings and descend on some smaller animal.

But the deacon waited patiently instead, in the Amish way, eyes narrowed at the approach of the sinner.

SIXTY-TWO

The police believed he had the child with him and they were probably right about that. Scotti thought that if he used one house, the Karpinksi house, to keep the child in, why wouldn't he use another one Homesafe watched over?

The only other house she knew he serviced was the one with the gutter hanging down, the one that belonged to someone called Ryan.

As soon as she dropped off Mario, she went out to Hydra.

Gus was tending bar and she ordered a souvlaki and a glass of retsina.

"Do you know anyone named Ryan who goes back and forth to Greece?" she asked him. "I don't think he lives here year-round, but he has a house here."

"A Greek?"

"Ryan doesn't sound very Greek, I know."

"I never heard a Greek called that."

"It could be our artist," Zoe piped up as she came to the bar with a check and cash to pay it. "Urian. He rides a dirt bike, makes an awful noise!"

"He rides a GS, right!" Gus waved his arms at the walls, where all the paintings were of a beautiful silver-haired woman with a black eye patch. In the lower right-hand corner, the tiny signature, Urian Simonides. "He goes to Athens all the time."

Zoe said, "He's a stockbroker in New York, and he's shortened his name for business. He has a place in Amagansett."

"In the book?"

Urian Simonides wasn't, but there was a Ryan Simon on Cranberry Hole Road.

"Hey!" Gus shouted at Scotti after she put a twenty on the bar and headed toward the door, "Don't you want your change? Don't you want a doggie bag for your food?"

She hadn't dared hope she would actually see him, but there was no way to miss Liam Yeats.

He was up on the roof of the house she was looking for, the sun spotlighting him there as he pulled an end of the gutter up with a lasso. A hammer hung from a wide leather tool belt around his waist. A cigarette hung from his lips.

She drove the length of Cranberry Hole Road and turned the Saturn around as Napeague Bay came into view.

On her way back she pulled into a driveway a few houses away from Ryan Simon's property. She was in front of a summer residence near Bendigo Road, which led down to the Devon Yacht Club.

He could not see her car from the roof. It was nestled in a grove of scrub oaks and pines. Fortunately, early that morning when she'd walked Baba, she had thrown on a pair of old jeans, a flannel shirt, and the parka she had given her mother for Christmas. She had no socks on to keep her feet warm inside her Merrell boots.

She had warm gloves tucked into her pockets and a wool scarf, which she wrapped around her head.

She sat a moment wondering if she should try to go the back way through the weeds and sand, or head down Cranberry on the pavement.

The latter was the better idea, she decided, and she got out, tucked her arms into her sides, and then headed up the driveway onto the road.

She chose the leisurely pace of a jogger.

He could see her then, of course, if he looked down. He would see her jogging along, head bent away from the wind, like anyone out for exercise. She counted on the idea that if he saw her, he would not expect she was doing anything else. And she also counted on the fact that at a certain point, if he stayed up there to hammer the gutter in place, he would not be able to see her go around the back of the house, then go up to whatever point of entry she could discover.

SIXTY-THREE

Scotti could hear the hammering above her on the roof. The white Ford was parked in the driveway, a cellar garage ahead of it, the door raised revealing a silver-and-blue dirt bike, skis, and steps leading up to the first floor.

She went quickly through the downstairs, calling softly, "Deanie? Deanie Lasher?"

If the child was there in the house, her mouth was probably taped. She was probably tied up.

At the sight of a bathroom, Scotti went in quickly and relieved herself. She had become accustomed to doing that ever since she had started dressing as a woman, taking advantage of a safe place so that her bladder wouldn't ever put her in a perilous situation. There was no way she could chance the sound of flushing.

As she arrived on the second floor, Scotti saw a chain connected to the trapdoor in the attic. A wooden plank rested against the wall.

She pulled the heavy wooden stairs down, thankful to Scott for his years of exercise and weight lifting. She saw the light at the top and went halfway up.

"Deanie?"

"Rona?"

She went the rest of the way, and saw the child sitting atop a blanket on the attic floor.

"Oh, Deanie, thank heaven you're okay!" She pulled the stairs all the way up.

"Who are you?" Deanie said.

"My name is Scotti House. You can trust me, Deanie."

"I don't trust anyone."

Scotti went across to her, bending over because of the low attic roof. "Right now you have to trust me. I'll help you. Otherwise you're at his mercy."

"How did you find out about me? Do my father and mother know I've been 'kidtrapped'?"

"Yes, they know."

"Do the police know? Is it on the television?"

"Deanie, the police know but it's not on the television. People don't know. Now I want to try and think what we can do to escape this place."

"He won't let us out of here!"

The hammering stopped.

"Shhh." Scotti put her finger to her lips.

The hammer sounded again.

"Listen carefully to me, Deanie," Scotti said. "We're going to get out of here together, before he takes you with him."

"Al's leaving me here."

"Did he tell you that?"

"Yes. He said he'd take the lightbulb with him if I made noise."

"We'll find a way out, honey."

The hammering stopped again. A minute . . . two.

Scotti crouched there while she listened to his steps right above her.

"I think he's coming," Deanie whispered.

Scotti crawled into the dark end of the attic, where there was fiber insulation lining the walls. She could feel cobwebs in her hair, and her hands came down on small beads of mice turds.

"Al will see you back there," said Deanie.

There were no boxes, no old furniture, none of the usual debris pushed into attics, nothing to hide behind or cover herself with. There was a Sound Off smoke alarm, a fan, and several large canvases leaning against one wall.

Scotti stood one of the canvases on its end, at a slant, so she could crouch behind it. There was the silver-haired woman again, a Urian Simonides painting, her eye patch half concealed by a large straw sailor hat. "How's that, Deanie? Can you see me?"

"The painting was on its side. He'll notice it's been moved. Al notices everything!"

They heard another thud. He had apparently jumped from the roof to a ledge or a porch.

"Keep your voice down, honey," Scotti cautioned.

"Put the painting back the other way."

"It won't cover me then."

"He's going to cut off our ears!"

"Shhhh."

A door slammed. Footsteps sounded inside the house.

The child was shivering—not from the cold, from fright.

They could hear him tramping up the stairs to the second floor, and then he caught the chain and pulled down the attic stairs.

Scotti felt her heart stop.

He shouted up, "Come down here!"

Deanie looked at Scotti, who signaled to go ahead.

"I'm coming!" Deanie answered.

Scotti nodded encouragement as the child went down the stairs backward. Scotti could see her eyes, wide with fear, tears starting to roll down her cheeks.

"Stop right there," the man said.

Then he said, "Stop blubbering! We're going to phone your mama now. This is what you say. You say, 'Mama, I'm all right but make sure

Delroy answers the phone in an hour because these men are dangerous and they could kill me. Make sure Delroy takes the Lucky We where he's told to and no police tailing him.' Can you repeat that?"

"Mama, I'm all right but make sure Delroy answers the phone in an hour and takes the Lucky We where he's told to and no police tailing him."

"Say these men are dangerous and could kill me."

"These men are dangerous and could kill me."

"Let's go over it once more, kid. Get it right if you want to grow up to be a big girl."

SIXTY-FOUR

As soon as Deanie had finished calling her mother on Liam's cell phone, she was ordered back into the attic. The wooden plank was put in place, locking Scotti and Deanie in.

"Delroy could get the instructions wrong," said Deanie. "He's not too swift. That's what my mother says. Daddy doesn't let me talk that way, but it's true."

"You don't have to be very swift to be the messenger. Delroy's really just the messenger."

"What if he goes to the wrong place? Mario's the one who knows his way around the Hamptons. Why didn't they choose Mario, I wonder? Do you know Mario?"

"A little. Don't worry. Delroy will know where to go. That will be made very clear to him."

"By the dangerous men?"

"I don't think there *are* any dangerous men, Deanie. I think he just wants your folks to believe there are."

"Because Rona isn't dangerous. He bosses her around."

"I don't know Rona."

"They're doing this to get the Lucky We," Deanie said.

"What is it?

"My parents engrave that on everything they give to each other. But Al wants my mother's ring, probably, because the real Duchess of Windsor owned it once."

"Is that what he said his name is . . . Al?"

"Yes. And she's named Rona."

"Where is she now?"

"I don't know."

Scotti tried to think of a next step, tried to act calm so the child would not know how panicky she felt. Damn! Why had Yeats stuck the plank there? They were trapped.

"Do you know about the Lucky We's?" Deanie asked. "*W* stands for Wallis and *E* stands for Edward, and they were a duke and duchess in London, England. My mother looks like the duchess."

"She must be very attractive."

"She is. And there's even a Lucky We 'lawnette.' It'll be my mother's. But she won't know about it until my father dies."

"A 'lawnette,' honey?"

"A black panther lawnette with emeralds for eyes. Daddy keeps it in a Tiffany box but it didn't come from there. Daddy bought it from a private person. It's very rare."

The pair sat huddled together in the cold attic while Scotti tried to pretend she was calm, talking with her in a casual tone although she could feel her heart beating under her shirt. It had been one of Scott's, a lovely soft cotton one from Paul Stuart.

"What does someone do with a lawnette?" she asked the child.

"Daddy says ladies used to carry them in their evening bags because they didn't like to wear glasses when they were all dressed up. They took them out of their beaded purses and looked through them at people on stage like dancers in a ballet."

"Ah! A *lorgnette*."

"Yes. In the olden days there were no contact lenses."

"I see."

"It's not as valuable as the Lucky We ring. The ring is the most expensive jewelry my mother has."

"Is it very beautiful?" Scotti had scrutinized the place very carefully. There was no exit, not even a single vent.

"I only saw it once and I was too little to remember it. My mother says it's too heavy. She only wears it at special times."

"That makes sense."

"Rona said my father owed money to Al and her which was why they have to steal it. That was a lie, wasn't it?"

"I'd say so. . . . What was Rona like?"

"She was dumb, too. She reads with her finger. Maybe I shouldn't say someone's dumb. My father said it was rude, and a nun I know said only God could judge a thing."

"She could be right."

"So maybe God did this to me for calling people dumb."

"Oh, I don't think God's that mean."

"He can be. 'The sword of the Lord is filled with blood.' And he smites people with it, too."

Scotti held the child close and said, "You're not God's enemy, Deanie. None of what's happening now is your fault."

"Life is just the way the ball bounces, Daddy says. You know what else he says?"

"What?"

"He says the way to make God laugh is tell him your plans. I'm not sure I get that joke but everyone laughs at it."

Scotti said, "It means not to always think things will turn out as you thought they would." She could not hear anything now but the wind. She had not heard a car start, either.

"Why would God laugh if your plans didn't turn out?"

"He might just smile, hmmm? Because he knows what's coming and we don't . . . I think I know one thing that's coming, though."

"Is Al coming back?"

"I don't mean Al. I mean I think I have a cold coming. I have the sniffles. I have to blow my nose." She searched the pockets of the L.L. Bean parka she'd given her mother for Christmas. All she found was a stale green Doggie Donut and a box of Good & Plenty candy.

"I'll use my shirttail if I have to blow my nose," Scotti said. "Want a piece of candy?"

"I guess so. Sugar gives you energy. I didn't sleep last night."

Scotti said, "Maybe this box is empty. It feels that way."

But it wasn't.

Myrna House had hidden three Camels inside, and three oven matches.

SIXTY-FIVE

Fina Merola believed in jinxes. Sometimes places jinxed you, sometimes weather jinxed you, sometimes people did. When it came to people, they were usually women, in Fina's opinion.

"That house in Greenwich was a pushover," she said, "but you had Nell Slack for a partner."

"She did the time. I didn't," Jimmy Rainbow said.

"I'm not talking about who did the time. I'm talking about how come there was time to do? I don't like to knock my own sex, but I wouldn't work with a female."

"What do you think you've been doing? Nell Slack is part of the team."

"Team," Fina said bitterly. "Liam swore he was never going to work with anyone again after that hijacking went against him."

"I'd like to know how either one of them got their hands on the Lasher child," Rainbow said.

"I would not! How clients get what they sell me is their business. But I don't like Liam's sudden announcement that she's not in the picture anymore."

"Was she supposed to do the snatch?"

"I told you: I don't ask. I don't care what their connection is with them."

Jimmy Rainbow said, "More than anything Nell fears going back to prison. Yeats wouldn't leave her. She must have gotten cold feet. I wouldn't mention this to your Mr. Smith. He might think the whole operation is a little sloppy."

"Jimmy, you don't get it. Mr. Smith doesn't even know anyone's name, doesn't know or care about any details. Mr. Smith is a collector. He does business the way I want to do it, and that's to just *do* it. Use the military rule for fags: don't ask, don't tell. . . . Even if I gave you Mr. Smith's real name, you wouldn't know it."

"So you said, Fina. He must be a very mysterious man, this Swiss."

"Who said he was Swiss?"

"You did. A rich Swiss collector, you said."

"He's way past rich. He adds to his collection by hook or crook. The only one who'd recognize his real name would be a representative of Winston, Cartier, et cetera. And a few, very few fences, like yours truly."

"This will be in the papers, you know. Lasher's a big deal."

"Mr. Smith doesn't read the papers. He doesn't watch television. He cares only about his collection."

Jimmy Rainbow strolled across the room of the cottage at Gurney's Inn to look out at the ocean. He was handsome enough to eat and Fina would probably do him that favor later that night, once they got back to New York with the Lucky We.

Her only regret was that Nell Slack wouldn't be around when Fina spread her square of black velvet and looked at the emerald and diamond ring with her loupe.

When they'd been in Haven together, Nell Slack had had more airs than the white-collar crooks, waltzing out of there for dinner dates with Jimmy, bringing back matchbooks from Union Square Cafe, Tavern on the Green, the Four Seasons, dropping them on the table in the lounge where she'd smoke her long, brown Nat Sherman cigarettes and look down her nose at everyone. She'd take out a purse atomizer and touch Shalimar to her wrists and forehead as though something around her smelled foul.

When Liam Yeats came on the scene, she pretended *she'd* ditched Jimmy. Everyone laughed behind their hands. They knew he'd had it with her way before she got to Haven. He was only seeing her out of guilt, because she'd taken the rap for him. He was biding his time while his real squeeze went up for her next parole hearing and got a nickel off her dime.

Now Fina had him, thanks to Liam. Thanks to Liam, Fina had something big to offer Mr. Bally, alias Mr. Smith. And who better to be her partner than Jimmy Rainbow?

She was ready to move into more distinguished circles, and one thing Rainbow had to propel her in that direction was class . . . something Josefina Merola was short of, thanks to having to hustle her ass since she was out on the streets from the time she was twelve years old.

It was Rainbow's idea to keep their partnership secret so they could surprise Liam and Nell. If Nell had chickened out, it wouldn't take Liam long to get past it once the cash was in his hands, all of it his. Forget Nell Slack! It was more than Liam Yeats had ever made for one job in his life, more than they all had.

What Fina liked most about Jimmy, besides the fact that he was tough, smart, and easy to look at, was that he knew what money was for. He reminded her of that old song about being able to tell the minute he walked in the room he was a big spender! *Hey, Big Spender!* . . . What did he do but take himself over to Amagansett Wines and buy the most expensive bottle of champagne he could find there, to take with him to the house on North Bay Lane, where Liam had told them he would bring the Lucky We. They'd all toast their luck in 1961 Krug, at $400 a bottle.

Fina called over to Rainbow, "If you're not doing anything, check the map again. I have no sense of direction, darling."

"I know exactly where the house is. I did a dry run this morning when I went out for the Krug. It's a gem, set back in the woods, big! How did Liam Yeats get access to it?"

"I told you that I don't ask questions. But he house-watches for people.

"It says Ned Frazier on the sign out front. I bet Mr. Frazier is someplace south, where I'd like to be."

"How does Miami sound to you? South Beach."

"Tacky," Rainbow snorted.

"How about St. Martens?"

"How about St. Barts?"

Fina was transferring the forty 1,000-dollar bills into his old pigskin camera case. She'd bought him a new one for Christmas.

"St. Barts is new to me," she said. So was St. Martens.

So were all those places the rich tooted off to that Jimmy knew about. She had a lot of catching up to do.

"I'll show you around, Fina."

"I might take you to a place you'd like tomorrow night," she said. "I might break one of my rules and take you with me when I meet Mr. Smith." She would never do it. There would be some last-minute excuse. But the anticipation of such a thing would sweeten the hours between now and then.

"First things first," Jimmy said. "First I want to get a look at Liam Yeats's face when he sees me."

SIXTY-SIX

Delroy did not need the map to locate Chatfield's Hole. Neither did he need the thirty minutes the kidnappers had given him to get from The Highway Behind The Pond to the trail, a few feet from the enormous rock marking Chatfield's Hole. It would take him only ten minutes, but he put off leaving the Lashers', and then drove slowly, to carry out the instructions exactly as the kidnappers gave them to him.

Lester Witt, lover of Sade and proprietor of Whale Hardware, had been a figure skater in his youth. Rare Sunday afternoons in winter, when he could escape his wife's insistent presence, he met Sade at Chatfield's Hole to show off his figure eights and sit with her in his ancient Oldsmobile, listening to opera while Delroy waited in Sade's Volkswagen.

Delroy headed straight down Newtown Lane, then made a left onto Long Lane, past the high school Delroy always wished he had attended. The Amish did not allow a child to go beyond eighth grade. Delroy had thought that once he got to Sag Harbor, he would go right through to senior year. After Sade's death, he did move to East Hampton, but he barely paid his rent working two jobs, and the only times he got to the high school were once for a performance of *The Sound of Music* and once when he drove the old Volks to a car wash there.

One of the secret games he played with Eelan was "Cheerleader." There was a high school near their farm, and sometimes they would pass the sports fields in the family buggy on Saturday afternoons. They would see the football players and the pom-pom girls, and Eelan would jump up and down in her seat and whisper, "When we get home, will you watch me do a cheer, Delly? Will you do a handstand?"

She would paint her cheeks with strawberry juice in the barn, and sometimes after "cheering" she would do one of her wild dances, hugging herself and scratching her bony little arms until they bled, going around and around in circles weeping, while Delroy caught her and held her close to quiet her. He would be afraid of the way she acted. He would remember his father saying Eelan needed protection.

After Eelan had run off with Bernado, it was Sade who told Delroy the Philadelphia police had finally found her when a stranger had taken her to a hospital. She'd been living in an abandoned building near a city park where she often recited scripture, singing hymns in German and setting fires. She had cut her arms with a razor, and she was pregnant. She claimed she did not know anyone named Bernado.

She was committed to some institution for children who were "mental," Harrell Davenport had told Sade. He would not say where. Her child was to be adopted when it was born. She was just sixteen then.

After his father's death, Delroy had tried to find out more about Eelan from a brother, who wrote that the family had moved to an Amish colony in Indiana. Harrell Davenport had gone to his grave without ever revealing Eelan's whereabouts, and they presumed that she was probably dead.

Fastened to the mirrors of bathrooms and bureaus, Delroy kept a small "souvenir" of his Amish life, a hand-painted bookplate his mother had made, which his father had put into his jacket pocket sometime before he rode away to the train station in the deacon's buggy. The bookplate was festooned with curlicue letters and small drawings of blue doves.

The printing was in a loopy style that was elaborate and difficult to read, befitting the message: LET US PRAY NOT FOR LIGHTER BURDENS, BUT FOR STRONGER BACKS.

When he had moved some of his things from the little house to the Lashers', he had left it behind, along with most of his other scant possessions.

Delroy drove along remembering how he'd gone from room to room and job to job after Sade died, until the Lashers had rescued him.

He went down Two Holes of Water Road, pulling over at the stone marking Chatfield's Hole.

He knew that well behind him was the black car that had been discreetly following, with the plainclothesmen inside.

He got out of the Jeep, noting the large stones that marked the trail he had been told to take.

He kept one hand on the small, black Sportsac, with the Lucky We inside. It was the same one that the taxi driver had brought to the Lashers', Deanie's gold locket sent from the kidnappers.

It was still light; Delroy could see the blue pond water on his right barely reflecting the trees overhead. It was very quiet, only the sounds of his own footsteps and some crows calling, a squirrel rustling the leaves.

Follow the trail, he had been told, and he did, wondering if the policemen had parked by the Jeep and set off on foot. There was a fork ahead, and Delroy did not know if he should go to the left or to the right.

Then, careening toward him on a silver-and-blue Kawasaki was a man wearing a cap pulled down over his eyes. He braked, kicking up soil and leaves.

He said, "Deanie will be home in time for dinner if you have what we want. Get on and hang on."

The Kawasaki sped to the left, up and across to Bull Path, along another trail, then down Mile High Road through the woods somewhere near the Grace Estate Reserve.

At the end of those woods was a large red brick house, nearly hidden by pitch pines, white cedars, and red maples.

There was no way anyone could have followed them.

SIXTY-SEVEN

The East Hampton branch of the Sound Off alarm company was next to the newspaper office of the *Independent,* which was published every Wednesday.

There was only one employee on duty, and he had slipped out to smoke a cigarette. Heading back, he heard the raucous drone of the alarm and he took the steps by twos.

On his board, No. 17 was lit up, and under it the name Ryan Simon, with the address on Cranberry Hole Road.

He knew it was a fire. A burglary beeped, while a low siren signaled a fire.

First he called the East Hampton Fire Department and then he tried to reach someone at the Simon house. There was no answer. Next he reached the Sound Off mobile truck, which was already on its way to Cranberry Hole Road.

He switched on the radio, turning the dial down to the Amagansett station that broadcast local bulletins immediately. The program was being interrupted at the exact moment for a news flash.

But it was not about a fire. It was about the death of Len Lasher, CEO of Lasher Communications, followed by a report of his only child's kidnapping. She was eight years old, named Deanie Lasher, a blue-eyed blond, reward for her return alive $500,000.

SIXTY-EIGHT

Fina was listening to Julio Iglesias, her velvet cloth spread out on the mahogany table, under the crystal chandelier in the Frazier dining room. Her loupe was attached to a long gold chain, which Jimmy Rainbow had given her for Christmas.

She had asked him to have something engraved on the tiny gold clasp, as proof they were a couple, since he had been so insistent that their romance be kept secret until the acquisition of the Lucky We was a *done deed*.

In tiny letters near the 14K stamp were the words: J TO F FOREVER.

Jimmy looked at his watch and said, "I'm going out now to meet them and be sure we get that thing inside safely. When Yeats sees me, it might throw him."

"It might. But Liam's trustworthy."

"You don't know that."

"I know who is and who isn't. If I didn't know that by now I wouldn't be where I am," and she couldn't resist adding, "plus you wouldn't be where you are, Jimmy."

She was humming along with Julio, who was singing "Paloma Blanca." Julio brought her luck.

Jimmy went through the kitchen, where his .357 revolver rested on the counter. He stuck it inside his trousers.

The moment he was outdoors, he could hear the dirt bike coming through the woods, and then he saw Yeats get off and walk the bike up the path, followed by a tall redhead in a leather jacket.

"Stop right there!" Rainbow called out.

"Mr. Frazier? That isn't you, is it?"

They stopped.

Jimmy Rainbow had on skintight thin leather gloves, a long overcoat with the collar pulled up, a fur hat pushed down past his eyebrows, and the goggles he wore spearfishing: no way to see his face.

"Now come ahead!" he said. "The redhead stays where he is. I'll cover him while you take the bag from him."

Yeats came forward, muttering, "No, you're not Ned Frazier."

He saw the .357 before he saw Jimmy, and even when he saw Jimmy, he couldn't see his face well.

"Someone you know is waiting inside," Jimmy said. "She'll want to verify the authenticity of the ring."

He kept the gun pointed at the redhead, who was visibly trembling.

Yeats began growling, "What the fuck is this?" Jimmy suspected it was slowly beginning to dawn on Liam Yeats what the fuck it was, and who the fuck it was. Yeats walked past Jimmy toward the house, holding the bag in both hands close to his chest. He closed the kitchen door behind him.

"Is Deanie in there?" the redhead had been inching toward Jimmy.

"Stay where you are. She's safe."

"Will she be coming out?"

"Just be patient, Red. Everything is under control."

He would have liked to hear Fina explain to Yeats that she had a partner, and who the partner was. He was looking forward to the expression in Liam's eyes when they came face-to-face.

The big redhead was standing there shifting his weight from one foot to another, rubbing his buttocks with his large palms.

Jimmy asked, "Have you ever been on a dirt bike before?"

"No, never."

"Hard on the ass, hmm?"

"Yes. You don't have to keep that gun aimed at me. I'm not going anyplace."

"I don't know that yet. . . . I hope the Lashers weren't foolish enough to try and substitute something else for what we want. My lady's an expert. She'll know."

"It's what you want," said Delroy Davenport.

They stood there silently for a while. It was beginning to get dark.

"Has Deanie had anything to eat?" Davenport asked.

"Of course!"

"It's getting cold, too."

"She's warm and she's been fed."

Finally Jimmy walked backward very slowly, then reached behind himself, pushing open the kitchen door. He shouted in, "Okay?"

"Yes! Okay! Let him go."

Jimmy said to the redhead, "Now listen carefully. The child is going to be released safe and sound near the Lashers' house just as soon as we can get to her, and so long as no one interferes with us, or comes here before we leave. No tricks! It's almost over! Don't spoil things now that you're this close to having her home. It wouldn't pay us to have anything happen to her, and nothing will if you walk back through the woods to your car. Go to the Lashers' and wait for her. If you do anything different, you put her life in danger."

He stood there looking at Rainbow, rubbing his hands together.

"This can be snow white clean or bloody dirty, it's up to you, Red," Jimmy said.

"I'll take the road," he finally said.

"You'll take the woods. It's not that dark yet. Go on."

"How do I know Deanie's safe?"

"You don't. But she is. We're thieves. None of us wants to hurt a child. We've got kids ourselves."

He watched while Delroy Davenport turned and trudged down the path away from the road and into the woods.

Then Rainbow went inside.

He stopped long enough to remove his hat and goggles, then grab the Krug from the refrigerator and carry it into the dining room.

Whatever Fina had said about him to Liam Yeats hadn't done anything to diminish the contempt Liam had for Jimmy. It was as clear in his eyes as the dark brown of his irises, hard little angry needles.

Fina said, "Give Liam his money. He wants to get out of here!"

Jimmy Rainbow looked at Liam and said, "We want to know what happened to Nell."

Fina said, "*We* don't want to know what happened to her. I don't *care* what happened to her. Pay him and he'll meet us in Manhattan for the second payment."

"What did Nell tell you yesterday?" Liam asked.

Rainbow answered, "I haven't talked to her in years." He set the Krug on the table. "There are three glasses right behind you, Liam. Let's have a wee toast, hmm?"

"You were in East Hampton last night, weren't you?" Liam asked Rainbow.

"Yes, of course."

"And you followed me to Maritime Way?"

Rainbow gave Liam a look. "What are you talking about?"

"I thought I saw you last night."

"Fina? What's he talking about?"

"I don't know and I don't care!"

"Then never mind," said Liam. "I have to go back for the child now."

"Where is she?" Rainbow asked.

"In Ryan Simon's attic up on Cranberry Hole Road."

"I do not want to hear this!" Fina said. "It's none of our business! Give him the money and send him on his way, Jimmy! . . . This is a beauty!" Fina was slipping the ring back into the Sportsac. "I can see why somebody becomes a collector."

Jimmy twisted the cork off the bottle. It popped and some of the champagne spilled from the neck of the bottle. "You know how you think Julio Iglesias brings you luck, Fina? I think a champagne toast does."

"I said 'no, thanks,'" Liam told him.

"Just pay him, Jimmy."

"OK. Put two glasses on the table for you and me then," Rainbow said. "I suppose you want to count your money, Yeats."

"Yes, I certainly do."

"Take your coat off. Sit down and count it." Jimmy put his old camera case on the table. "It's all there."

Yeats took off his jacket, reached in his pocket for a pack of cigarettes, and looked around for an ashtray.

"Uh-oh," Jimmy said. "I guess Fina didn't tell you this is a smoke-free house."

"Ha ha, very funny," Fina said.

"Gun smoke's allowed, though," said Jimmy. He flipped his gun out of the top of his trousers, aimed the gun at Yeats, shot him through the head, then fired a second shot at Fina.

He was a good shot.

They were both dead.

Fina sat at the table bloody facedown, but Liam had thrown back his head and it hung to one side dripping blood on his Members Only shirt. Two crystal wineglasses were between them and the bottle of Krug. A little mystery scenario for the police to ponder.

Then Jimmy picked up the Sportsac, put the camera case inside, and, smiling, went out the door.

Fina and Jimmy had never gone anyplace in the same car. Her Toyota stood beside his Audi down near the road.

He had not checked in at Gurney's so he didn't need to check out. He had already packed the few things he'd taken to the little bungalow at Gurney's that Fina had rented for them.

There was just one last thing to do, and Jimmy Rainbow removed his gloves, put them in the glove compartment with his gun, turned the key in the ignition, and took off to do it.

SIXTY-NINE

*The Crepidula fornicata is one hundred percent male when young, but once
it has reached sexual maturity this slipper snail reverses its sex status and
becomes totally female.*

After the police left her apartment with Nell Slack in tow, Dr. Loeper
returned to her research, grateful for the simplicity and ingenuity of mol-
luscan life.

Whether she was describing the Crepidula, or the common garden-
variety land snail, a gastropod possessing both male and female sex organs,
capable of reproducing autogenetically, any anxieties she might feel were
swept away by this far more intriguing and compelling subject matter.

People were so often disappointing.

Whatever explained a Nell Slack, it had become impossible for Ginny
to excuse her or think of her any longer as a friend.

Ginny wished she had never run into Scotti House at Metamorphs. It
was distressing to have become a part of this kidnapping, however small
her role in it. Yet that serendipitous encounter may well have been the cat-
alyst for Nell Slack's arrest.

"Another species has no male members," Ginny continued writing.
"Their eggs develop without fertilization, a form of—" but the clock in
the corner began the count to six.

Ginny usually waited for prime-time news at six-thirty.

But finally, enough curiosity about the real world seeped into her consciousness, and she saved and exited her Apple.

She turned on the TV and went into the kitchen to make another cup of tea, stopped by the words:

"Good evening! A report just in from Suffolk County police . . . "

She turned the heat off from under the kettle and went back into her living room, in time to see none other than Scotti House herself. She had her arm around a child whose face was covered by a blanket. They were being rushed through a small crowd by several policemen.

"The only child of the late Len Lasher, of Lasher Communications, was rescued from kidnappers thanks to a smoke alarm in the house of artist Urian Simonides, who calls himself Ryan Simon. A local East Hampton house watcher named Liam Yeats is wanted by the police in connection with—"

SEVENTY

"... the crime. A reward of $500,000 was offered for the safe return of Deanie Lasher, whose father died of a heart attack last evening without ever knowing his child had been abducted . . ."

Lara lowered the volume and put the remote beside her on the couch. "$500,000?" She looked at Jack Burlingame. "Who said?"

"You said. I asked you if there shouldn't be a reward when the police lost track of Delroy and you said okay. I said we'd better make it big, better do $500,000, and you said okay."

"I was out of my mind at that point."

"Well, it's on record now and my God, Lara, we have Deanie back!"

"We don't have her back yet. Why won't they let me go to her?"

"Abrahams says it's too chaotic. The press is all over the place. It's better to have her brought here. As long as you're worrying, worry about Delroy."

"I am worried about him. It's just that I have no recollection of offering $500,000. When I add up what the past twenty-four hours have cost it boggles the mind!"

Jack said, "What happened to 'now is a good time to lose the ring what with Len gone' and so forth? Do you remember saying that?"

"Don't be a bastard, Jack! I know you're good at it, but try to hide your talent for it right now. I just want to see Deanie come through that door."

"And so do I, Lara. Followed by Delroy."

"Don't group Delroy with my daughter!"

"They could have killed him, you know."

"For what?"

"For being able to identify them. When he went to meet them, they still believed they were getting away with it."

"Just who gets this $500,000?"

"I'd say the woman who rescued her. That House woman Mario was taking out."

"How did she get involved in all this? Wasn't her mother the one Delroy was always visiting?"

Before Jack Burlingame could answer, Deanie burst through the front door.

"Daddy? Mother?"

Jack resisted the impulse to ask Lara if it wasn't worth $500,000 to hear that?

SEVENTY-ONE

Bound for Manhattan on 495, Jimmy wished he could call Bally on his cell, just to have someone to tell that all was well, since there was no one else he could tell. But Fina had been right about Bally: he didn't want blow-by-blow accounts of how he came into possession of his stones.

Now that it was all over the news, Bally would probably still not know anything about it. He was famous not only for removing himself from the whys and wherefores of his business, and from the few fences he trusted, but also for supposedly removing himself from the world at large.

Jimmy had been right in guessing that Bally could not quite trust Josefina Merola. She was not in a class with the providers he was accustomed to. Besides that, why pay out more than necessary? Jimmy Rainbow was not a greedy man. He would sell the Lucky We to Bally for $1,000,000—the $800,000 that would have gone to Liam and Nell, and another $200,000 in memory of Fina. That would be a good deal for Bally, one he might well remember if he should ever have occasion to do business with Jimmy Rainbow in the future.

Fina had been careless. From the moment she made her deal with Liam, and then invited Rainbow into a partnership with her, it never occurred to her that Jimmy would be able to discover who "Mr. Smith" really was.

The less curious Jimmy Rainbow pretended to be, the more Fina bragged to impress him, mentioning that "Smith" lived in Zurich, that he kept a suite at the St. Regis, on and on until all Jimmy had to do was make a few inquiries of the right people.

Like any collector of his ilk, Anton Bally knew who was in possession of all the Windsor jewels. Bally's forte was knowing what had become of the world's priceless estate jewelry. What he could add to his own collection he did, usually arriving on his Gulfstream IV to take possession personally.

Although a collector like Bally was rarely visibly rich, his name seldom recognizable in society or to media people, representatives of dealers in rare and precious gems knew him indeed.

It hadn't taken Jimmy very long at all to learn his name and how to contact him.

Jimmy had telephoned him to say, "If Fina were reliable, she wouldn't have let me know your identity. I'm more reliable and a lot less expensive."

Bally did not need to be persuaded any further, just as Fina would wave away details of the nuts and bolts involved in acquiring what she fenced.

The deal was set in a perfunctory but cordial verbal agreement. Jimmy would be at LaGuardia Airport early in the morning, after a brief overnight stay in Manhattan.

Jimmy turned off the car radio, deciding that Anton Bally's modus operandi had more finesse. Shut it all out. There would be no one, nothing to connect him with what was taking place in the Hamptons. Wherever Nell was, she would not have a clue, either, that he had teamed up with Fina. Fina Merola would be the last person anyone would imagined involved with Jimmy Rainbow.

He shoved in a tape, a string quartet playing Mozart.

He thought about St. Barts. He'd never have taken someone like Fina there. The kind of woman he was looking for would own the Lucky We, not fence it. The last time he had visited St. Barts he'd stayed at Guana-hani, but this time he would prefer a place less flashy, subtler: the Hôtel Le Toiny.

Yes.

He smiled as he raced through the night, imagining himself in the sun, or a sandy beach, nearly naked, far away from winter . . . rich.

SEVENTY-TWO

His face was scratched from stumbling through the woods as it grew dark, knees bruised from falling, feet blistered from walking until he reached the road. A truck driver took him to Le Reve. There the police were waiting for him, along with Abrahams, who was hell-bent on finding Liam Yeats.

Because Delroy had remembered the biker asking, "Is that you, Mr. Frazier?" they had taken Delroy to the house in the woods at the corner of North Bay Lane.

Yeats seemed to have slumped from the Fraziers' table to their floor, in a bloody heap, while a small brunette sat facedown in blood before a full bottle of Krug and two blood-spotted, fluted glasses.

The police could identify Yeats, whose wallet was tucked in the back pocket of his black Dockers. Not until they found the registration of the 2006 Toyota behind the Fraziers' were they able to surmise that the female was Josefina Merola.

What happened to Delroy next was all he needed to change his mind about keeping the lorgnette.

It was not the angry tone of the questioning that frightened Delroy. It was not even that he was grilled so persistently and unfeelingly that he almost began to believe they would somehow implicate him as an accessory. None of what he suffered at the hands of the police, in the grim headquarters on

Pantigo Road, was responsible for his decision to return the sleek panther lorgnette with the tiny Lucky We inscription.

It was something else.

It occurred to Delroy that somewhere there could be a bill of sale for the lorgnette, a record of some sort, even though the Mister did not believe in insurance. If Mrs. Lasher came upon it, she would set out in her relentless way to find it.

What if Scotti showed it to her mother, or what if someone saw her using it? She could very well end up in that same police station. With a double murder to be solved, and a discovery of this second Lucky We, Scotti could be submitted to the worst kind of brutal treatment. Delroy would not have been surprised if she had been strip-searched . . . and the thought of Scotti enduring that humiliation horrified Delroy. In his mind's eye he saw the pathetic, stubby penis she had held between her long fingers on the night they first met.

It was early morning when they finally finished with him, dropping him off at Le Reve.

Immediately after sneaking up the back stairs, he returned the lorgnette to the bureau drawer along with the last note Len Lasher had written to his wife.

While Delroy was in the bathroom of the master bedroom applying hydrogen peroxide to his various cuts and scratches, he heard Deanie crying out from her room. He heard the Missus leave the guest room where she had been staying through the Mister's illness and go in to comfort her daughter. Then Delroy went into his nook, and, as he had so many times, slept in his clothes, leaning back in the recliner.

SEVENTY-THREE

Thursday, Friday, the media was filled with speculation about how many kidnappers there were, and which one was the murderer. There were photographs of Nell Slack, Fina Merola, and Liam Yeats in the newspapers and on television.

Delroy had been called in a few more times to be questioned, but he had not actually seen any of the kidnappers' faces. As the police began slowly to fit together some of the puzzle (Merola had rented a cottage at Gurney's Inn; the Slack woman had verified Merola's connection with Yeats), there was a less hostile ambiance during the proceedings. But Delroy could not bring himself to respond good-naturedly. What he had imagined would be his triumph was nothing of the kind. He had received perfunctory thanks from Lara Lasher, at the same time she had seemed annoyed that he had left the Jeep at Chatfield's Hole.

"What do you mean you couldn't find your way back there?" she'd actually hollered that at him.

While Scotti's photos appeared on television and in the newspapers, no cameras had been aimed at Delroy; nor was his name mentioned, only a passing reference to "an employee who delivered the Lucky We."

The first thing he had seen when he had arrived at the little house Thursday afternoon was a sheet of the pale blue Le Reve stationery on the coffee table.

The note was written in Mrs. Lasher's large script, the T-bars flying off the stems, the upper and lower loops fat and expansive.

Delroy, my husband would have been so proud of you, as I am. and grateful, too, for your part in Deanie's rescue.

I am not reneging on my promise to let you live here rent-free (but you are responsible for utilities and upkeep) until Memorial Day, and this is your proof of that.

I do think the trim should be painted the moment the temperature is consistently mild enough in early spring, and yesterday would not be too soon for the kitchen.

We will need you at Le Reve through summer and possibly fall, depending on what I decide. You will be our traffic manager and general helper-outer at the same pay, with no deduction because of the living situation arranged for you.

At noon on Saturday in the library, Mr. Lasher's lawyer will read that part of the will which pertains to the help, and of course you are included.

With thanks, Lara Lasher.

It had been in the police station on Wednesday night, as well, that Delroy had made another decision. He wanted to leave Le Reve. The letter from Mrs. Lasher made him all the more determined to go. There was nothing left of that life; there had never been as much to it as he had thought.

He could not bring himself to ask the Missus for the $300 she had left in the envelope on the cherry chest, which had been gone when he returned to his nook. He had looked everywhere for it, imagining that he'd pushed it aside in his hurry to return the lorgnette.

Jack Burlingame, the one person at Le Reve he might have mentioned it to, had left for New York early on the morning of Deanie's return.

Saturday morning Deanie appeared in the kitchen as Delroy was eating his breakfast.

"I miss my daddy," she said. "Do you miss my daddy?"

"We all miss him, Deanie."

"Is that why you're packing? Are you going back to live at the little house?"

"No, I'm leaving, Deanie. I'm going to find another job somewhere."

"Leaving?" the cook exclaimed as she set a plate of buttered toast in front of him. "When?"

"This afternoon."

Deanie said, "We're going away next week. My mother wants to get hold of herself. Is that what you're going to do?"

"Yes," said Delroy.

The Missus had decided against a funeral and all that the Mister had planned. There would be no mourners flocking to East Hampton, staying at the inns, gathering at Guild Hall and then going by limo to the Green River Cemetery, no enormous luncheon at The Point—none of that. Not now. Maybe a memorial service later in New York City, the Missus said.

Delroy was surprised that he felt disappointed. He realized that he had been expecting the Mister's death for so long that at times he believed he had faced it already. He hadn't, though. At odd moments he would find himself teary, remembering small things about the Mister. The way he had worked to master the voice synthesizer, and the first time it had spoken to him in its eerie tone: "Dale Roy L O!" while the Mister had grinned: "L O Dale Roy, L O."

But more often when they were alone together Mr. Lasher had jabbered away in his own strange language while Delroy had leaned forward, listening so carefully, learning how to hear him.

"Dok e, L oy" (talk to me), and Delroy would, telling him about the Amish, his life before he had left Pennsylvania, all that he could recall, and always his memories of Eelan.

One day, early in his illness, the Mister had made Delroy promise to keep him clean, never to let him smell or drool, to always help him to keep his dignity, his eyes fixed on Delroy's, "Pwamis me. Pwamis."

He had needed Delroy.

Who else ever had except poor Eelan?

Delroy would join the servants' memorial gathering at noon, as Mrs. Lasher had asked everyone to do, and there he would announce his decision to leave Le Reve.

The only one he sought out to tell was Myrna House.

Delroy had not seen Scotti since all of this had happened, but he had asked her mother that morning, "Will Scotti still be going to the opera?"

"What a memory you have, Delroy! Yes, she's already left. Tonight, perhaps, you'll come for dinner with Baba and me."

The only item Delroy had not packed was the Lautrec poster that said L'OPÉRA. He would take it with him to Tulip Path, and tell Mrs. House it was his way of thanking Scotti for rescuing Deanie. He had been knitting frantically for the past two days, to calm himself through the police questioning, so he had finished the sweater for Baba, too.

Deanie helped herself to a piece of toast and said, "Will you do me a favor and give my mother the lawnette? I want to show it to my newest best friend before I go away."

"Your father told you about it, did he?"

"Yes. It's her last surprise from him ever."

"I know, Deanie. I've kept it in a safe place."

"It's a Lucky We, too. But not the one the kidtrappers took."

"Yes, I plan to give it to your mother this afternoon."

The cook asked Deanie, "When did you get time to make a new best friend? I made that toast for Delroy, so don't eat it all."

"My new best friend is Scotti House," said Deanie. "She got us out of the attic and she knows who you are, Delroy, so I guess you know who she is."

"I do know who she is," Delroy said.

SEVENTY-FOUR

"Can I meet her?" Emma said.

"I'd like you to meet her," Scotti said, "because we've become good friends."

"Did you meet her in that attic you set on fire?"

"We set your grandmother's parka on fire, and then we held it up to the smoke alarm. It was the only way we could call attention to ourselves."

"Was this little girl scared to be kidnapped?"

"Very."

"Could I be kidnapped?"

"No, sweetie, we're not rich."

From the kitchen Jessica hollered in, "You're a lot richer than you ever were, though. Rich enough to take us out to dinner."

"Can we go to dinner with your award money, Daddy?"

"*Reward* money. Practice saying Scotti instead of Daddy, honey."

"Can we go out to dinner, Scotti?"

"Tonight I have to go to the opera, but we'll do it next Saturday if you want to."

"Can Deanie come?"

"We'll see . . . and Emma, we have to talk about something if you're going to meet Deanie. We have to pretend to Deanie that I'm your aunt."

"I don't think that's a good idea." Jessica had walked into the living room.

"I do!" Emma said. "I want to meet Daddy's new friend."

"You see what I mean?" Jessica said. "She'll slip and call you Daddy."

"I will not!"

"You just did!" Jessica said.

"Because no one's here!"

"Scotti?" Jessica said. "Would you come into the kitchen and look at the cookies I'm baking? They're so hard!"

Scotti got up and went with her, saying, "You have to take them out as soon as the chocolate bits start melting. Otherwise you'll have chocolate rock cookies instead of chocolate chip. . . . Em, honey, open your present."

In the kitchen Jessica said, "Put a hold on that meeting with Deanie Lasher. Emma's not ready."

"She's as ready as she'll ever be. There's going to be some trial and error, Jessie."

"It's too soon, darling."

"I don't think so. This $500,000 reward could be a mixed blessing, too. I worry about being outed with all the media hype going on."

"Who'd do that?"

"Someone who could use some extra money from the *Examiner* or the *Star*, the *Post* or *A Current Affair*."

"But who knows?"

"Our ex-neighbors and all the Metamorphs at the institute. I'm going to make an appointment with Dr. Leogrande fast, now that I can afford it. And we'll stash plenty away for Emma, hmmm?"

"But what about Sheba Samitses? You were going to help me nail that gang. She'll be at the Annabel Spa in July."

"That's why I want to get Leogrande to set a date for the surgery," Scotti said. "If I get a March date, I'll be fine by July."

Scotti opened the oven door and smoke poured out. She put on oven mitts and pulled out the burning Nestlé Toll House cookies. She turned the sink faucet on, and Jessica put the mess there.

"I've got to tell my friend Mario," Scotti said. "I've decided that."

"Is he the one who took you home Thanksgiving night?"

"No. That's Delroy. He already knows, remember? I don't have to tell Delroy. And I'm not worried about him anymore, either."

"He sounds a little strange, though."

Scotti laughed. "And I'm not?"

"Mom? Scotti?" Emma called. "Come hear my fortune!"

They went back into the living room. Emma was holding the white-faced doll with the purple hair and red eyes.

The small, mechanical mouth popped open.

You're going to make a new friend!

"Deanie Lasher!" Emma said. "Right, Aunt Scotti?"

SEVENTY-FIVE

In ten minutes the servants would gather in the solarium, where they would be told what Len had left each one in his will.

Deanie kept insisting there was something coming that Lara knew nothing about. Deanie said the only ones who knew were Delroy and herself. Lara could not pry out of her whatever it was, nor could she seem to distract Deanie from the subject of this Scotti House.

Scotti this and Scotti that and Scotti hung the moon!

It was one more reason Lara had decided to book a reservation at Hôtel Le Toiny in St. Barts, where they could swim and sun themselves, and Deanie could have fun showing off her French. They would leave there after two weeks, the same time the Invictus School would be returning from the Mexico trip. That should be enough time to delete this Scotti from memory, for Lara had no intention of allowing them to meet again. Dr. Mannerheim had agreed with Lara that there was no point in allowing the kidnapping to become an event in Deanie's memory, no reason for her to befriend her rescuer, who was to be amply compensated for the rescue.

After Delroy had confessed Len's suicide plans and explained about the half-acre grave site at Green River Cemetery, Lara had told him again there would be no memorial service, no luncheon afterward for close friends.

"But the Mister planned everything so carefully."

"Things were different then, Delroy. I know what Mr. Lasher would want now. Deanie and I will take his ashes to Green River by ourselves and very quietly say our good-byes. That's how he would want it. Don't you think I know my own husband?"

Why was she suddenly defending her actions to the help?

She had had her fill of everyone, and certainly of Jack Burlingame. He had left almost immediately after Deanie had come through the front door. They had had a most unpleasant disagreement over the fact Lara had decided to pay the extra $300 she had promised Delroy after he painted the little house. He was living there rent free until Memorial Day! A summer rental could fetch her thousands! And what other guarantee did she have that Delroy would do the painting? She wanted to have the little house ready for realtors to show.

When Bud Deigh walked into the library, Lara looked up at her lawyer, surprised, for she had asked him to wait in the solarium. He would read the will himself to the small gathering. He was top man at Deigh and Cobb, the law firm Len had dubbed "Pay and Sob."

"Mrs. Lasher? There's something I have to mention before we begin."

"What is it? Is this the something Deanie said was coming?"

"This has nothing to do with your daughter. No one knows about this. It's a codicil, Mrs. Lasher."

"The codicils don't pertain to the help."

"This one does. You see—"

She interrupted him. "I know all the codicils."

"Not this one. This is one which was there from the time Len was in the wheelchair, but Len wanted it kept private until after his death."

"Kept private?"

"Kept secret, Mrs. Lasher."

"From me?"

"From everyone." He shrugged. "I guess it's a special case. It has to do with a Delroy Davenport."

"Are you sure?"

"Oh yes. He's described in Len's will as the principal caretaker during his final days."

"I hope he didn't leave him more money."

"Not exactly. I'll read it to you, Mrs. Lasher." Deigh took a sheet of paper from his briefcase, and put on reading glasses. "It says, 'For Delroy Davenport, my principal caretaker during the last days of my life, one thousand shares of stock in Lasher Communications, to do with as he sees fit, with thanks and the hope he will one day find Eelan."

"Who?"

"It's spelled capital E, small e-l-a-n."

"There must be some mistake. I've never heard that name!"

"There's no mistake, Mrs. Lasher."

"My God! One thousand shares!"

"Yes, ma'am."

"What is the stock worth?"

"At yesterday's closing bell it was worth $104 a share."

"So that would be?"

"That would be roughly $104,000, Mrs. Lasher."

"Let me see that!" Lara Lasher said.